DON'T MESS WITH ME TEXAS

Based on the Satanic Panic, Child and Domestic Abuse and the Children's Underground Network in the 1980's

SATAN SLAYER SERIES

COMEUPPANCE #1

By

SKYE RYTER

DON'T MESS WITH ME TEXAS

Based on the Satanic Panic, Child and Domestic Abuse and the Children's Underground Network in the 1980's

Copyright © 2022 by Skye Ryter
Business Name: SKYERYTER PRESS
Email Address: skyeryter@gmail.com
ISBN: 9798825502458

All rights reserved. No part of this book may be reproduced, scanned or distributed in any printed or electronic form without permission. Please do not participate in or encourage piracy of copyrighted material in violation of the author's rights.

Book Cover Design and
Formating by Word-2- Kindle

This work is a memoir/novel based upon actual and fictitious events. Some characters, towns/cities, events are real and others are fictitious. Any resemblance to real people, living or dead or to any actual event is unintentional or coincidental. Some of the main characters' actions did not occur. The author is offering her personal perspective on the subject of protecting children from their abuser(s). This is not an instruction manual for putting a child(ren) into hiding, circumventing the courts, interstate laws, or any illegal means to keep a child(ren) safe from abusers that include ex spouses, relatives, CPS, Foster Parents, FBI, Judges, police, et al. Furthermore, this memoir/novel is not intended to give legal advice and the author is not responsible for adverse consequences for decisions made by readers of this memoir/novel. Those readers who are in need of such services are advised to seek local resource remedies for their unique situation regarding protecting a child(ren). The author is gender neutral in her attitudes recognizing that both genders, including LGBTQ identifiers can be victims or abusers.

DEDICATION

To my daughter and all survivors of abuse and the parent(s) who rescued them from abuse.

I also dedicate this to the woman who's organization helped with rescues and the families worldwide who provided aid.

I also dedicate this to victims still being tortured and the courageous people who have defyed the odds and escaped.

CONTENTS

FORWARD

***B**y April, whose West Coast case coincided with the authors during the 1980's without them having spoken until 2022. April bravely went public and her and her daughters' case made National and International headlines.*

We hope other moms who were victims like we were during that era feel brave enough to contact us at skyeryter@gmail.com. We need to support each other. We need to talk!

To the Reader,

Go ahead. Go to Amazon. Look up Satanic Ritual Abuse Survivors. Almost 100 books written by courageous people who experienced the indoctrination of a cult and came out the other side to tell their horrific stories. Horror after horror. Children taken to church basements, to the woods, to a relative's house to be ritually abused. Killing babies, killing animals, chanting to the devil, locked in cages with dogs, snakes, spiders,adults dressed up as devils, altars, candles, knives, ... unbelievable stories but they are true. It is hard to read one of these books and see what people will do to control another being. It is especially hard to read when you find that it is one parent or both parents who indoctrinate children. FEAR Instill fear in a child and they will do what you want them to do. Threaten them with their own death. Tell them if they tell someone they love will be killed, tell them if they tell they will be living this nightmare forever, tell them if they tell no one will believe them anyway. Who would believe a child who says, "I was married to the Devil when I visited Dad last time?"

I did. My daughter was satanic ritually abused, sexually abused, physically abused and emotionally abused by her father and his cult. I have drawing after drawing of the horrific terror she experienced. She spent months drawing these pictures of what had happened to her after I was able to get her away from her father. Satanic Ritual Abuse is REAL EVIL. She had been told over and over that if she said anything to me that I would be killed. She had been told that if she said anything that she would be dropped from the roof of her father's house. It was so hard to believe that this man that I had "fallen in love with" and had married was now terrorizing my child. What had I missed? How come I had no idea? These questions still torment me. My heart was broken. My daughter had experienced evil and I could not protect her.

Oh believe me, I tried numerous times in court to have her protected from visiting her father/abuser. I had no idea about the "good ole boy system" in courts and how the patriarchal system works.

I first met the author of this book just a couple of months ago. We shared drawings that our daughters had done of their cult experiences. It was the first time that I could talk with another mother who had experienced what I had been through. We had been fighting in courts to protect our daughters at the same time. She in Texas, and me in California. Both learning that it didn't matter what kind of evidence you had to stop visits with the father/abuser that the patriarchal system looked the other way. There were so many times reading this book that I gasped and thought "that happened to me too". This book is totally creditable. These horrible atrocities really occur. I know.

April

PREFACE

One mom's traumatic dealings with the state of Texas during the 1980's to protect her baby and herself from an abusive husband and his family's alleged involvement in Satanic Ritual Abuse (SRA) and Kiddie Porn Abuse.

There is the very real probability he was also a victim. But he was too far gone to be saved so we needed to be saved from him. They used mind control torture methods to keep the children afraid to talk. These were the same methods and experiments used by Nazi Satanists and subsequently the U.S. and Canadian governments to create super spies during and after the Cold War. MkUltra was the name of the project and experiments were carried out unethically from 1953 until it was stopped in 1974. Allan Dulles, head of the CIA, approved the project and after WWII, hired and brought Dr. Josef Mengele, the Nazi 'Angel of Death' to the U.S. to teach mind control techniques using LSD, electic shock and torture on non-consensual citizens in both the U.S. and Canada. The objective was to produce alternate or 'split personalities' in spies to infiltrate China, N. Korea and the Soviet Union. When someone has "split personalities" or Dissociative Identity Disorder, they essentially have no memory of what the alternate identity knows or experiences and therefore won't reveal the government secrets if captured. The Satanists used "splitting" torture techniques and drugging on the children they used in their rituals and kiddie porn businesses in order to keep the children from telling caretakers what the Satanists were doing. Like sacrificing people and animals and filming children who were killed, raped and tortured for their lucrative hard core pornography trade with the rich and powerful. Apparently very wealthy people pay big time money for films and magazines of children being killed, raped or tortured. What's the saying 'absolute power (and wealth) corrupts absolutely'. The mind control techniques used on the children made their accounts of abuse sound unimaginably absurd and unbelievable.

It's no surprise then that the 1980's produced the 'Satanic Panic'. All those trainers and their victims were let loose into the public by 1974 having been introduced to Satanism and learning there's a profit in torturing others while filming them. It's no secret Mengele and Hitler were Satanists. My child and undoubtedly her father were victims of the government's clandestine experiments. Thanks alot Director Dulles.

This is a story of resilience and courage waging a constant uphill battle with CPS, the courts, archaic and harmful Texas laws, the police and FBI getting them to believe what my daughter was telling them about abuse done to her and get protection for both my daughter and me. Some might say, "No way, this don't happen, not in ma 'Merica," if you're from the South and "Holly shit, I didn't know this was going on. We need to do something about it!" everywhere else.

This story includes years of abuse; years of hiding, good Samaritans and despicable evil doers. It exposes problems with the state welfare agencies and lack of funding and resources. It includes vigilante justice when necessary, intended and unintended comeuppance to bad characters.

Texas isn't the only state with a broken down child protection system but it is one of the worst. It is a wild ride. It has to be to equal the wild west of Texas.

Part 1

CHAPTER 1

I had a long drink of water from my thermos and after blowing my nose for the umpteenth time that day, I went back to looking out over the barrel of my rifle, waiting for my target to drive up and get out of his car and go up to his house. I figured I'd get him while he was standing on the porch, fumbling with his keys to unlock the door. I had been sitting there for hours and had gone through a half a box of Kleenex already and copious amounts of flavored water. Having a runny nose and being uncomfortably thirsty while pulling the trigger would cause a sure miss.

While sitting there, I forced myself to remember why I was doing this. I say forced because the emotions those memories generated were ones that were still too close to the surface and could be exposed if the dirt got kicked around too much. I wanted them buried; six feet under.

Up until this moment that endeavor has been impossible to achieve consistently because just when I'm riding high on the happiness meter, whoosh...down I plummet with those gaping mental wounds. They hurt like the pain you get when you trip and land on your elbow and knee cap and your skull hits the cement sidewalk. Just when you least expect it, pain happens. You just want those pains to stop as quickly as possible so you can get back to the bell at the top.

It's no different with mental pain caused by festering memories. It eats at your gut and leaves you gasping for air. The painful realizations have not diminished long after you suffered from them. Mandatory minutia of life can hide them for years but eventually torture recall comes to the surface presenting as rage, PTSD, DID (Disassociative Identity Disorder) and...pain. Psychiatrists have known for years about it's root causes but somehow that info hasn't reached the masses unlike body diseases have. Society still is just stuck with the aftermath mopping up and doing a piss poor job of it in my opinion.

Abusive mates are still getting away with violence. Children harmed by caregivers are still not being believed. Judges are still uneducated on Cluster B's; Psychopath's, Sociopath's, Malignant Narcissists or the adverse effects of spousal abuse on family members. FBI and cops are still going after the wrong person and gender, fueled by prejudices and zero mental health training. And very few of them believe Satanic Ritual Abuse (SRA) is a real thing. This later group does know how to mop up and does an excellent job of it.

I didn't enjoy thinking about any of these nagging injustices but doing so had become an important routine ritual before deciding to exact justice from anyone. They kept me focused and intent on the eradication of the people who have been and still are causing pain to others, including me. Somehow the blast from the gun and the falling body made the hate dissipate. Mainly because there wouldn't be anything left to hate.

I hadn't always hated. In fact I had been the opposite of hate, always comforting, always caring, always thinking good thoughts no matter what. Even about bad people. I would treat my enemies in school with kindness no matter how much they bullied or smeared my name. One fact was evident, however, they always got their Comeuppance.

One senior in High School hated me because, as a Freshman, I took her place as lead singer in our all girls choir. She would purposely crash into me in the halls or slap my books out of my hands. She spread rumors that I was a slut, her word for me as she passed by me. I would just smile and send sweet thoughts her way. This went on my entire first year of high school until her Senior Graduation night. That night her drunk boyfriend took a corner too fast in his daddy's convertible. They crashed into a billboard and she was instantly decapitated. I sang at her funeral with an angelic smile on my face.

Somewhere in the Bible it says to be kind to your enemies; your goodness will burn like hot coals on their heads. I stopped using that technique a long time ago. I learned the nicer you are to some bully's, the meaner they get. I want them gone by my hand...now. Am I saying prayers and kindness don't work? Let's just say I don't like giving control of my body and spirit over to anyone, real or unreal. I have seen it work, however it's too random and unreliable. I want quick results.

Also, patience can turn into an excuse to not act. Let someone or some god take care of the problem. I guess you could say I've crossed over to the other side, but these are evil people we're talking about here. In my mind, I'm the good guy. Girl, actually.

OK, I need to get back to concentrating on my personal pain. I have a particular disdain for this mark and want to be sure and send that bullet with all the physician's precision I can muster.

CHAPTER 2

He was washing his car in the parking lot of the barracks I had just come out of on a beer run to the little market on post. As I passed by he gave me a warm hello as he stood to hose off the roof. I smiled, taking in his tall physique and handsome face. "Hello," is all I said as I crossed in front of his car heading for the store, smiling to myself the whole way.

Once in the store I quickly purchased a six pack, hoping I'd pass him again before he had finished and left. I tried not to walk too fast as I headed back to the barracks and saw he was still there.

Oh good, I thought, what should I say? Should I just ignore him and see if he says anything? Should I stop and ask who he was, where he lived, would he like to go out? I chose the later, however, a much watered down inquisition. He saw me approaching and stood still as I came near and said, "You must have just arrived. I know everyone here but I don't know you, but I'd like to."

Thank goodness, I didn't have to break the ice and his question was an easy one.

"Yes, I just got in yesterday," I said.

"Are you going to drink all those beers by yourself?" he said grinning.

"No, I'm going to share with some people I met this morning," I answered laughing.

"Wow, here only one day and you've already made some drinking buddies," he countered.

I chuckled and considered inviting him to join in but thought better of it. "I'd invite you to share but I see you missed a spot on the fender so you still have cleaning to do," I said grinning, as I turned to leave.

"My name is Scott McConnell and what's yours," he asked.

"Mine is Kiftin, or Kif," I said, "Kiftin O'Tool."

"That's an unusual name and there's a lot of Scottish in there," he observed, adding, "I guess we have that in common," at which we both grinned.

"Well, I'd better get these to the party before they get warm. I don't want to make enemies on my first day. Nice meeting you."

"I'll see you around, I'll make sure of that," he said. I turned and left for the barracks, energized with the excitement of a potential connection.

The four people I'd met earlier were busy playing poker at a table when I walked in with the beer. Two males and two females noisily teasing each other and all smoking cigarettes. The air was thick with smoke and the smell of dirty socks. The walls had nudes and beer signs. This must be the boys room, I surmised as I put the beers on a bureau.

I had been invited to this get together by one of the girls I had met in the bathroom that morning so I didn't know if the foursome were two couples or just friends. Either way, they didn't stop their game when I entered or acknowledge the beer I had brought.

I was bored already and a little put off. They were ignoring me so I opened a beer and sat on the edge of a bottom bunk bed. They were probably from some part of the country where acknowledging newcomers wasn't called for in these kinds of situations.

After being introduced to more sophisticated social scenes in my previous years, beer and poker parties ranked very low in how I liked to spend my time. The young man I had met in the parking lot gave me hope that I wasn't surrounded by immaturity. He was well spoken, polite and oh so charming.

I sat and finished my beer and then headed for the door, still unnoticed. Oh well, I thought, I have unpacking to do anyway so I walked out and headed to the staircase that led to the women's rooms on the third floor.

CHAPTER 3

I hadn't gone into the military intentionally. It was the last thing I thought I'd be doing with my life. I had already had many experiences by the time I was given an M16 rifle, starting with joining in protest marches against the Vietnam war and for women's rights in San Francisco where I moved after high school and a year of junior college in my hometown.

Having worked at company's where the men had control over all the women including how long our skirts should be in S.F.; banning me from smoking a tobacco pipe in Cambridge, Mass.; being used as sexual window dressing for a Boston furrier; being blatantly asked for sex or blow jobs in order to keep my job while working in Europe after my husbands death. The military was just one more male bastion of control I would have to deal with. By then I knew the drill; don't make waves.

My run-ins with men had started with my father who openly called me stupid, ugly (I'm not) and voiced his dislike of me to everyone within earshot whenever he saw me. He did this because, unlike my mother, I bristled at his control by gender. He knew that I knew he was an ego driven, selfish tyrant with little empathy or desire to understand or nurture his only daughter.

I prayed he would die. He did die when I was 20, still living in San Francisco. Comeuppance? Who knows... possibly.

CHAPTER 4

After living in Europe and the East coast after my years in San Francisco, I moved back home with my mom to attend college and try to get some sort of connection with her.

My mother could never understand or relate to a daughter who would never be satisfied with settling down, having children and keeping her opinions to herself. She kept her mouth shut while my father verbally bashed me and hid when he came home raging drunk instead of standing up to him and protecting me. This didn't win her any points with me either. Our mutual dislike of each other was obvious to us both; but at least I wanted to try to fix it.

Once back with my mom, I attended a semester of college and a year of cosmetology school and eventually got my beauticians license.

I thought I would enjoy the artistic aspect of it but my back would be in excruciating pain by days end. After a year of popping pain killers and drinking copious amounts of alcohol, I started considering a new career.

I eventually moved in with two roommates in a house where they had pool parties and drugs galore, which were all illegal at the time. I had learned from my time in San Francisco to steer clear of the hard stuff after a few friends died from taking mystery pills or shooting up heroin.

So I had already packed a lot of living in by the time I was 26. This was the age Uncle Sam took over my life. I'll tell you how it happened. It's funny now, but back then I thought my life was ruined.

CHAPTER 5

One of my roommates was a girl named Sherry. She was my age, originally from S. CA, and worked at a clinic in town. One of the doctors at the clinic kept her supplied with drugs and I suspected she was perpetually high on cocaine, along with marijuana.

She and the owner of the house were always either talking about smoking or dealing marijuana, while I spent my free time out drinking with my hairdresser friends. I didn't like cocaine, it made me sleepy, (it does have that effect on some people) and marijuana made me sensibly paranoid.

Six months after living in this house that could be raided at any moment, Sherry asked me if I would go with her to Oakland.

"Why on Earth would you want to go there?" I had asked.

She said she wanted to go see a recruiter about joining the military so she could get her nurses training for free. I had told her earlier that I had lived in San Francisco and she offered to get a hotel room there and I could show her the city after she saw the recruiter.

Why not, I thought. Where's the harm? Besides, I did want to visit S. F. and see it through more mature eyes. Mine, not hers.

"Alright," I told her, and we coordinated our days off from our jobs.

I really had never connected with Sherry, mainly because she talked in short bursts of nonsensical musings, along with inappropriate laughter (which I attributed to the pot she smoked nonstop) that had nothing to do with anything around us. Her mind was perpetually in Alice's wonderland.

I hadn't spent much time as a passenger in her car and was a bit worried about her driving the four hours it took to get to

Oakland. I needn't have as she insisted I drive because I knew the way and if we got pulled over, she wouldn't get arrested. Her talking gibberish alone would have gotten her arrested.

We arrived at the huge, all services recruiting facility around 11:00 on a Friday and headed for the Army recruiter. She had been told the Army was the best military branch for getting nurses training.

While she sat close to the recruiter, practically sitting on his lap with cocaine enthusiasm, I found a comfy chair and started reading a magazine.

It wasn't long before they both got my attention and asked me to come over and listen in. The recruiter was especially eager and said the words $10,000.00. I don't need to tell you I pulled my chair closer.

Sherry was bursting with eagerness to tell me the good news, but she did let the recruiter explain.

"I can get you both in on the buddy system. You would go in together and go through boot camp and training and then you'd be stationed wherever you wanted, together. How does Hawaii sound? Plus we'll throw in a $10,000.00 bonus just for joining."

"Oh no, the military is not for me," I said. "I'm a confirmed hippie liberal and don't believe in wars. I also don't take orders very well."

"Well, as a woman you're exempt from combat but you can take advantage of bonus money, getting an education and free travel," he reasoned.

Now Sherry is practically on her knees begging me to go along with this out of body experience.

The recruiter said, "Well, it's lunch time so I tell you what, here's $10.00 for each of you. Go have lunch on me and you can talk about it and meet me back here in an hour."

He told us about a bar right across from the building we were in that had great food and of course lots of alcohol. So we crossed the street and commenced to having a liquid lunch along with a plate of nachos. I'm sure the bar got kickbacks from the military for their service of getting candidates drunk enough to enlist.

Sherry could barely contain herself gushing about how great it would be to go to Hawaii, get our education paid for and get $10k. It was like winning the lottery! She was capitalizing on my telling her on the way down to Oakland that I needed to find another line of work because of my back pain.

"Yes, and think of what good shape we'll get in from boot camp," she gushed.

Well, I did need to shed some liquor acquired fat from all the drinking I was doing at my job. I was thinking this as we slammed back our third Jim Beam and coke and another order of nachos.

Once back at the recruiters, things went so fast it was all over before I knew what hit me. The recruiter hadn't taken his lunch at all because he'd been busy typing up the contracts with our names on them to sign. He had Hawaii brochures laid out on the table and he got right down to brass tacks. He cranked up the sales pitch because after all, we owed him.

Sherri was the first to scribble her name on her contract while I sat there smoking cigarettes, inhaling them like they were pure oxygen.

I insisted he go over everything and he said he would but that the swearing in ceremony was only 15 minutes away and if he couldn't get us in there we'd have to come back the next day. Sherry pointed out we couldn't do that because we had San Francisco to explore.

What the hell! I signed and before I could put the pen down he was hustling us off to the swearing in room down the hall. I took the lead and they walked behind me, Sherri talking, no doubt rambling on about something totally unrelated to what we were about to do.

When we got to the room an MP was standing in the doorway and said, "Single file, walk in and stand in line and no smoking or talking."

People were lining up vertically instead of horizontally in a loose formation. I figured Sherri was behind me.

After the room filled up a Sergeant came in and said, "Raise your right hand and repeat after me…and the rest I tuned out. I solemnly swear, blah, blah, uphold the Constitution… blah, blah, and it was over in one minute.

We were told to go upstairs where we would pee in a cup and be examined by a doctor to make sure we were healthy enough to die in war.

I turned to talk to Sherri but she was nowhere in sight. I figured her cocaine had propelled her out the door after the swearing in and that she was either way ahead in line or she was way behind me.

After following the line to the doctor's exam room, a man in a lab coat, who looked like he lived on Skid Row, listened to my heart and passed me. I went searching for Sherry. She was waiting for me at the recruiters desk looking like she had been told of a death in her family.

"Well Sherry," I said, "It's you and me off to Hawaii." She knew what she had to tell me would really piss me off and it did.

"I didn't swear in," she said, "The recruiter told me they do drug testing and if the test comes up positive I can't go in the military."

I was livid. "Did it occur to you to tell me this before I gave my life for government use," I said angrily.

"The recruiter wouldn't let me," she wailed.

"Oh goddammit," was all I could say.

I would have gone ballistic but there were MP's everywhere and I didn't want to get court martialed on my first day.

Once in her car though I cried out like a wounded hyena while she sat as far from me as she could get, the silly, perpetual, drug addled grin she always wore wiped clean off her face. "No S.F. for you," was all I could say as I headed for the freeway back to Redding.

I had signed up for delayed entry to give myself six months to get my affairs in order and to plan where I could bury Sherry's body before I became cannon fodder.

In hindsight I should have been kinder to Sherry. She would have been a lamb to slaughter in boot camp. The Army also dodged a bullet by her not enlisting as her reality-departed brain would have gotten whole squadrons killed in battle.

CHAPTER 6

As I sat on the plane for the four hour flight to Hawaii, compliments of Uncle Sam, I reflected on my life so far. I had lived a very 'fly by the seat of my pants' kinda life up until joining the Army. I had lived by my wits and knew that I could always come up to the surface when thrown overboard.

I was either fearless or stupid but I knew I would survive. My ability to adapt would soon be put to the test. A very hard test whose passing would mean life or death.

But for now I would soon be in paradise with three months worth of basic training and two of AIT already logged. It was Spring and it was gorgeous. I had gotten into the best shape of my life and wore my long blond hair down on time off work so I was ready for adventure.

After dropping off my backpack and changing into shorts and a crop top, my bunkmate came into the room. She was friendly enough, but only after I assured her I wouldn't rat her out when she had her boyfriend sleep over, which was a dischargeable offense.

I was eager to look around so I went downstairs and explored. There was a small PX, 20 yards from the barracks I was in so I went in and bought items for my 'room'. I got a popcorn maker that could also be used as a makeshift hotplate, since rules and regs I had to read and signed said, No Hotplates. Microwaves hadn't been invented yet. I could use it to cook with when the mess hall was closed. I also bought beer and a cooler and headed back to the barracks.

The first floor of the barracks had a rec. room, another room with an unstocked bar and pool tables and the mess hall that served both the barracks I was in and the one next door. The remainder of the post was houses and duplexes for married couples and officers. There was also the Full Bird and Generals mansions high on a hill, overlooking the cannon fodder below.

When I reached my room door I heard someone say, "Hi." I turned my head and it was Lauren, the girl I had met that morning in the bathroom. She stopped at the door two down from me and said, "Hey, where'd you go? The game broke up right after you left."

I said,"I'm not a card player." to which she replied,

"Well, thanks for the beer. I'd be glad to drive you around the island and show you the best hangouts."

"That would be great, how about now." I said.

She laughed and said, "You're bored already, huh? Come on down to my room and we'll figure out a way to unbore you."

I smiled and said, "OK, let me get this contraband in my room and I'll be right there."

Before we left for a drive, we went to the mess hall for lunch. As we were about to leave, who should walk by but Scott.

He stopped at our table and said, "How lucky can I get, seeing you twice in one day." I laughed and introduced him to Lauren, finding out later she knew who he was. "I'm headed over to the field for a tag football game if you want to come watch," he offered. Lauren neither said hello or smiled at him. The first 'red flag' I ignored.

"Lauren is taking me on a little driving tour. I can't wait to see the island," I said. "Well have fun and take your camera," he said and sauntered off.

"How did he know I'm an avid photographer?" I said after he left.

"It must be kismet," she smirked. "Actually, everyone who comes here takes copious photos. It is Hawaii after all."

Lauren and I went to her car and drove off post headed for Highway 1 that goes around the whole island. She took me to downtown Waikiki and showed me the military's hotel, The Hale Koa which is on prime real estate right on the beach. We parked there and she took me to a patio bar where we ordered drinks and looked at the Diamond Head view and the ocean. Lauren filled me in on her job as a secretary at Company Headquarters and told me about her boyfriend Lenny. She had been stationed in Hawaii for over a year and she and Lenny had been together for almost that long. By the time I told her my enlistment story we were both half drunk laughing and knew we'd be friends. We had a pu pu platter then headed back so she could see Lenny who had to work that Saturday.

On the way back to the barracks we passed the field where the football game was being played and I spotted Scott right away. My first day in Hawaii wasn't even over but already I was having those excited crush feelings. "Hey, slow down there," my brain said, but I argued with it and said "Why should I?"

CHAPTER 7

My MOS, or job, was driver and I was assigned to the motor pool on post. I soon found out that I had been lucky being assigned to Ft. Shafter Headquarters instead of Schofield Barracks. Headquarters was where the officers lived; the higher ups in the circle of mansions that all faced a helicopter pad so they wouldn't have to walk too far to get to whatever war was going on.

The cars in the motorpool were unmarked and looked like civilian sedans. That's because we mostly were assigned to pick up world dignitaries and officers. Many of our pickups were at the Oahu Airport and the Hale Koa Resort where they would be staying while in Hawaii when they arrived. I quickly learned all the shortcuts to take to do my pickups, was friendly and helpful to first time visitors and soon had requests from repeat visitors to be their driver while they were on the island.

There were many days I would circle Oahu numerous times as it only takes 2 hours to drive around the whole island. Oahu has a base for all military branches so it wouldn't be unusual to go to all four in one day. There was also TAMC, the big pink hospital that sat high on a hill that all military branches used. I really enjoyed my job as I was able to be out and about and meet people from all over the world. I always acted professionally, saluted when I needed to and was a safe driver.

The carpool Master Sergeant and I became good friends and he and I could laugh together and were always teasing each other. He started giving me fun assignments like sending me to do pickups at luaus and award ceremonies where I would be fed while waiting for my passengers.

One such assignment he gave me was picking up a full bird colonel on a Saturday. I said I'd be glad to do it and bought the officer a lei while waiting for him at the airport. I told him I'd be happy to drive him around the Island and show him all the posts after he told me he would be in charge of all transportation for all branches for the Pacific Rim. We spent the day together, telling each other about ourselves and having a good time. His last assignment had been Washington DC, and he said he had never been to Hawaii. He was a lifer, and I figured he was probably around mid 60's. I showed him where he could shop but he told me he had been assigned a cook and a housekeeper. They were civilians working on post. Must be nice for him, I thought.

When I arrived at the carpool on Monday morning my Master Sergeant called me into his office and said the colonel had requested I be assigned to him full time and would have a small office next to his at headquarters. Not too shabby, I thought, entering the inner bastions of HQ. I had lucked out.

CHAPTER 8

My luck with getting something started with Scott was up and down. I wanted it to get past the small talk and really get to know him. He hadn't asked me out yet and it had been two weeks since I had arrived. We would bump into each other occasionally but each time he'd just say hi then go back to talking to whomever he was with or just keep walking. Oh well, so much for that.

One Saturday, Lauren and I went to a cookout on the North Shore where there was a secluded beach designated for military R&R. There were cabins that could be rented and a large park-like area with BBQs. Lauren's boyfriend met up with her and to give them time together I went on a walk down the beach. As I passed a group along the way, someone called my name and as I turned, Scott was by my side, walking with me. I was elated. What a perfect day in paradise! We spent the rest of the day together and he asked if I wanted to ride back to post with him and his friends. Would I! We sat in the back seat and talked and laughed and then he kissed me. It wasn't a passionate kiss, more like a 'I like you' kiss.

Back at post, it was late so we had to go our separate ways because 10 o'clock was cutoff for visitors of the opposite sex in the rooms. He lived in the barracks next to mine and we lingered in the parking lot between them, where we had met and he finally asked me out. We made plans to go to the drive-in the next weekend and he gave me another kiss and we parted.

CHAPTER 9

Ahhh, glorious Saturday, the day I would finally spend time with Scott. I spent the day shopping with Lauren for something to wear and having lunch and a drink in downtown Oahu. We got back to the barracks at six and I went about getting ready for my date at eight oclock.

When he showed up at my door we hugged and he took my hand and led me downstairs. I felt like a princess and completely at ease and happy. He told me Oahu was really big on drive In movies and the one we drove to had back to back screens. There were long lines so there was a long wait to get in and Scott was visibly irritated and impatient. He even honked his horn like that was going to make the line go faster. Once through the ticket gate he once again grumbled that the only spaces left were on the outside perimeter. He drove up and down the lanes, determined to get closer. I told him to just pick a space in the last row, but he ignored me. The movie started and we hadn't even parked yet. "Scott, it's OK to park in the last row, we will still see it." He finally parked and opened his door and without a word headed for the concession stand. 'Well, that was rude', I thought. He came back with beer and popcorn but we ate and drank in silence, his mood setting the tone for our date.

The movie was Body Heat with Kathleen Turner and William Hurt. It turned out to be a very memorable film for me that I referred back to many times in my life. Life can truly imitate art. The woman's character ends up with all the money and escapes to an island after disposing of the male character.

First dates are always a little awkward and a lot stressful. We probably should have opted for a drive so we could talk. Luckily, the movie was good and had lots of sexual tension so I could gage his ability to control himself. He did, but he also became very uncommunicative.

When the movie was over he drove to a beach parking lot where I was hoping we could talk but he acted very distracted and uncomfortable. I started getting frustrated and uncomfortable myself and when I asked him if everything was on, he got angry and blurted out, "I'm just thinking about something, allright, so stop questioning me."

Oh crap, I thought, a wacko! I responded by getting out and walking towards the road where I hoped to catch a ride back to base. He started the car and I assumed he would drive away but he came alongside me and stopped the car and got out. I just kept walking and he walked alongside me apologizing and asking me to get in the car. When I didn't stop he ran in front of me and blocked me and said, "I'm sorry, I'll take you back."

I stopped and said, "You had better take me back because people know I'm out with you and if you try anything and I end up missing, the MP's will have your name," and with that I got in the car.

Once we were on the road he spent the entire way back apologizing while I said nothing but just sat there, disappointed and terrified. When we pulled into the parking lot he drove up to the stairs to the barracks and I jumped out and ran upstairs, glad I was away from him.

For the next few weeks I layed low, barely speaking to anyone at work or afterwards. I was thoroughly annoyed with myself that in spite of Scott's behavior, I couldn't stop thinking about him. I was very sexually attracted to him and every time I saw him either on post or in the mess hall, my heart would skip a beat and I would feel flushed and excited. It was like his very being had this power over me I couldn't control.

On more than one occasion when we would pass each other in the hall he would slow down approaching me and very gently say, "Hi, how are you?" I was sure he could see my knees buckle when this happened and that he knew I knew we weren't over yet. It was like this animal magnetism that was at once exhilarating, yet terrifying. For the next few months

I tried to meet other men on post to get over him, occupying my time with Lauren and other female friends I was making. I found myself getting obsessive about looking for his car in the parking lot to see if he was on post and looking out the window of my room to see if he was playing football in the field in front of the barracks.

CHAPTER 10

A few weeks after my tumultuous date with Scott, I went with Lauren to see a popular band at the island's football stadium. It was jam packed but Lenny was holding seats for us and after much row searching we finally settled in for the show. Everyone was drinking beer and the atmosphere was electric with the sexual tension of thousands of enlisted personnel. The band was one of my favorites and the female lead singer was as famous and popular as you can get.

I was there, but my mind was elsewhere. I figured Scott would be there and I spent the entire time scanning the audience to see if he was. It was senseless, really, but I couldn't stop obsessing about him. I was angry with myself over this because I was channeling an unrequited school girl crush devoid of the reality that we weren't meant to be. Then that all changed with a visit to the bathroom.

As I made the long stadium mountain climb up to the restrooms I forced myself to stop looking for him and concentrated on getting myself ready mentally for a new love interest. This meant retreating back to my core belief that I was worthy of someone being as into me and I was into them.

All these thoughts flew right out my window of resolve when I came face to face with Scott. He pulled me out of the stupidly long girls line to the bathroom and propelled me forward to the mens restroom. As usual, there was no line and I decided to take advantage after he told me he would stand guard outside my stall. As copious amounts of beer pee drained out of me, I was simultaneously filled with an overwhelming feeling of being special and cared for but also raw anxiety. Like someone standing before an oncoming train, I knew I would be helpless to move out of the way of the animal attraction Scott and I had for one another. I had to find out about him; his past, his hopes and dreams, and how I could fit into it all.

By the time I was ready to open the door to the stall, I had made a plan. I would tell him I wanted a date do over. After exiting the restroom we both instinctively headed for a secluded area nearby and he said, "I can't stop thinking about you, please see me again." We were standing very close and looking straight into each other's eyes, right into our souls, and I leaned in and lightly kissed him and said, "That would make me very happy. Come by tomorrow night at 7 and we can talk then," I continued as I backed away and headed for my seating section.

"I'll be there," he said.

Back in my seat, I got Lauren's attention and said, "I can't believe what just happened," and proceeded to tell her why I was positively beaming. The expression on her face was not the smile I was expecting.

"You have been saying all week that his anger really frightens you. Why are you willing to see him again?"

I couldn't explain in words how he made me feel but I could sense that Lauren didn't approve. She had reminded me earlier that day that he was the first man on post to show me any attention but there were plenty of other men around and I should look around more. I explained that Scott and I hadn't had a chance to talk on our first date and I wanted to know more. The concert continued but I was in a dreamworld and barely paid attention.

CHAPTER 11

When Scott came to my room, I was dressed in shorts and a loose button blouse. I was intent on finding out more about him. I decided to invite him in and we could have some beers and talk. I liked to draw portraits and had a sketch pad and pencil ready and asked him if he would like me to draw him while we talked. He came in and sat in a nearby chair while I sat on my bed facing him.

As I began drawing I asked him where he was from and how long he'd been on the island. He said he was from Lubbock, Texas and had six months to go before being discharged. He answered no when I asked if he was going back there when he got out. "No, I want to live on the island," he stated emphatically. My face flushed with joy at this information. If he had said yes, there wouldn't be much point in continuing on with him. It's not like you can just go up to your superiors in the military and say you're quitting so you can follow your love interest around.

We ended the night at 10 pm and we hugged and kissed for a while before he left for his barracks. Like 10 year olds, the military wants it's children tucked in bed sleeping so they can be refreshed and ready for war the next day. We all hated the rules associated with living in the barracks and we all knew the only way off post was to marry and either get housing on post once you came to the top of a long waiting list, or receive COLA and live off post. Some made agreements to marry to do just that, then get an annulment once they were restationed or ETS'd out of the military. It was highly illegal to make such an agreement but many made the choice and took the chance of getting caught.

According to Ben, a coworker I knew, Scott was married in just such an agreement. Ben had early on expressed his interest in me and had asked me out numerous times. I had always turned him down. I thought he was making things up about Scott so I would date him, not Scott. Ben went on to tell me one day at work that he had bunked with Scott and knew all about him. I was gobsmacked by the things he was telling me. Ben saw my alarm and continued on. The girl Scott married and was living with accused him of abuse and turned him into his Master Sergeant and also JAG for marrying her under false pretenses. She claimed he admitted to her he had only married her in order to live off post. She was reassigned to Germany after getting an annulment and Scott had been arrested and questioned with conspiracy to defraud the government. "This all happened just before you got here," Ben told me. He went on to tell me that somehow Scott hadn't been prosecuted or discharged. "I've seen Scott in action," Ben said, "he can smooth talk and lie his way out of anything. He always blames somebody else."

That evening when Scott came over, I confronted him with what Ben told me. Scott quickly stated he was innocent and the girl he had married was crazy and he was the one who was getting the annulment. He told me he had loved her and his attorney had told him there was no way the military could prove what she claimed. I was suspicious but I found myself believing him and defending him. This was probably why he had acted so erratically on our dates. He was stressed out from being falsely accused.

The weekend after Ben told me of Scott's marriage, Scott took me to a couples' house off post. They were gone and Scott said he was house sitting for them. We made dinner after grocery shopping and Scott and I talked into the evening. He laid out a plan to be together. He was to ETS out of the military in 4 months and he would go back to Texas, live with his dad, and work at a meat packing job in Lubbock that paid good wages, save money for six months and return to Hawaii and we could marry. He said he knew I wanted out of the barracks and he didn't want me meeting other men. Oh how sweet, I thought. I told him I would think about it.

Back in the barracks I did think about it and they were not positive thoughts. Besides the accusations against him, I also thought about one weekend when he said he'd be babysitting this four year old girl for a single female friend of his from work. I said I could come over and keep him company.

He hesitated and said, "I don't think my friend would like that, I'll have to ask her." I knew where this coworker lived because once Scott said he had to take her something when he and I were together. When we arrived at her duplex he said he'd be back in a second, but 30 minutes went by while I sat waiting in the car.

When he returned he said, "Sorry I took so long, she kept talking." That weekend he went to her house to 'babysit' and I couldn't help myself. I bought a six pack and went to her house.

When Scott opened the door he said, "What are you doing here?"

"I want to keep you company," I told him. "Well, we'll have a beer but then you have to leave," he said.

The little four year old girl was shy with me at first but acted very frightened around Scott. She was actually clinging to me whenever he came near. He made no attempt to engage with her and I thought it very strange a grown man would volunteer to babysit a child. Another red flag I chose to ignore.

I finished my beer and left, feeling humiliated and disappointed in myself for chasing after him. Three days later while I was coming back from the PX, I saw an MP car stop Scott who was driving, about to enter the parking lot. I went around the back entrance so I wouldn't be seen and went to my room and watched out my window that faced the street. The MP's were walking around his car looking at the tires and at first I thought they stopped him for some illegal turn or something related to driving. After writing down information they got looking at the tires, they left and Scott pulled his car into a parking space in front of the barracks.

I had a feeling he was coming to my room so I picked up a book so I could act like I was reading. Soon after there was a knock at my door and I knew it was him. I let him in and went and sat on the bed and offered him a beer. He acted like it was just an ordinary day, making small talk and sitting next to me. I played along for a while and finally asked, "I was coming back from the PX and saw the MP's pull you over, why?"

Without hesitation he said, “Oh, you know that couple whose house we were at when they were gone?” he said, “Well they have accused me of stealing their tires,” he said nonchalantly.

“What?” I blurted out, standing up. I had been there when he took all his tires off his car and put on the new tires stacked up in the couples garage. I could have been an accessory to a crime.

“Well, they had told me I could have them but now they’re saying I stole them.”

“Did you steal them?” I asked, shaking.

“The MP’s let me go after I told them it was their word against mine.”

“But did you steal them?” I sputtered. After thinking, he decided to stick to his story, saying ‘No’, with his words but his body language screamed, ‘YES, I stole them’!!

Omg, who is this guy?

CHAPTER 12

Although I continued with our, or rather his, plan of going to Texas than coming back to Oahu, I was starting to get a sinking feeling concerning Scott. Then, the hammer fell. A month before Scott was to ETS, he was court martialed for using his mess hall card while living off post with his first 'wife'. The story he gave me was that he didn't know he wasn't supposed to use it after moving off post. He told me the military was releasing him anyway on a dishonorable discharge because the coworker who's little girl he 'babysat' accused him of stealing from her also. The only charge that could be proven was the mess hall card use but the accusations against him were piling up so the military found him unfit to serve. On top of that, Ben took me aside at work and said, "You don't want to hang around Scott, that dude is into really bad shit." Within a few days, Scott was flown off the Island back to Texas in a military transport plane. I was devastated and in total shock.

I was determined to forget about him but it was hard, especially because he called me everyday from Texas. There was only one phone booth on every floor of the barracks and it was answered by whomever passed by or sat there waiting for an expected call. The first week I would tell whomever came to get me when he called, to tell him I wasn't there. He kept calling anyway.

I'm ashamed to admit it but I was obsessed with him. Everything inside of me was telling me to help him. To love him into decency. It could be my purpose in life to show him how to behave responsibly.

If I had known then what I know now of Narcissists, capable of domestic violence, I would have shielded my heart. Or would I have? My father was abusive, especially to me, his only daughter, and was run out of our hometown after he beat up a man, almost killing him. The man had been his best friend, had helped out when our family had moved from Los Angeles when I was four, pulling strings to get jobs for my father. He was paid back with a concussion and disloyalty.

I have since learned that when a child is abused by a parent, they will unconsciously seek out a mate who produces similar high anxiety. Having an overwhelming desire to 'fix' the mate is really a deep desire to fix the relationship with the abusive parent. That and high anxiety is a familiar emotion and while destructive, it's what the abused person knows and is used to. It was this mindset that led me to start taking Scott's phone calls.

CHAPTER 13

Initially, when I took Scott's calls it was mostly him doing the talking, mostly about how sorry he was. He sounded so sad and alone that I slowly developed deep empathy and forgiveness and soon our talks were back to making plans to be together.

He said he was saving his money and would be back on the island in six months. He asked me to marry him and I said yes, I will. I was elated and was so ready to get out of the barracks and to live off post and fix this man.

I started making plans for my wedding. I bought material to make my own dress with a borrowed sewing machine and worked on it each day. I made arrangements with the on post pastor to officiate the ceremony and booked a story book castle that was part of a children's amusement park for the wedding location. I reserved a cabin at the military's private beach for our honeymoon, the same beach where we had walked on the sand months before. I did all this with some of the bonus money I had gotten when enlisting.

When I asked Lauren to be my bridesmaid and Lenny to be best man they had looked at each other with concerned faces. They knew Scott had been thrown out of the military and were rightly shocked that I was willing to marry him. After I told them he had changed and learned his lesson, they both agreed, although totally lacking enthusiasm.

CHAPTER 14

Time passed quickly after Scott left. He and I talked on the phone almost daily with him calling me from a payphone. I was happy at work, knowing I would be out of the barracks soon and knew I had an exciting future.

In January, Scott returned and I picked him up at the airport in a car I had bought while he was away.

Seeing him again exiting the plane ramp made my whole body tingle and the joy I felt was indescribable. He saw me and hurried over, hugging me like there was no tomorrow. We kissed deeply and long, oblivious to people around us.

We picked up his luggage and headed for my car, talking excitedly. I told him about the arrangements I had made for our wedding, the dress I had designed and sown and the date I had reserved the castle and the chaplain. I had picked mid January for our wedding, just two weeks after his return. We would have to take a chance with him staying in my room until then. I was glad my roommate had her boyfriend sleeping over most nights. I won't tell if you won't, I told her. Luckily, the Army didn't go so far as to search our rooms every night at 10:00 and escort people out.

CHAPTER 15

The wedding was only attended by a few people, mainly because the park charged for each guest and it wasn't cheap. It was attended by mostly personnel from the motor pool and my friends. Scott had no one. I thought about inviting the motor pool Master Sergeant and my Colonel, but decided not too, although they both knew I was getting married. I had hired a photographer, a friend who lived in my barracks and had a reception set up in the room with the bar and pool table I had seen the first day there.

It was a fun day and night, culminating with Scott and I going to our favorite night club, still wearing our wedding attire. I had rented a traditional Hawaiian white shirt and slacks for him, along with a red waist sash and a red and white flower lei. I was dressed in a floor length taffeta dress with off the shoulder pouf sleeves and a red flower head garland and carried a bouquet of red and while flowers. We were quite the spectacle at the nightclub and were bought numerous drinks along with well wishes.

The next day we headed to the cabin on the North Shore I had reserved to start our honeymoon and our lives as husband and wife. We had the cabin for the weekend and I had gotten a week off by my Colonel. We needed that time to look for someplace to live off post. I had found out there was a long waiting list to get a duplex on post, compliments of the Army. The COLA money was very generous anyway so we got a one bedroom apartment in downtown Waikiki.

Part 2

CHAPTER 16

Like all newlyweds, Scott and I had to learn about each other's preferences, habits, what TV shows to watch and if mayonnaise was better than Miracle Whip. I learned he drank copious amounts of sweetened iced tea while I drank an equal amount of Diet Pepsi. I learned other things about him in those first six months, things I didn't like.

One was that he confessed he hadn't saved any money while in Texas. He said he had to borrow money from his dad to pay for his plane ticket. The look he saw on my face was both disappointment and anger. I had used money I had saved for the wedding but thought he would at least have money to buy me a ring. I ended up having to buy my ring with my money, to which he reminded me it was now our money. The way he said it put me in a very bad mood.

Another thing I didn't like was that he didn't try very hard to get a job. It took three months before he finally got a part time job making pizzas. His hours were in the evening so he would take my car. I really didn't know what he was doing all day but our joint bank account was soon being depleted of money, fast. He claimed he was looking for a new job because he had gotten a warning from his boss at work that if he didn't start getting to work on time he would be fired. I told him I would take him to work and pick him up and I could tell he was not happy about that arrangement. I wasn't happy either because that meant I had to stay up late to go get him.

With our work schedules we didn't see much of each other, only two nights midweek. He always worked Saturday and Sunday evenings, the days I had off. We really couldn't go too far because his weekend schedule was between mid afternoon until midnight.

We both started feeling the pressures of marriage and both of us were drinking way too much alcohol. I had quit smoking at his request, on our wedding day, so I didn't have that habit that had always calmed me down in the past. Tensions were very high the night we decided to go to our favorite nightclub and the fun we had there on our wedding night had vanished into the past.

Scott, I found out, had a jealous streak in him. When he was in the bathroom, I was asked to dance and since it wasn't a slow dance, I accepted and went a few feet on the dance floor from where Scott had left me. When he returned he was not happy. In fact, he was livid. He came on the dance floor, grabbed my hand and pulled me out the door. His grip was very tight and I complained to which he said, "It serves you right, now get in the car."

We drove home in silence until we pulled into our parking stall. As he turned the car off, I apologized. Truth be told, I was very flattered that he was jealous.

Without a word, he got out of the car, came around to my side, pulled me out of the car and slammed me up against it. I reacted by punching him in the chest so hard I broke a bone in my hand. I stood there crying while he stalked off towards the building. I ran after him and asked him to take me to the hospital to which he yelled, "Take yourself." I began to cry and said, "I think my hand is broken." His demeanor changed and he gruffly said, "Go get in the car, I'll take you."

At the hospital my hand was X-rayed. I had a broken bone. The intake nurse and doctor who came into my cubicle wanted to know how it happened. He told me the bone that broke can only be gotten by a clenched fist, a boxer's break, he called it.

I could have been brought up on charges if I told the truth so I made up a story about reaching for the car door handle to open it, misjudging the distance and had rammed it into the door. That seemed plausible, the doctor said and went on to tell me I would be getting a cast from my hand to my elbow.

I had a moment of panic, realizing it would be very hard to drive with a cast. The doctor said he would get me time off driving until it healed but that I would still have to report daily to the motor pool and do paperwork or whatever I was capable of. I was afraid my Colonel would replace me as the cast had to be on for 6 weeks.

Once discharged from the hospital I told Scott I was going to drive us home so I could see if the cast would interfere with my driving. It didn't hurt if I just used my thumb and index finger, but driving my own car and driving a military vehicle were totally different. I had had defensive driving classes before being stationed and was taught how to do a 360 turn around in case the enemy was coming at us. I couldn't do that maneuver with a broken hand, and because my Colonel was in charge of transportation for the entire Pacific Rim, it would look really bad if his own driver was incapacitated and could be a target. He needed a reliable driver.

CHAPTER 17

When I reported to the motor pool with my left arm in a cast and a sling, I had no idea how I would be handled by superiors. I really couldn't drive and so I was put on sick leave. There was really nothing I could do other than sit in the room where drivers waited for assignments if they had made me report everyday. I couldn't manage a broom so cleaning was out and paperwork and scheduling was handled by the Motor Pool Sargeant. After a week, my Master Sergeant told me to just stay home

Scott didn't like the idea that I'd be home all day. I found out why a year later.

The cast was making my arm and hand so itchy, it made me practically insane. I would slip a straightened wire coat hanger down into it and end up making bloody gouges into my arm. Scott did not sympathize and told me more than once, it was my own fault.

During this time, I also developed an allergic reaction to mango pollen. I had sinus infections constantly and would end up at TAMC Hospital totally suffering on numerous occasions. For this, I was assigned a TAMC doctor who became our family doctor. He met with both me and Scott who had driven me there during one of my flare ups.

Looking at my cast, he gave Scott a look that said, 'Hey bud, I have a feeling you had something to do with this'. Scott got a look on his face of surprise and innocence. The doctor asked Scott a lot of questions about whether he was employed, if he was under psychiatric care and if he had been with me when my hand was broken. The doctor had my file in front of him and must have read about how it had happened. He was also reading between the lines.

I could tell Scott wanted to tell him to f off and mind his own business but gave the same story I did about smashing it into the car door. I really wanted to say, 'Doc, what really happened is he slammed me up against the car and I reacted by punching him. And, oh by the way, can you save me and get me out of this marriage.' The doctor could tell something wasn't quite right about us.

Scott became very caring after our doctor's visit. I think he knew our doctor was on to him and that he didn't want to mess with the military if one of their investments was harmed

During my time off we actually had some fun times. We explored restaurants in Waikiki, went to watch the surfers on the North Shore and went fishing one evening with a $10.00 fishing pole meant for a child. We bonded that evening when three locals, who were fishing next to the pier we dropped our line in the water from, began laughing at us. "You won't catch anything with that pole, brah," one of them said. We both laughed and threw the line out again. All of a sudden, Scott got a bite and brought up a two foot long fish, which neither of us could identify. The locals were in shock and soon were running up to the pier asking about our bait. We had used oysters from a can we had bought along with the pole. We came home happy and I took a picture of him fake kissing it. That day was only one of a handful I could say I was happy being with him.

CHAPTER 18

Our time together seemed like it was finally beginning to gel and I thought I could playfully tease him. I was wrong. One day as we were sitting up in bed talking I said something as a joke. Right after, I went into the bathroom. While I was sitting there he came in and punched me in the chest so hard I could barely breathe. After I got up he ran into the bedroom, put his clothes on and raced out the front door. I was in shock, but I soon was crying both from pain and betrayal.

When Scott finally returned that afternoon before he had to go to work, he had a big bouquet of flowers. He found me in the living room still stunned and motionless. He came over to me and sat down and apologized. All I could say was, "Why did you hit me?" A flash of anger appeared on his face and he said, "Don't you ever insult me again." I was about to say, 'Fine, and you never hit me again', but thought better of it. Instead I apologized for insulting him, which was crazy. He was the one who needed to apologize. He threw the flowers on the couch and stalked off to the bedroom.

I should have divorced him immediately but that very week, I discovered I was pregnant. It dawned on me that he had hit me while I was pregnant. Oh my god, what should I do? I couldn't raise a child alone while in the military and without a mate. I called the number to the Military Oahu Women's Shelter and spoke with a woman who told me they had a lawyer on staff and that I should come in and talk to him. I thought I would have to go through JAG so she told me to find out but that I needed to divorce him. She said, "He will do this again, they always do. Promise me you will get away and stay away from him."

I was so torn. I had such strong feelings for Scott and knew he needed help and I was determined to find out how I could help him. I told Scott I was pregnant, hoping this news would at least keep him from hitting me.

He was ecstatic about it, which was not what I had expected. He held me and kissed me and patted my stomach while I just stood limply still, not knowing how to act. I was afraid to make him angry again. He sat down on the couch next to me and asked if I was hurt. Oh my god, is he insane? Of course I'm hurt because you hurt me!

For the remainder of the week he took me out to dinner, to the movies and exploring the North Shore as if nothing had happened. He told me he was going to be a good father and he couldn't wait for the baby to be born.

I said we'd need a bigger apartment and he agreed. We spent all our free time looking at apartments and even some houses. I also met with our doctor at TAMC and he said he would be delivering the baby.

We found a two bedroom, two bath apartment on the 16th floor of a highrise not far from my job at Fort Shafter. It had a pool and a children's playground. We moved in and spent the next few months buying furniture and household items. I was always more at ease with him out in public. He would get seriously arrested if he was seen hitting a pregnant woman. We also bought a muscle car he had seen. He worked on me relentlessly to buy it until he finally got his way. We had to use my good credit and money to purchase it because he had just started work at a fast food restaurant as a manager. He had bad credit and no credit cards even after being in the military for three years.

CHAPTER 19

My pregnancy was difficult and by month six I was ordered to bed rest by our doctor.

During this time while I was at home, a series of very upsetting events occurred. First, there was a knock on our door and when I opened it, there was a young woman who asked for Scott. I told her he was at work so she said, "Can you tell him I have the stuff?"

"What stuff?" I asked but she soon realized I wasn't in on any of this. She turned and ran to the elevator.

I knew from George that Scott had a cocaine habit but he had told me he quit when we got married. I had a hunch he was either using again, or worse yet, dealing.

My instincts directed me to his underwear drawer and after lifting up a stack of t-shirts I found a tie off hose and a syringe. I put the stack back in place and sat down on the bed, paralyzed with fear and anxiety.

When Scott came home early, he had more bad news. He had gotten fired, having been accused of stealing from the safe at work. How had he not been arrested, I wanted to know. He claimed it wasn't him but that he and the other managers were the only ones who knew the combination to the safe and the theft had occured during his shift. He did it, I knew it for sure. I knew it because he bought himself some new clothes, an expensive watch and stereo system in spite of losing his job. I knew it because I was the one who managed our money, paid our bills and gave him cash when he needed it. I hadn't given him the kind of money he was spending on himself.

I sat on the bed, dazed and pregnant and afraid to say anything. Scott meanwhile, went into the kitchen, made himself a sandwich, grabbed a beer and turned on the TV. I decided to tell him about the girl's visit earlier, hoping he would fess up. He didn't, instead made up some story about parts for his new car this girl I didn't know was going to give him. Probably stolen parts...or more than likely, cocaine.

CHAPTER 20

When Christmas was approaching Scott got a job working at a factory. He came home one night with a coworker, Kevin. After dinner, as I was cleaning up, Scott said, "I've told Kevin he could stay with us. He and his girlfriend broke up and he doesn't have a place to stay." I was furious he asked me with Kevin present but knew better than to confront him so I sat down and asked Kevin questions about himself. I instantly liked him. He was funny and sweet and very outgoing. I was relieved and by the end of the evening I told him I was happy to have him stay in our second bedroom. Kevin put his backpack in his room and I actually had a sense of safety, safer than I did with my own husband.

Christmas arrived and Scott bought me a plethora of gifts, no doubt bought with the money he had stolen. I was stunned, figuring I'd be lucky to get anything. The glow of Christmas wore off fast however, because Scott's tolerance cycle had lapsed and he was once again ready for a fight.

The fight we had was about him continually parking his car in the tow zone of our apartment building. Each time, it would mean having to go downtown and pay $150.00 to retrieve it.

By the third time we had to do this in one month, I couldn't take it anymore and scolded him like he was a toddler. His reaction was swift. He approached me and put his hands around my neck. I kneed him where it hurt and ran down the hall towards our bedroom. He caught me in no time and drug me by the hair back into the living room where he threw me on the floor and began kicking me in my back. I was screaming in pain and terrified I would have a miscarriage. Just then the front door opened and Kevin came in.

"What are you doing Scott?" Kevin yelled as he helped me off the floor.

"I don't know Kev, I came in from the bathroom and she was on the floor crying in pain." he lied.

"That's not true Kevin, he beat me up, please take me to the hospital." At this, Scott said, "I'll take her Kev, she's on medications and not making any sense." Kevin looked at me and said, "Is that ok with you?" I nodded, hoping to have Scott arrested at the hospital.

At the hospital I was put in a wheelchair because of the pain and because I was seven months pregnant. At the intake desk Scott tried to tell them he came in from the bathroom and I was on the floor moaning in pain. I called out as loud as I could manage that he was lying, that he had beat me up. Because he was a civilian, the MP's couldn't arrest him and when I was called into the exam room they actually allowed him to wheel me in. Once in the exam room he loudly said, "You'd better keep your mouth shut if you know what's good for you." Luckily, two male orderlies heard him and came into the room. One of them immediately pushed Scott up against a wall and told him to stay away from me, while the other stood by me and asked if I was OK. When I said yes, they escorted him out.

After getting checked out by the doctor I was released. I wasn't even sure he'd be waiting and had a moment of panic as to what I would do to get home. He was there waiting and looked miserable. The orderly who had helped me wheeled me out to the car, telling Scott he was lucky the Honolulu Police weren't called and then gave me the phone number for the military's Women's Shelter. I should have insisted that the police be called.

Once we were on our way home, Scott said he was, "Sorry, but you just make me so angry. You need to not make me angry." Spoken like a true abuser.

CHAPTER 21

When we got back to our apartment, Kevin was in the living room talking to his girlfriend on the phone. I had planned on taking my car and going to the shelter, but with Kevin there, I felt safe from Scott.

When Kevin hung up the phone, he confronted Scott and said, "Wow man, you beat up your pregnant wife? What are you thinking, brah?" Scott went into his song and dance about me making him mad and if I would just not do that he wouldn't have to hurt me. He then said, "Let me remind you Kevin, I'm giving you a place to live." I spoke up and said "Kevin can stay here as long as he wants. Let me remind you Scott that I pay for this apartment with money I make." With that, Scott left, angry but not wanting to beat me up with Kevin there.

Kevin was very sweet and made me some tea and sat and comforted me while I cried and asked over and over, "What am I going to do." Kevin suggested I call the police and at least report him. Kevin also said he'd stay until the baby was born but that he and his girlfriend were going to try to get back together. I was so relieved. Kevin and I hugged and he said he'd spend nights at our place but he'd be gone at work during the day. I went to bed, exhausted and drained emotionally, but relieved Kevin was looking out for me.

Scott didn't come back until three in the morning. I pretended to be asleep in case he wanted to fight. He was still sleeping when I got up and after reading an apology card he had left for me on the bathroom vanity I drove myself to the military hospital to see my family doctor. The card did make me feel like I would be safe coming back home after going to the hospital.

My doctor examined me, took an ultrasound and said the baby's heart was still beating, then told me I really needed to go to the Military Women's Shelter if Scott wouldn't leave. He then gave me a card with the shelter's phone number. I needed it because Scott had taken the one given to me by the staff at the hospital when my hand was broken. The doctor also wrote up a report that I had been the victim of domestic abuse and after examining me and taking X-rays. He told me I had bruised ribs, a huge knot on my head, bruises on my throat where he had choked me and a massive bruise on my back where he had kicked me. He also told me he had to report it to my Colonel. I asked if JAG could help me move on post but I already knew there was a waiting list a mile long and it would take a year. He told me JAG couldn't touch Scott because we didn't live on Post and he was now a civilian. He said he was very concerned for my safety and that I should call an attorney for serving Scott annulment papers.

My life was swiftly becoming unbearable. I was sick through most of my pregnancy and I was married to a psychopath, plus, even if I did divorce Scott, I would have no help moving or having the baby. I did everything I could to not be home with him. I utilized the art center on post and stayed till they closed almost every evening at 9. I made Christmas ornaments out of clay and clocks out of wood. Scott always went to bed at 9 so I was lucky there. I'm a night owl. He was usually getting ready for bed by the time I got home.

CHAPTER 22

There was an unspoken truce between us and I eventually was lulled into a sense of trust. Scott would accompany me for prenatal office visits and got very excited when the ultrasound showed the baby's heart beating. He fainted when a long needle was stuck in my navel so the nurse could draw out some amniotic fluid for testing. He also agreed to Lamaze classes but he didn't understand it after the second session so he quit.

When my due date came around, my mom flew over to help me and I was so relieved she did. I knew she could sense the tension in the house but neither of us discussed it. My water broke the weekend after she arrived and off we went to the hospital. It was a horrific birth. It took 23.5 hours. Had it gone to 24 they would have sent me for a C Section. I had gone into labor at 11:00 in the evening and so had already been awake for 12 hours before labor even began so I hadn't slept for 36 hours. Instead of laying my daughter on my stomach they had Scott whisk her away for testing while I passed out from exhaustion and slept for nine hours straight. I woke up, aching all over. My baby was almost 10 pounds and I felt like I had been ripped open by a chainsaw. I developed an episiotomy infection and was sick for weeks. Scott and my mother were very attentive but I was too out of it to do much except hold and nurse my baby in bed, then conk out for long stretches of time. Kevin was staying with his girlfriend while my mom used his bed and when Kali woke at night she would bring her to me. Scott was also caring and made most of our meals. I didn't know if my mothers presence forced him to behave but I suspected as much.

I found out the answer as soon as my mom flew back home to California and Kevin moved back in. He had been putting on a show for my mom.

I had to have an operation to deal with the infection and to repair the large gash left by the episiotomy. I had six weeks off to be with my baby after I healed. Scott and I earnestly looked for a sitter. It was a daunting task. We finally found a mom who lived in our building who had two toddlers. I found out later that she was also being beaten by her husband. After a year, she finally divorced him and moved back to the mainland with their children. That meant we were on the hunt again for a new sitter. Scott was working at a flip flop kiosk in downtown Waikiki making minimum wage and we finally decided he would stay home and take care of her.

The honeymoon Scott and I were having tending to our child ended four months after her birth. Scott and I argued in the triple story parking garage when it was discovered he had left the windows open and the doors unlocked to his vanity car and as a result my Nikon SLR had been stolen from the back seat. I wasn't so angry about the camera but the bag it was in contained all the film of pictures of our baby that hadn't been developed yet. To say he didn't react well is an understatement. Going down the stairs of the parking garage he pushed me from behind and I fell down the last three steps of the stairwell. He was holding our daughter and I had grocery bags. The groceries went everywhere with some bottles breaking and I hit the concrete wall face first. He acted concerned and said "Are you OK, you must have tripped." 'Nice try sicko, you pushed me', I thought.

By this time I had gone back to work and I had to wear dark glasses to hide the huge bruise on my left eye and cheek bone from the fall. My Colonel was suspicious when I kept the glasses on even in the building and he asked me to take them off. The makeup I had used to try and hide the huge purple bruises apparently wasn't working and he asked me point blank if I had been hit by my husband. I truthfully told him I fell down a staircase, I just didn't tell him I had been pushed.

You're probably wondering why I stayed with this man hell bent on killing me. I'll tell you why. After the garage incident and after my Colonel insisted I take steps to protect myself, I told Vince I wanted an annulment, divorce, whatever, I wanted him gone.

His reaction added an extra layer of chills down my spine that I already had just being with him. He said, "Fine, you go ahead and divorce me but while you're at work one day I'll take Kali with me and we'll fly back to Texas where you'll never find us. You won't know when I'll do it and you'll come home to an empty apartment and an empty bank account." He knew the military wouldn't allow me time off to pursue him and I knew then I was screwed. He had me held prisoner.

I did take the advice of my Colonel and reported all the abuse incidents to our family doctor who pleaded with me to divorce Scott. When I told him what Scott had told me about taking Kali to the mainland where I would never find them, he sat silent. He knew and I knew that I was indeed screwed.

CHAPTER 23

Realizing I had no one to turn to for help other than the shelter, some part of me died inside. It was the optimistic, happy, trusting part and all my behavior became that of a hunted animal. I was at his mercy and he was gaining more and more control over me everyday. I no longer laughed or expressed myself. I felt weak and powerless and did not like what I was turning into. I had lost my voice, my will to defend myself. He had beaten me into submission. My body was living in Paradise but my soul was living in hell. My Colonel was very kind to me but he knew I was only going through the motions at my job. I told him of Scott's threat but outside of the military he had no authority to help me.

Kali was a little over a year old when she and I went to our first Battered Women's Shelter. It was the first of many. We ended up there after Scott got angry when a friend of mine from the barracks was at our apartment visiting me to see Kali. Scott hated my friend because she knew about the abuse and wasn't afraid to tell him what an asshole she thought he was. He went after her on this occasion and she threatened to call the police, to which he ripped our phone out of the wall and threw it at her. It landed at her feet so she threw it back and we ran out the door. I had been holding Kali and we ran down the hall with him in pursuit. Luckily, the elevator opened right away and we made it downstairs where we ran to her car parked in the road. She took me to a payphone where I called the shelter. They said they had room.

The shelter turned out to be like most we ended up in. In Waikiki, it was in an old military barracks that had literally gone through our war with Japan. It was a concrete slab of a building with a big rusted entrance door that looked something like the door of a bank vault.

Inside, it was dark and filled with cigarette smoke and mothers watching soap operas while their children played on a rug that looked to be 50 years old and never cleaned. There was an empty olympic sized swimming pool in the center of the courtyard, that we weren't allowed out on. That was the only view from the window. The place felt haunted and full of the misery of broken hearts.

Kali and I were led to a room down the gray corridor. The single bed was made up of donated mismatched sheets and an old comforter. There was a crib, but I wanted my Kali next to me. To comfort her. To comfort me.

In the evening after dinner, The Burning Bed was either shown by the shelter staff on VCR or it was just coincidentally on a tv station. I don't know which but it was the story of all of us women in that shelter. It starred Farrah Fawcett who was so abused and controlled by her husband that she lit the bed he was sleeping on, on fire and killed him. Of course she had her kids taken away from her and went to prison. Never mind the fact he had beaten her and the children on a daily basis.

During the movie I was called into the office next to the living room. I was told I had a phone call. Huh, what? The only one who knew where I was was my friend who had brought me here but she didn't have the number. It was Scott. I remembered he had the number that was never published anywhere but that was only given to an abused woman. He began screaming at me to bring his daughter to him. Without a word, I hung up on him. He called back again, but this time he was crying and begged me to come home. He was for sure faking, but I listened to his sad pleadings and promises he would change and things would be better. He finally said the magic words; that he would grant me a divorce and move out. He asked me to meet him at the park downtown which was close to where I was. He didn't know where the shelter was and the shelter staff were not supposed to admit I was even there by calling me to the phone, but he got through to me, nonetheless. I agreed to meet him at the park the next day. Apparently, The Burning Bed hadn't taught me anything. I was living in the unreal world of a Narcissist who had a power over me. I wasn't strong enough to fight. Unfortunately for me...I loved him and the psychic connection between us was made of steel. I was determined to fix this person, not realizing I couldn't.

CHAPTER 24

At the park, Scott was waiting with flowers and a toy for Kali. I put her in the baby stroller he had brought with him and we went over to a nearby bench.

As usual, he apologized and made promises he had no intention of keeping. He took my hands and looked into my eyes and said he would change if I would only come home with Kali. Oh Christ, I realized, the spell was softening me. I didn't want to but like I said, he had a spell over me, a spell I had asked the universe, or god, or whatever is in charge of Universal Order to break. Not that day it wouldn't be broken.

Life did settle down from high alert to stand-by alert. Kevin had moved out and there were nights of tension when I would sleep in the single bed next to Kali's crib.

Scott obtained and lost numerous jobs but my income kept us afloat. I had gone into the Army as an E-3 because of school credits I had earned at various junior college semesters I had accumulated. Those, plus the fact I got a 99 on my ASVAB, put me at an advanced pay grade. My colonel told me he was retiring six months after my ETS date and said if I stayed in the military an extra six months he would make me a Sergeant. That meant an additional pay raise. I was saving secretly all I could before my tour was over so I readily agreed.

My plan was to pretend Scott and I were well on our way to complete reunification. He was still reminding me that if I filed for divorce on the occasions we did argue, he would take our daughter home with him to Texas where he would move in with his mother who would raise her. Just the fact he would still threaten me with that told me I would never be able to trust him. My plan was to have our furnishings shipped to a mainland locale closest to where my mother lived. I would find a place to live near her and divorce him, sending him on his way, out of our lives. He had always been enamored with California and said he was excited to finally get to live there. Not for long, I'd think as he waxed poetic about the state.

We sold his very expensive muscle car and my little Toyota and bought a new Honda. It was under my name because of his still bad credit so I would have a car, $2,000.00 in US Savings Bonds I had secretly accrued, final pay from the military which would be $4,000.00 and $1,000.00 left from my secret savings account. It would all set me up nicely in an apartment or house and he would have...nothing. Oh, I might give him a few bucks to take a bus to Texas or wherever as long as it was away from me and our daughter. I didn't want him anywhere near her.

CHAPTER 25

Before leaving Hawaii, I booked us a room at a hotel right on the beach near the Hale Koa Resort that was always booked years in advance.

It had a small fully stocked kitchen and a lanai that overlooked the ocean and had a good view of Diamond Head. After getting settled, we went to the Hale Koa to sign up for their luau that evening. I wanted to have an enjoyable last dinner and pretend all was well with my marriage. We had fun, or at least Scott did, happy he wasn't paying for any of this, and Kali was her precocious, inquisitive self who charmed and entertained all the guests seated at the long table. I have pictures of her trying to hula with the dancers and running in between them, laughing and happy.

We stayed for three days while our apartment furnishings were being boxed up and shipped and on the last day, taking our car down to the port where it would be shipped back to California. I also went to TAMC on my own and got all my medical records, making sure the reports on abuse done to me were included.

In truth, I had wanted to continue on in Hawaii in the military. However, my MOS had been eliminated by the Defense Department. All transportation jobs had gone to civilians. If I was to remain in the military I would have had to select a new MOS, go back through AIT training, which meant living on post in barracks with all the other soldiers, and then be sent wherever the military wanted to send me. The military is not set up for single moms.

I also thought about staying in Hawaii, getting a job and going through the court system there to divorce Scott. There were two problems with that idea. One was Scott could still threaten to take

Kali off the island to Texas and he had refused to tell me where his mom lived, so I'd have no idea where to even look; and two, he had 'Island fever' a psychological condition people can get living on a small island. It's like claustrophobia on steroids. He wanted off the island and said so daily. No, my best bet was to move back to Calif. near my mother so I would have help raising my daughter. I would pretend to stay with him until I reached my mothers and there I would tell him to leave.

My mom didn't know about the abuse. The truth is, I was ashamed. Ashamed of myself for picking out the wrong man to father a child with. The wrong man to love me the way I knew was really love. But I was also ashamed to admit to anyone how unlovable I must have been for someone to abuse me. Shame can cripple you. Shame can kill you if you are too ashamed to ask for help. Truth is, I didn't really think anyone could help me.

CHAPTER 26

Once we reached Oakland where we were put up in a family barracks for the night while we waited for the car to arrive by boat, we talked about our relationship. I told him we could stay with my mom until we got a place of our own. I told him I wanted to attend a 4 year college there and asked him what he wanted to do in the way of work. I didn't want to deprive his daughter of a father but so far in her young life, all she knew of him was how long he could scream at me and how hard he could hit me. My plan was to get an ironclad visitation schedule set up, ideally with him getting supervised visits.

In answer to my question he stated he had no idea what he wanted to do in the way of bringing in money. He had relied on me to provide for him.

By the time we reached my mothers his anxiety turned into anger and blame and we entered her home while still arguing. He had met my mother in Hawaii and she had ended up staying with us for two weeks. They had seemed to get along, but now he was downright rude to her, complaining about how small her house was and bossing her around.

What happened next was like a slow motion nightmare that causes total panic and has you jerking awake. I told him he couldn't stay in her house if he couldn't behave himself. He said "Fine," and with that he picked up Kali and walked out to the car. He had the car keys because he had been driving. I followed after him and told him to stop. He said "I'm heading to Texas tonight so take your last look at your daughter." While he put her in the car I ran out and stood in front of it. He got in the driver's seat and said, "The only way I'll stop is if you go with me."

I almost fainted with fear and anxiety but pulled myself together and said, "Just let me get my purse and suitcases." I went in the house and my mother was just hanging up the phone after calling my brother who lived nearby. I went up and hugged her and said, "Mom, I have to go with him." She nodded, started to cry and helped me take the luggage out to the car. Her and Scott didn't say a word to each other and I barely got out "I love you," before he sped off down the street.

Now in hindsight, what man in his right mind would want to drive cross country with a crying baby in the back seat? Also, he had no money. I had it all. He only wanted me on this trip so he'd have a baby caretaker and money. I should have called his bluff. But should you really chance a man backing down when there's a 1 year old child's life on the line? No mother would take that chance. I certainly wouldn't.

CHAPTER 27

Something pleasant happened on our drive down the California coastline. However, the pleasantness sent chills down my spine. It was like he was a different personality.

Immediately after we drove away from my mothers and the town I wanted to live in, Scott's personality completely changed to a happy go lucky, talkative, engaging man who couldn't be nicer.

Oh god...I thought, he either shot something up in the bathroom he went to while getting gas before we left town, or he was exhibiting a split personality. It made my neck hurt from the whiplash this change had caused.

I had learned from experience that his behavior could turn on a dime. I sat still, afraid to move or talk, just quietly having a nervous breakdown. I was still in shock over what had transpired at my moms, feeling totally traumatized and abused, yet I dared not tell him my feelings for fear he would drag me out of the car and leave me beside the freeway. I felt like I was being given a ride by a madman, the father of my child.

We got as far as Santa Cruz before stopping for the night. We got a hotel room on the beach so Kali could play in the sand.

Scott had shown annoyance that I wasn't playing along with his happy couple routine so I dredged up the bubbly personality I had had when we first met. It was an act. An act, I hoped he bought. I had gotten a new camera after mine had been stolen, thanks to him, and made a big show of taking pictures and pointing out interesting scenes, anything to keep his mind from going to the dark side. It worked, for the time being and my daughter's joy and the joy she gave me temporarily made me forget I was with a very sick man.

We decided to drive all the way to LA and go to Disneyland. It was my idea, hoping to give him a goal to occupy his mind. We actually had fun along the way and after a while I let my guard down enough to act like a happy person. We managed to make it to LA with no fights.

We got a hotel room close to Disneyland and settled in for a good night's sleep after our long drive down the coast. As I was laying with Kali next to me sleeping, Scott called his mother in Texas. After talking to her for about 10 minutes, he hung up, turned to me and said, "My mom got me a job at a manufacturing company in Waxahachie. This man at her church is a foreman there and he said "I've got the job if I want it." Well this was a surprise, I thought. He's been planning this all along with his mom. He never had any intention of living in California. He's been talking to her since we left Hawaii. I pretended I was happy and went to sleep dreading living in Texas.

CHAPTER 28

Disneyland was a welcome diversion for all of us. We had to limit the rides because of Kali's age so we mainly hung out in Fantasyland and stayed away from the thrill rides, my personal favorites. We stayed till after the nightly fireworks, then headed back to the hotel, exhausted but recharged mentally. I thought, 'if we could only live at Disneyland, I'd be safe and happy."

By noon the next day, we were back into the black of reality and reality was hot and tedious. We couldn't take the dessert nothingness for long and stopped in Las Vegas for dinner. Scott didn't argue when I told him we needed to spend the night. I did resent him going down to the casinos by himself however, leaving me to stay with our daughter who had been sleeping for most of the trip. I had visions of Scott going up to shady characters on the strip asking for speed or pot or whatever he took. I imagined him soliciting prostitutes that hung out in front of the casinos. I had no doubt in my mind he would do those things without even a second thought.

He didn't return until 2 am, drunk and waking up Kali. He wanted sex, but she wanted my attention and so I got out of it that night. I didn't know how long I could put off being intimate with him. Ever since that first time he had hit me right after we had sex, I could never really enjoy it. He had successfully turned me off although I'm sure if I tried to explain why he would just get angry and accuse me of trying to make him feel bad.

When I tried in the past to bring up his abusive behavior when we argued, he would almost growl at me and say things like, "If only you hadn't made me so mad," or, "It was all your fault," or, "Jesus, get over it, let it go."

I had stopped asking him to explain to me why he had to resort to violence long ago and knew better than to question him.

He was successfully training me. Training me to conform to his will, to bend myself into a pretzel to avoid punishment. I was slowly becoming a prisoner, a prisoner with Stockholm Syndrome; a bird in a cage, a cage he liked to rattle and a bird he liked to poke at. I couldn't dare to be my true self around him. I was being forced into Texas against my will, a state I detested from afar for its braggadocio, it's holier than thou church fanaticism, but mostly for it's male chauvinistic attitudes toward women.

CHAPTER 29

When we arrived at his mothers house in the small town of Riverton, Tx. It was around 3 o'clock on a Sunday. His mother answered the door and hugged him, looked me up and down and stated that her and her husband, Leroy, were headed to their church, that they'd be back in a couple of hours. Texas church fanaticism was on full display. This woman hadn't seen her son in over 3 years, nor had met her daughter-in-law and her grandchild, yet she couldn't even miss a church get together even for this occasion? She hadn't even acknowledged we had made a very long trip with a toddler and had failed to tell us where we'd be sleeping or offered us something to eat or drink.

All we could do was sit and wait. Upon their return, Bertha and Leroy breezed past us into the kitchen without so much as a hello. I felt like I was no more important to them than a stranger sitting waiting for a bus. Scott also looked peeved and shook his head, indicating this was typical behavior on their part. Bertha finally came into the family room where we were sitting after getting herself a cup of coffee and stood over us, taking a sip with one hand and waving the other at the room. "You can stay in here on the fold out couch," she said. "Karen, you can come help me in the kitchen."

"Her name is Kiftin mom, not Karen," Scott said.

"Well, I've just never heard of a name like that before," she Southern drawled with a tone that my name was unfamiliar, therefore unacceptable. I told her I'd be in later but right now I had a diaper to change. She whirled about to say something, thought better of it, then lit out for the kitchen.

While pulling Kali's diaper bag closer, Scott said, "You haven't seen what's up on the shelves all around us near the ceiling have you." "No," I said absently. "You'd better look so you won't scream later on." Scott knew there was only one thing that could make me scream, besides him hitting me; spiders. I slowly raised my head and I saw wall to wall jars surrounding us on shelves. Looking closer I saw that every jar contained a spider. Spiders of every size and color. The tarantulas were in quart sized mason jars, that's how big they were.

Bertha was a thin, hyper woman who I towered over. Her bossy attitude, however, towered over me. In her kitchen she put me to work washing their lunch dishes. When I asked where the dishwasher was she turned toward me and drawled, "We ain't spoilt around here, we wash by hand," and threw down the peeler she was holding and stalked out of the kitchen. I could hear her complaining about me to her husband who was sitting in the living room. The words "California" and "useless" reached my ears before she came back in to again attack the potatoes she had been peeling. We did our chores in silence but we both may well have been screaming "Bitch" to each other. I finished washing, then without a word went back to be with Kali and my abuser. To say I felt surrounded by danger on all sides, including the spiders, is an understatement.

Bertha shouted from the kitchen that they had bought a tri-tip for dinner and ordered Scott to help Walter extend the dining room table because Leroys' two adult kids and Scott's younger sister would be coming to dinner. Scott asked when they were coming and Bertha said, "Leroy's son and daughter are in their rooms with Stormy Gayle and Philip, and your sister is out with her boyfriend."

So there were people upstairs who hadn't bothered to come down when we had arrived? Did Scott know them? Were they hiding or just not caring? I thought I'd heard noises from upstairs but couldn't imagine it was Scott's relatives.

It was only after Scott and his mother set the table and put the food out that everyone appeared out of the woodwork. Leroy's daughters' children, Stormy Gayle and Philip were ages 6 and 3. I was shocked seeing them. I hadn't heard the children upstairs. Jennifer, Scott's little sister, a sophomore in High School came in the house with her boyfriend. They sat down, ready to be waited on and Jennifer talked all about the movie they had just seen, A Nightmare On Elm Street. That's exactly how I was feeling, only I was in 'A Nightmare on Main Street'. Jennifer told us all about the blood and gore in the movie with gleeful squeals, to which I said to myself, 'I thought you people were Christians, why would you approve of your young daughter seeing that horrific movie?' Baffled, I silently ate the tough meat and gave all my attention to Kali, sitting on my lap.

I noticed, as the meal progressed that the children didn't talk at all. Her mother slapped Stormy Gayle's hand so hard tears sprang to her eyes when she tried to reach for a biscuit. In a harsh tone Bertha pointed an accusing fork at Stormy Gayle and said, "You will eat only what we give you and no more." I observed that the poor kids were both dangerously skinny and had terrified looks in their eyes. Something was very wrong about these people.

CHAPTER 30

Could I really sleep in that room with those spiders? After dinner I let the others take care of cleaning up. I had Kali to tend to and stayed in the family room we were assigned to. After they were finished in the kitchen, the whole group ascended into the family room where a football game was put on the TV. I was stuck there with them and forced to watch a game I absolutely don't like for many reasons. One was that Scott and I had many arguments about his obsession with watching every single football game that was played while we lived in Hawaii. The sport literally kept Scott from spending any family time getting out of the apartment, going to the beach or exploring all the beautiful parks of Oahu. During football season I was basically a widow. Kali and I were on our own. I would take her to the mall, to the Aquarium on the leeward side and the beach where we could splash in the waves. I felt utterly alone at those times. I got little comfort realizing at least I wasn't being abused.

So here I was, having to sit through a game that had literally divided us. During a commercial, Leroy proudly pointed out the spiders and told us how he had collected them. He was a long haul trucker and as he was driving through the vast badlands of desert that makes up the southern state, he would get out at truck stops and go spider hunting. Charming.

After everyone finally got up off the couch we would be sleeping in and went upstairs, Scott and I tried to get comfortable and get Kali to sleep. I hoped and prayed Scott would fall asleep fast leaving no chance for an argument to take place. I had no doubt this family, including him, would put me out of the house if he and I fought.

The next morning we were woken up as the sun was just coming up by Leroy, who was banging around in the kitchen, getting ready to go out on the road in his truck.

Soon, the whole family was downstairs milling about, oblivious to the fact we were out in the open, unable to get out of bed because both Scott and I always slept naked. I had to pee so bad I could cry but Leroy's daughter had walked past us into the bathroom off the family room so unless I wanted to run upstairs naked to use the bathroom up there, I was screwed. His son was, no doubt, using that one anyway.

She finally finished, walking past us without a word, and I took my chances of Leroy seeing me naked and bolted to the bathroom. While in there, I sat with my hands covering my face and thought, "What have I done getting myself into this miserable existence?" I was unhappy to my core.

Scott opened the bathroom door and threw me my clothes from the day before. 'Well at least we're weathering this ordeal together,' I thought. Maybe we can make this work.

CHAPTER 31

Once dressed I traded places with Scott and tended to Kali and folded the bed back into a couch. Bertha was in the kitchen but I made no move to join her and when she did come out she headed for the living room, oblivious to me and Kali sitting there. I found it odd that she had not once, since our arrival, come over to her granddaughter to hold her or do the usual baby talk and smiley faces people naturally do with a baby. That's alright, I thought, I didn't want her bonding with my daughter anyway.

When Scott came out of the bathroom his mom called him into the living room and said she wanted to talk to him. He obeyed and went in. I couldn't hear what she was saying but figured it was her giving him the name of an attorney he could call to get rid of me. Instead, she told him about the job in Waxahachie her friend from church had told her about. She gave him the number to call and then went upstairs.

Scott was very happy and said we would go get breakfast somewhere and talk about where to live. I was just glad to get out of the creepy old house we were in.

Because I didn't know the towns around us, I left it up to Scott to choose for us. He didn't want to live in either Waxahachie, where the plant was, or the town we were in. He didn't say as much but I got the impression he didn't want to be close to his mom.

He said we should look in Waco, where there would be a better chance of me finding work. I reminded him that I had at least six months unemployment we could use from my military service. I really didn't want to go through the trial and error of finding child care and besides any job I could get would get eaten up by childcare expenses. He agreed, so we left the restaurant and drove to Waco.

I found out later that Waxahachie is over an hour's drive from Waco. That fact and the shifts Scott was assigned were disastrous for our already flailing marriage. We should have moved to a southern suburb of Dallas which was 45 minutes away from where he would be working. Woulda, coulda, shoulda.

We did look at three houses for sale in Waxahachie but found out why all three owners wanted to sell; fire ants. Those tiny little creatures have a big sting and if you get stung enough times, they can kill you. All the yards were saturated with them and because Kali was only a year and a few months old, we couldn't move there.

The house we rented in Waco was partially furnished but we still wanted the furniture we had accumulated in Hawaii. So, three days before Scott was to start work, he flew out to Sacramento, rented a UHaul and got our furniture that the military had stored for us. That expenditure wiped out my enlistment bonus.

CHAPTER 32

While Scott was at work I felt relief and somewhat at peace. But when he was home, I was a nervous wreck, always waiting for the other shoe to drop. It didn't take long and it wasn't a shoe but a big, pointy cowboy boot.

It took only three months for him to start unraveling and the shift work he was on contributed to his agitation. He worked a full seven nights from 11pm to 7am; then had four days off before working evenings from 3pm to 11pm, 7 days straight; then four days off finishing with seven straight morning hours from 3am to 11am. This rotation was grueling for both of us. Plus, he had an hour commute each way. His job was also exhausting, working in the warehouse.

Both of our circadian rhythms were destroyed in no time and on the shift where he worked nights and slept during the day were torture. The slightest noise would wake him up and he'd come out of the bedroom like a hibernating bear, growling and cursing at me. I tried my best to keep Kali quiet but that's impossible with a 1 year old. Scott didn't want the TV or radio on so we had to either go to the backyard or just leave and go to the park. The closest one had fire ants so we'd end up just driving around or wandering around the mall. On Scott's days off, he spent most of them sleeping, or watching football. Kali and I were on our own.

As the months passed, Scott began going to his moms, taking Kali with him. I was never invited. On those times, they would spend the night, coming home around noon the next day. We only had the one car so I would basically be stranded in the suburbs until their return.

Kali, of course, had royal tantrums the times he took her and her sobs of "Mama" trailed off as they drove away. I would practically be left hyperventilating. I always had an ominous feeling when he would drag her, kicking and screaming, out to the car to go to the spider house and her stone cold grandma.

During one of these occasions while changing the sheets on our bed, I opened the drawer in the hall pantry and lifted out the sheets and tucked between the layers I found a magazine. The cover literally made me gasp. It showed what looked like women being tortured. I looked through the magazine and page after page had unspeakable sex acts and one picture had the title "Snuff". I had heard about films being made where victims are actually killed during the sex act, but was skeptical that really happened. Now I was convinced, seeing women being strangled while men would be either raping them or standing around masterbating or having sex with each other. I had heard these women were either hookers or women they picked up hitchhiking. A woman no one would come looking for if she went missing.

Towards the back of the magazine were pictures of very young girls, some looked as young as four or five who were chained in cages. One picture was of a young girl on what looked like a concrete table with a young man kneeling over her, raping her while other young and old men, all naked, masturbating on her. The girl had her eyes closed. How and where did he get this magazine? I contemplated removing it and presenting it in court once I filed for the divorce I was sure we were headed for. Then I froze. Knowing him he would say it was my magazine. There'd be no way for me to prove otherwise. I also knew that confronting him would cause a real knock down drag out fight. I meekly put it back and tried to control the disgust and panic I was feeling. After opening the drawer again, I dug deeper and found what I was looking for. The tie off rubber hose and the box with needles plus white powder I surmised was cocaine. He was using again.

CHAPTER 33

By November, the other boot did drop. I had gone in to use the second bathroom because he was taking a shower in the hall bath. I had flushed the toilet and was entering the hallway when he came flying out of the bathroom yelling at me. He had knocked Kali out of the way to get to me. She immediately began crying but I ran into our bedroom to get away from him. He slammed me up against the wall and put his hands around my neck and began choking me. I began punching him first in the stomach and then slapping him in the face. "What is wrong with you," I gasped.

"You stupid bitch, you flushed the toilet and the water turned cold."

Kali was hysterical by then and her screams brought Scott back to reality and he left me to pick her up. "See what you have caused," he screamed. Then he really capped it. He said, "That's alright sweetie, mommy was being bad but daddy's here to protect you." He put her back down and went back into the bathroom.

As quietly as I could, I got my purse, got the car keys out of his pants lying on the floor, picked up Kali and went out to the car. I had just sat back in the driver's seat when he came running out of the house with a towel wrapped around his waist. I locked the door, started the car and backed into the street with him running after me. I didn't have anywhere to go but ended up at a gas station phone booth where I called the police.

The cops met me at the gas station and took my statement. I asked them if there was a Women's Shelter they could take us to, but one cop said, "Before we do that we need you to take us back to your house to get your husband's statement."

I did not like how this was going down. Scott was a smooth talker, tall and handsome, but more importantly a good ole' boy Texan. I reluctantly agreed and drove back to the house.

They got out of their patrol car and knocked on the door. Scott came out dressed and holding a kleenex to his cheek. I could hear him telling the cop that I had attacked him and stopped so the cop could see a cut on his left cheek. The cop approached me and asked to see my neck, presumably to see bruises but finding none he put me on the defense and said, "Is that true ma'am, did you start this fight?"

"No, I already explained what happened," to which the cop said,

"Well, let's just arrest both of you and we'll call Child Protective to come get your daughter." Both Scott and I backed down and after being made to apologize to each other, the cops left.

Scott knew he had gone too far and came over and hugged me and after getting Kali out of the car, we went back into the house of horror.

CHAPTER 34

I really loved Scott, but I was equally just as afraid of him. I was also afraid of living in Texas. I knew instinctively that the culture, the men and the women, the police, the churches, the rattlesnakes and spiders did not like outsiders. Outsiders like me, a blond woman from California who they probably thought ran along the beaches naked and smoked pot.

Texan's don't like any outsiders, especially from California and 'Northerners' from states like New York and Vermont and anywhere else non confederates lived. Texas cops were famous for pulling over visitors from 'up North' and California over made up infractions like not signaling a full one minute before changing lanes or going through yellow lights the cops claimed were red.

I had heard, while living in San Francisco, that a black California man, traveling through Texas, was pulled over, probably for being black. Unfortunately for him they searched his car and found four rolled joints of marijuana. He was arrested right then and there and when he came before the criminal judge in Waco, he was given a year sentence for each joint. Four years in prison for four joints. I made a mental note to myself at the time to never go to Texas, yet here I was living there, in Waco no less.

Before asking someone you meet there what your name is, Texans ask what church you belong to. And you'd better come up with one or they'll shun you as being unsaved, meaning you might lead them into temptation, or worse, they'll try to convert you and save your soul from damnation and hellfire. It's best to say Baptist just to be safe.

Scott's mother and stepfather were Church of Christ. That particular sect doesn't allow musical instruments because there is no reference to them in the New Testament. They also don't allow any hymns sung that were written after 1965, which was probably when their hymnals were printed. Anything newer than that wasn't considered true gospel music and was blasphemous to Jesus. "Don't the angels have harps," I asked, but I could never get an answer. I think the question stumped them.

Scott wasn't religious and I had left the Christian Science church I was raised in as soon as I left home. I attributed my goody two shoes behavior growing up to it's teachings and I could swear I could heal wounds just by praying but that all ended when I was raped just before moving to San Francisco. Raped by my boyfriend who wouldn't take no for an answer on his last day at college in the town I was from.

CHAPTER 35

When Scott was working, I spent my time teaching Kali how to read with a clever game I had gotten her right after we moved to Waco when she was 16 months old. It was a wooden board with the alphabet and numbers carved into the wood, along with plastic letters and numbers. I showed her how to put the plastic letters and numbers in the matching ones on the board, sounding them out as I put them in place. She blew me away with how fast she mastered learning. Within two weeks she could name all the letters and numbers while picking up each one and putting it into it's space. She was only a year and a 4 month old but began being able to read simple words by the second month using this method. It also didn't take her long to write. By age 2 she could write all the letters and by 3, using phonics, she could write words.

I shouldn't have been surprised because she had a 26 word vocabulary by age one, most of them two syllables. Her first word, momma, she said at age 10 months, This was the age she began walking and swimming wearing water wings. While sitting in her stroller or in a grocery store cart, she would reach out to passing babies and say, "Hi baby, I'm Kali." Her greetings were always met by blank stares from the babies, many much older than her, and astonished mothers. Her intelligence would play an important part in our lives in the coming years. We would both be required to be at the top of our game mentally at all times.

I found out much later, after taking a course on Child Development, that when children are born into an abusive home where potential violence can occur on a regular basis, their survival instincts kick in very early. They learn faster than children born into a peaceful environment. In her case an additional factor of heredity surely played a part. Her father's IQ was in the genius range of 155. Like all good con artists he was too intelligent for his own, or anybody else's good. Perhaps he had also had to learn survival skills at an early age because of his childhood beginnings. From what little he remembered or told me about his childhood, it was certainly plausible.

CHAPTER 36

As the months passed, Scott and I instinctively avoided each other. His schedule at work affected both of us negatively. I had to constantly acclimate to it or pay the price. Waking him up accidentally during the day on his nightshift weeks would mean certain punishment.

The weeks he worked late nights to mid morning were especially bad for my sleep because he demanded I be awake and ready to feed him when he got home at 4 in the morning. I could never get back to sleep in those weeks and would be a wreck by the time Kali woke up at around 8. Those weeks I slept in her bedroom so that when she did wake up, she wouldn't make noise and wake up her father. I had to have my clothes, shoes and accessories picked out and put in Kali's room because getting dressed in our room would wake up Scott.

The only weeks where I got enough sleep were when he worked days or had days off. Kali and I couldn't watch her favorite show, Sesame Street, on those days because even at low volume he would wake up and come roaring into the living room threatening to smash the TV if I couldn't learn not to use it while he slept. I would try to be gone as much as possible, although Waco isn't rich in exciting things to do.

His schedule was causing unnecessary strife and was an outright danger to my physical and mental health. I meekly asked him to find a job in Waco. He was making very good money working where he was but I would take not being beaten over money any day.

I felt isolated and lonelier than I'd ever felt in my life. I was surrounded by young families who had all known each other since childhood. There were large BBQ's always going on around us that, as outsiders, we were never invited to. We could smell the food and hear the laughter while we sat, miserably eating our food at the kitchen table. I didn't have any friends, I didn't have any family and I didn't have a loving companion for a husband.

Scott didn't have to quit. He was fired for sleeping on the job. I was only mildly surprised given his inability to keep a job for very long. I would have been thrilled if I hadn't been so mentally depressed and physically exhausted, but my attitude was more like, "What doesn't fall apart in this relationship?"

Scott did manage getting a job in Waco at a manufacturing plant driving a forklift during the day. I began having hope that our lives would change for the better. My mother came to visit and I was so happy to have her, although Waco is much like Redding, Ca., there is very little to do or places to see. I should have taken her to Dallas or San Antonio where we could sightsee, but I didn't want Scott along for the ride and both options would have meant spending the night.

I didn't want my mother to know how bad our marriage was or how I couldn't stand to be with him. She surely must have known though. The last time she saw us I was being dragged off to Texas while she stood in her driveway, crying. While she was visiting we had days with just us and Kali while Scott was at work.

I should have talked to her about my feelings but whenever I had in the past, she would get so uncomfortable she would either change the subject or just get up and do busy work like cleaning. She knew the vacuum cleaner would successfully drown me out. I never thought it was disinterest, more like she couldn't deal with the realities of pain. Her method for dealing with strife was to just ignore it.

There was one weekend Scott had off when we took her on a drive around Texas but she was soon just as bored as I was by it all. She was only there a week and when her plane took off, I felt lost once again with no answers for what I should do nor comfort for how I was feeling.

By February, life with Scott had not improved, despite the fact we were now living hours compatible with the normal circadian rhythm humans need to thrive. It all reached a crescendo of events that forced me into taking action.

Scott had taken Kali to his mother's house without me twice in the month of February. The second time they had spent the whole weekend there and didn't return until late Sunday night. I was left behind with an ever growing anxiety.

Call it mother's intuition but I had an overwhelming sense of doom and dread concerning my child's safety. Maybe it was related to the creepy house she would be in with the spiders on the walls and her ice cold grandmother.

My fears were not allayed on their return. Scott came in with a look like he had just witnessed a fatal car crash and Kali looked like a beaten up rag doll. She pushed out of his arms as soon as she saw me and began crying in huge gulping sobs. Her hair was sweaty and matted and her clothes were stained and damp. They were the same clothes she left in because he had said they'd be back that evening on Friday night. It took me a half hour to get her calmed down after I filled the bathtub to clean her up. I was alarmed when she panicked being put in the tub. She clung to me with all her might and kept saying, "No, no, please don't."

"It's alright sweetie, you love the bathtub."

She responded by crying and whimpering, "No, no, it will hurt." I was puzzled and alarmed. I didn't find out why until a year later. Bertha would hold her head underwater in the tub and then lift it up and tell her if she told anyone what was being done to her, Bertha would not let her up and she would die.

CHAPTER 37

The following week, I made plans to take Kali and I far away from her father, her grandmother and Texas. I phoned the Women's Shelter in Waco and asked to speak to whomever was in charge. When a woman got on the phone and asked if she could help, I told her about the abuse from my husband and my concern about Kali's visits to her grandmother's.

I asked her about how I could take her to California without being arrested for child kidnapping. She gave me the number for the attorney the shelter always used in family court and said that as long as I left Scott a letter stating where I was and how he could reach me, I would be safe.

I asked if I could file divorce papers in Ca. but she said that because I was considered a resident of Texas after living here for six months, I wouldn't be able to file divorce in Ca., only Seperation papers. She advised me to stay in Texas and file for divorce. She said I could get a restraining order on him if I had proof of abuse and he would have to leave the house.

I hung up the phone racking my brain for what to do. I had spent almost all the money I had saved on furniture, car payments, getting our possessions moved and on top of that my unemployment had run out. I only had about a thousand in my secret checking account.

How would I pay rent and afford child care if Scott left. Knowing him, he'd strong arm me for the car, which was in my name, and leave me stranded. I only had one credit card, but he was on it as well. After calling and checking the balance on the card I was told it was maxed out! I hadn't been using it but apparently Scott had been. I was still the primary on it though and I was responsible for paying the bill.

In hindsight, I should have gone and stayed with Kali at the shelter and filed for divorce from there. Then I remembered the Shelter Director telling me there were no rooms available at the time and I'd have to keep checking back. I didn't want her going with her father to her gandmothers ever again. I had to take action that week.

Luckily Waco is a headquarters city for the VA for the Eastern part of Texas and I found out I could get my military records from there. I had gotten my abuse records before leaving Hawaii but they were in a storage unit for which Scott had the key.

I told him I was going to take him to work and use the car for shopping. He reluctantly agreed because by then his control over my activities was becoming tighter and tighter along with his suspicions. He wanted me home, isolated and under his thumb. He should have known me better than that.

By the third day of the week, I had purchased plane tickets to Redding, gotten my records and packed a small suitcase for both Kali and me. The next day, I drove Scott to work, went home to get our suitcases and left the note where I was going and my mom's phone number on the kitchen counter. The note also told him the car was at the airport with the keys under the mat. I called my mom and told her when she could pick us up at the Redding airport.

CHAPTER 38

The day after we arrived in Redding, I called a divorce attorney and filed separation papers.

I was told I couldn't file for a divorce because technically, I wasn't a resident. That technicality proved to be disastrous. Scott, in the meantime filed divorce papers in Texas. I had been banking on him just giving up. It would have been nice to know before I left that divorce trumps separation. I was served by the end of the week.

Scott called and said he was flying out to pick up Kali... without me. I only had the weekend with her when two Sheriff's showed up at my door to get her. I went hysterical and they had to pry her out of my arms.

"Where are you taking her," I cried. The female sheriff said, "Your husband is at the sheriff's office waiting for her." I took my mom's car and got to the sheriff's office right after they did.

Scott was sitting down in the only chair in the waiting area when I approached him and as quietly as I could said, shaking, "You won't get away with this," to which he calmly replied like a villain in a Bond movie, "Well it looks like I have," and stood and pushed past me as the female sheriff came in with Kali and handed her over to Scott. She kept looking around not knowing what was going on. Scott said, "I'll give you five minutes to say your goodbye," as Scott sat back down and held her close with an evil smile on his face.

"You'll never see her again so make it good." I sat down and with tears streaming down my face, said, "Don't worry baby, mommy will see you again," to which Scott said, "OK, that's it, if you say one more thing like that and don't stop crying, we're leaving."

As I rose to my feet I said, standing over him, "This is not the last you'll see of me asshole," and turned and drove back to my mom's.

I couldn't stop hyperventilating and once at my mom's I called the Women's Shelter in Waco and got the number for the attorney they used. When she answered I blurted out all that had happened, gasping for air the whole time. She said she would take my case but I would have to send her a retainer fee of $200.00. I got her information for sending the money and went into the living room to tell my mom I needed her help.

The attorney had told me to wait until the court date before coming out to Texas. The date on the Divorce paper I had been served was to be in one month from the day served. She said that he would have custody up until then.

In telling my mom all this I practically fainted telling her about my impression of Scott's mother, the spiders, and how he had to work so no doubt Kali would be at her house an entire month. My mom had been very quiet the whole time, seemingly unconcerned but said, "I'll help you," and went back to reading her magazine.

CHAPTER 39

In hindsight, I should have cleaned out my secret bank account before leaving Texas. I wouldn't have been able to access our joint account without his signature. I went to the local bank branch to access my money but was told all the branches were independent and I couldn't get it out.

In a state of panic, I visited my cousin, who was like a sister to me and crying on her couch she gave me $200.00. I told her I might not see her for a long time but would pay her back as soon as I got to Texas.

In the month leading up to going to Texas, I still had my hairdresser license so I applied at almost every shop in town. I also got a job right away with a cab company, driving drunks home from bars in the evenings. I got a job working at a chain salon so by the end of the month I had the money for the attorney and money to fly to Texas.

Having no place to live, once I got to Waco, I called the Women's Shelter and explained my predicament and after considerable consideration on the Directors part, she said I could stay until after the hearing and if I got custody, Kali could stay with me until I found a place to live. I was so relieved, I sat and had a long cry after we hung up.

The time couldn't go fast enough. I was so stressed out my hands began to peel and the face looking back at me in the mirror was haunted.

A week before the hearing I was lying on the bed and I thought about praying to God like I had in my youth and while crying, I got on the floor kneeling and begged God to help me.

Astonishingly, as soon as I did, the phone rang. My mom answered it and came into my room and said, "It's Scott." I gasped, got up off the floor, wiped away the tears and ran to the phone.

"Kif, I'm going to let you talk to Kali but you can't cry or tell her you will see her."

'Fuck you', I wanted to say, but I agreed and he put the receiver up to her ear. I said "Hi baby, it's mommy, are you ok?" When she realized it was me she whimpered, "Mommy, where are you, I miss you. I don't like the spiders and..." Scott took the phone from her and said, "Ok, that's enough, you go play now."

I could hear her start to cry and say "I want my mommy, let me see my mommy."

Scott said harshly, "That's enough Kali, you can't see her." She began to really cry loudly so he hung up the phone. I was at the same time happy to hear her voice but raging inside at Scott.

Once I calmed down after the phone call, I decided I would do as the Texans do...I'd get religion. I knew I would need many tools at my disposal to fight them. I instinctively knew I couldn't go before a Texas judge as the pegan I was sure I'd be made out to be. I would be the most buttoned up, prim, wholesome woman I could possibly manage.

In fact, I was going to join the Church of Christ, Bertha's church, as I was sure she would be lurking around behind Scott's decisions and financing his efforts to destroy me.

I had passed by a church four blocks from my mom's house, never paying attention to it, and walked down to see if anyone was there and what I'd have to do to belong. I stopped once in front of it, gaping at the name over the door. Church of Christ it read.

Omg, was this a sign, was god really real, and leading me to this place? I opened the door and a man approached me asking if he could help. I said, "I've been led here by god, can you tell me how I can give my life to him."

After telling me I needed to declare that Jesus was my savior and after being baptized I would belong. Easy peasy, just like that. Sign me up. He gave me a bible and told me to read the New Testament and come back later and he would baptize me.

I told him I knew the New Testament having been raised in the Christian Science church but that CS doesn't baptize, to which he said. "Well alright then, come back in an hour so we can prepare the baptismal bath and we'll get this done today. We need to get you saved as soon as possible." Amen, brother!

CHAPTER 40

I spent the whole plane ride back to Waco brushing up on the New Testament, determined to fight fire with fire.

Once on the ground, I took a cab to the Women's Shelter and after signing in, looked in the paper for used cars for sale. I called a few numbers but the prices were too high, so I went for a walk to get out of the dark old house that was the shelter.

After walking a few blocks, I came up to a driveway that had an adorable Toyota station wagon with a red crayon sign on the windshield that said FOR SALE, $200.00.

My generous cousin was about to buy me a car! I knocked on the door and a man answered with good ol' Texas hospitality and got the keys and started the car for me. It sounded great. He said they didn't need it and he was selling it real cheap to any Christian who had the money.

"I actually have it and I'm a Christian and I'd like to buy it." Was there something to this Jesus thing? You tell me. Before I left, he wanted me to come in and meet his wife and their little girl, the pageant queen.

The house was filled with trophies the child had won at beauty contests. The man's wife came out and met me and insisted on showing me her daughter's pageant dresses and costumes.

After marveling and freaking out a little at all this attention to physical beauty, (after all, I had been part of a protest to the Miss California pageant another cousin was in six years earlier), the man said, "We should go to the DMV and do the paperwork right now and you can drive it home today." It was Friday and there was just enough time. First though, the mom wanted us to gather in a circle and say a prayer, thanking god for making this sale. Amen.

Once I had the car, I made plans to go to his mother's the next day, a Saturday, when I knew Scott would be off work and probably at his mom's. I didn't know what I would do there. I was just hoping for a glimpse of my child.

I had parked down the street to watch for Scott and Kali. It didn't take long for a car to pull in front of his mom's house.

He got out and at the same time a young woman got out on the passengers side. Scott opened the back door and got Kali out of her car seat. He was walking around the front of the car when I impulsively got out and called to him.

He turned and saw me, said something to the girl, who got into a car parked behind his and drove off, and approached me quickly. He extended Kali for me to hold and said, "Let's go sit on the grass and talk." I followed him and we sat facing each other.

I let him talk and he took my hands and said, "I am so happy to see you." I was shocked at how well this was going.

He went on to tell me how unhappy he was with his mom taking care of Kali while he was working. He said he had moved to her house after I left and was working locally. He told me this with a thick Texas accent. I had asked him after we met why he didn't have an accent and he said he hated it and by high school no longer 'talked in twang'. So who was this person speaking to me? Was it pre HS Scott? Strange.

I told him I was at the Women's Shelter in Waco and he said "We need to get you a place here, I'll help you find one." He went on, "There's a boarding house a few blocks over that's really cheap so let's go see if there's a room available. We need to go soon before my mom get's home. She'll be really angry if she sees you here."

Before I could respond something very strange occurred. It was like he suddenly became a little boy. In a panicked voice he said, "Momma why are your hands all bloody and who is the bloody girl in the chair sleeping?" He was looking off into the distance while saying this with his face all screwed up and pale.

I said, "Scott, are you alright, what are you talking about?" He snapped out of whatever dream he was in and gruffly said, "We need to go now, but we'll take my car so she won't wonder why my car's here but Kali and I are gone."

I knew it wasn't the time to remind him it was actually my car he was driving and I basically kept quiet, afraid of saying something that would make him change his mind about helping me.

CHAPTER 41

The boarding house was actually an old house carved up into very small apartments. The owner lived there and answered the door after Scott rang his doorbell. He said he had one apartment available and after getting his keys he let us in.

The studio he showed us had a bedroom, a very small kitchenette and a bathroom. It had the smell and vibe of all the down and out people who had passed through it. I was now one of them.

Scott paid the first and last month's rent making the decision for me that this was where I wanted to live. He drove me back to my car so I could go back to Waco and get my meager possessions. He took Kali back into his mom's house so she wouldn't get suspicious when she got home.

On my way back to Waco, I wondered why we had to sneak around his mom when we were Kali's parents. I wondered why she had so much control over her son. Then I thought about what he said when we were sitting on the lawn. I was afraid if I asked him about it he would deny it. He had definitely been in another time or reality and had even sounded like a young boy, like another personality. I thought about the huge mottled burn scar he had that covered half the top of his chest and wondered if she had anything to do with it. He had told me it was caused by spilled coffee but hot coffee doesn't cause melted skin.

I knew by reuniting with Scott I was putting myself back in danger but at this point it was my only option if I wanted my daughter back. After getting my suitcase and thanking the staff at the shelter, I drove back to face my doom or my salvation.

After I let myself in and put my clothes in the bureau, I had little to do except wait for what would happen next. I had to remain there in case Scott brought Kali over.

I needed to eat but had nothing and had forgotten to stop at the Sonic on my way into town.

An hour after my arrival Scott finally arrived with Kali. He had brought me food from Dairy Queen, the de rigueur fast food staple in every Texas town. He had Kali with him. "I'm going out tonight and know you want to have Kali with you. If you go for a walk, don't go past my mom's house because she doesn't know you're back." He saw my face fall and said, "I'm dating that girl you saw me with. I'll be back later to get Kali."

I tried my best to act like I didn't care, so all I did was nod as he turned and left. I still had an enormous attraction to this man who could give me hope in one sentence, then dash it immediately with the next.

I still loved him, dammit! But for now, I turned my attention to Kali and tried to imagine my new role as a single, soon to be a divorced, glorified babysitter so Kali's father could be with a new mate. I knew I should have just accepted we were not meant to be but right now it seemed impossible.

It was impossible because when Scott returned at 2 in the morning, smelling of beer and womens perfume he said he was spending the night with me. He wanted sex and I was too weak willed and honestly afraid to not let him have it. As we laid there afterward, he turned on his side and said, "I want us to try again."

"What about your girlfriend?" I meekly asked.

"She's moving back to England in a month. She wants me and Kali to go with her but the court wouldn't allow me unless you will sign your right to her over."

"Is that what you're asking me to do?" I asked, sitting up now and distancing myself from him. I started to panic and he could tell I was getting upset.

With frustration he angrily said loudly, "I honestly don't know what to do. I still love you, but I love her too."

Kali woke up and called out to me. She was in the crib the manager had gotten out of storage for me so I went and got her and put her between us in bed.

"You know I can't sign her away. She's my life now and she needs me. Let's sleep and figure this out tomorrow."

He agreed but only because he was too drunk to stay awake so we spent the rest of the night nestled in bed like an average loving young couple. I barely slept, too afraid and too panicked about the days ahead.

CHAPTER 42

Apparently Scott's mother didn't watch Kali during the day. Scott had a babysitter for that and insisted on taking Kali over there so as to avoid suspicion by his mother who always picked her up after work there. Scott informed me of this as he got up to go to work and picked up Kali and headed out the door.

Panic once again rose up in me because he didn't tell me where she would be and because he might not choose me going forward. He was totally in control of my life and I didn't like it. It felt like being a passenger in a car about to careen off the side of a cliff.

After dressing I decided the best thing to do was get work. I drove to a market and bought a newspaper for the want ads. Scott had told me where his mom worked and told me not to go near the place for fear she would see me.

This hiding out was getting old real fast. Why wouldn't he just tell her? Was he afraid of her? What power did she have over him?

I bought a paper and looked at the help wanted ads and there was an ad for a waitress at a bed & breakfast in town. I went to the phone booth in front of the store and called.

The woman who answered said the job was still available so I drove over and was hired that day. They needed someone immediately for the lunch crowd so I put on the apron she gave me and began taking orders in the dining room.

The room had eight tables and as I was the only waitress, It was quickly evident to all the diners that I had never waitressed before. I didn't know the specials, I didn't know where the extra cutlery were and I got everyone's order mixed up.

I was tempted to pick up a glass, take a knife and hit it a few times to get everyone's attention and say, "This is my first day, I don't know how to waitress. My abusive husband has control of my life and our two year old, so please forgive me and give me a break."

Instead I muddled through until everyone was cleared out after the lunch hour and then the woman who hired me said there had been complaints about my service, but she would give me one week to prove I could do the job. In the meantime she would help me bus all the tables, throw the dirty table linens in the washer and show me where to find what I needed.

I was expected to waitress the breakfast and lunch crowd but be off work by 2 pm. I had gotten tips from most of the diners so that was encouraging. I made enough to buy a bag of groceries and put a little gas in my car so even though I hated waitressing, it would suffice for the time being.

CHAPTER 43

After returning to my hovel, I tried to make the place livable. It was crammed with furniture, almost like it was the owner's storage room. There was barely any room to walk around and the four highboys were useless to me because I had very little to put in them.

There was a tiny kitchen stocked with various patterns of plates, cups and silverware and a frying pan that looked like it had been dug up from the Civil War. It had the tiniest stove I had ever seen, so narrow it only had 2 burners. The oven would cook a chicken but nothing bigger. The refrigerator was tiny also, the kind students use in the dorms.

One thing I did do was get out the can of Raid I had bought and sprayed every square inch of the kitchen. I didn't want another night of cockroaches running over my and Kali's faces. After doing this, I left so as not to die from the fumes and went for a drive to explore this hellhole of a town I was forced to live in.

Riverton was so small it only had one market. The downtown area consisted of the requisite square that the massive courthouse sat on. Surrounding the square there were shops and cafes that only extended 2 blocks in every direction. None of it was charming or cute. It was run down and looked like the buildings had been constructed during the wild west era.

I did find the Church of Christ not far from the town square. My plan was to attend this church in order to be accepted as a good Christian instead of a California hippie that I was sure Bertha referred to me as.

I would sit near Bertha and her spider man husband and dare them to reject me. Once again, God would help me deal with my enemy. I say enemy because I'm sure Berths was behind the financing for having my daughter taken away and for Scott's divorce attorney. She was probably also behind the reason my husband was a raging alcoholic abuser. I wanted to know what she had done to him.

I drove the length of the main street until I reached the freeway. This was where the new action took place. Truck stops, fast food restaurants, motels and another Church of Christ. Jackpot. Why were there two? Now the question was, which one did Bertha and spider man attend? The town only had 1,000 people tops, not enough Church of Christers' to fill even one, let alone two. My plan was to attend both churches and have connections on both ends of town. I needed to find friends and allies fast. Being isolated made me vulnerable. Vulnerable to the abuse I knew would erupt soon.

CHAPTER 44

It took three days of Scott popping in and out, whenever he felt like it, sometimes with or without Kali, to blow up in anger.

I had attempted cooking some chicken on the stove, having gotten sick of fast food, when it happened.

It was around 4 o'clock when Scott let himself in. Kali wasn't with him and Scott worked until 5 so I was surprised to see him. He was drunk and said we needed to talk. He pulled me into the bedroom and sat me down and said, "I'm going to go live in England with my girlfriend and Kali's going with me and you're going to write a letter giving her up for the divorce judge." He had been standing over me, but now I was mad. I pushed him back and stood up. "And what will you do if I refuse?" I shot back.

"I'll show you what I'll do," and he punched me in the chest twice, so hard, it knocked the wind out of me. Just then the room began filling with smoke. It was the chicken on the stove. We both ran into the kitchen, me in front, and as I reached to turn off the stove, he hit the handle of the frying pan and it went flying, the whole thing landing on the floor near my bare feet. A piece of sizzling chicken fell on my foot and hot grease splashed all over it. I screamed in pain. I was still afraid of Scott continuing beating me so I turned to run out the door into the hall. He grabbed me before I reached it and pulled me towards himself, hugging me and saying over and over, "I'm sorry, I'm sorry, I'll take you to the hospital." He picked me up and took me out to the car and gently put me in the seat and drove me to emergency care.

The doctor on duty came in and took one look at my tear stained face, ravaged by terror and said, "Let's take a look."

I told him what happened, leaving out the abuse that led up to it. He treated and bandaged my foot and then sat on the bed next to me.

"You have two purple bruises on your chest and on your arms. How did you get those?" I gave him a look that said, 'I really want to tell you but I can't because I'm powerless right now and have to keep anyone from knowing so Scott won't get arrested. His mother will bid for custody because she has connections here and probably knows all the judges and lawyers in town, so I can't tell you.'

The doctor asked me, "Did that man waiting in the hall for you do this to you?" Glumly, I said "No." He stood and picked up my file and said, "Well, I think you're protecting him, so I'm going to put in this diagnosis that I think you're a victim of spousal abuse in case it happens again." I nodded and he escorted me out to my abuser, shaking his head.

When we returned to the apartment, Scott took me inside, then left to get Kali. The doctor had given me a pain pill and sedative so I fell asleep until late in the evening.

When I woke up, the first thing I thought of was if I could do my job with my foot banaged to the point I couldn't put on a shoe. In addition,the doctor had also told me not to walk on it for a few days.

I was still very hungry having not eaten all day, so got up and hobbled into the kitchen. Scott had picked up all the chicken pieces and the pan and they were back on the stove. I threw them in the trash and made a peanut butter and jelly sandwich and went back to the bed to elevate my leg. After eating, I went back to sleep until early the next morning.

Once awake, I tried walking on my foot but after only a few steps, the pain was unbearable. I took another pain killer and wondered how to contact my employer. I would have to drive to a phone booth, but instead I decided to drive to the B&B and tell them in person.

The doctor had given me crutches to use so I got them out and hobbled into the B&B back door and knocked. The cook answered the door and quickly assessed my condition and called out, "Mary, come here." The woman who had hired me came to the door and after seeing me with my crutches said, "You can't wait tables on crutches. Can you walk without them?"

I answered, "I was told to stay off my foot. It's burned and very painful. I just came by to tell you I won't be able to work for at least a week, and I'm really sorry and want to thank you for giving me a chance but you should hire someone else."

Martha nodded and said, "Well thank you for coming here to tell us instead of just not showing up. Y'all get better now." and she shut the door.

I went back to the apartment and laid back down after taking another tranquilizer and slept.

I woke up when Scott and Kali came in. I thought I was dreaming but fully came to after seeing the flowers Scott was carrying. After Kali asked me why my foot was all bandaged and had crawled up next to me, Scott sat down in the overstuffed chair next to the bed.

"I'm not going to England and I'm going to drop the divorce," he said. I just sat there, shocked. He continued, "Let's look for a house together and tomorrow we'll go talk to my attorney in Waco." I was overjoyed. Wait, why was I overjoyed? I shouldn't be happy about this. This man could someday kill me. He was very capable of doing so. My mind reached for the fastest and easiest way to survive. "Ok," was all I could muster, but thinking, I'll go along with this plan until I can plot Kali's and my escape from this very unstable jail of a marriage.

CHAPTER 45

It didn't take me long to realize I had been Scott's second choice as a mate. He confessed to me that his girlfriend from England had broken up with him because I was back in his life and we weren't divorced, and besides she was moving back to the UK. He told me this as we drove up and down the streets of Riverton looking for houses with For Rent signs.

We finally found a nice house on a quiet street with a landscaped yard. He pulled up in front and went up to the door to ask about it. He came back saying there was a note on the door with a number to call. He drove us down to the phone booth in front of the market and came back to the car saying we could meet the owner there in two hours.

Encouraged by our find, more so with me as this might be a start over for our marriage, we went to dinner. He didn't seem as optimistic as me while we sat and ate at the Golden Corral, all you can eat buffet. His attitude was one of a spurned teenager who was out to eat with his mother or sister. He was no doubt bummed about his girlfriend dumping him. He wouldn't get any sympathy from me.

After eating he drove us to a children's playground where we took turns taking Kali to the different play equipment. She joyfully laughed as she went down the slide and breezed back and forth on the toddlers swing. She was probably also subconsciously happy her parents weren't fighting and were together.

We went back to the house for rent and waited for the owner to arrive. An older, paint peeling sedan finally pulled up into the driveway. The car was filled almost to the ceiling with boxes, clothing and tarps. The woman who got out wasn't too steady on her feet but managed making it to the door of the house. She was very disheveled and dirty and reeked of alcohol. I wouldn't have cared if she was naked; I wanted this house.

After letting us in, she slurred out the cost for rent and staggered after us as we went from room to room. It had two bedrooms and a large living room. The whole house was furnished except the second bedroom. Scott told me our furniture from the house we had shared was in storage in Waco and we could get Kali's four poster bed with all her Rainbow Bright bedspread and accessories and anything else we needed from it.

The woman took us to the backyard which was lush with trees, shrubs and flowers. There was a large lawn that would be perfect for Kali to run around in.

"You have to take care of this yard," the woman said. "If I come over here and my plants are all dead, I'll kick ya'll out." I looked at her face for a good natured grin, but she was dead serious.

Scott laughed his phony, 'I have no intention of doing so but I'll tell you I will' laugh and said, "No problem there. When can we move in?"

She didn't hesitate, "Today, but I'll need a cash deposit of $100.00. Can you get that for me?"

Scott, surprised, said, "Can you wait here while we go to the bank?" "Well, you better hurry, it'll close soon." she answered. I followed Scott to the car holding Kali. I didn't want to be stuck there with this woman who could barely walk or talk. Besides, I wanted to see where his bank was and more importantly get access to the money in there. After all, I was still his wife and I assumed Texas laws would give me that right. You never know though, with Texas.

I wanted to go in and add my name to his account but Kali was asleep in the backseat so I waited in the car. I could take care of finances later, like I always had before our separation.

Scott had the money, including the first and last month's rent and we went back to pay her and hopefully move in immediately.

When we returned the woman was using the washing machine. She took the money and stuffed it into her dirty jeans pocket. We asked her about signing a lease but when she shook her head no we let it go. Not the smartest thing to do but we didn't want to put any roadblocks in front of getting this house.

She handed Scott the keys then went out and got in her car and drove off, with the clothes still washing. She never did come back for her laundry which turned out to be a sleeping bag and a frayed and holy blanket. We found out from a neighbor that she was an alcoholic and lived in a homeless camp somewhere in her car. She had enough faculties left to rent her house out to pay the mortgage so she wouldn't lose it but having no income it really was her only option.

CHAPTER 46

After moving in Scott confessed he still hadn't told his mother we were back together. He tried to figure out a way to lie to her about why he was moving out of her house and why she didn't have to pick Kali up from daycare any longer.

He wanted me to help him figure out how to get around telling her but I wanted no part of their mother/son dynamic. He told me he didn't want to lose his babysitter in case we didn't work out so wanted to continue taking Kali there during the weekdays. He was calling the shots and I knew better than to object.

The next day we went to Waco to see his attorney and go to the storage unit. His attorney was a small, highly hairsprayed, auburn haired spitfire. You could tell she took no prisoners and could fight tooth and nail with the good ol' boy lawyers she came up against in court. We followed her into her office to the sound of her noisy high heels clicking on the floor tiles and sat down on hard wooden chairs.

It was this woman who had initially filed the paperwork to have my baby ripped from my arms by the Sheriff in California. She would not be my friend. I didn't care how syrupy her Southern drawl was.

After asking Kali if she remembered her and shoveling some phony lighthearted bs, she asked what Scott needed. She was his attorney after all, not mine.

Scott had told me he was going to drop the divorce but being true to his psycho personality, he told her he wanted to schedule the divorce six months ahead to give us a trial reunion. He may as well have said, 'I want to keep this divorce hanging over her head to keep her in line and keep control over her'.

Together they looked at her calendar and picked out a date. It felt like they were casually, calmly, in front of me, deciding my date of execution. I kept my mouth shut like a good little Christian wife who let a man decide her fate.

"I'll tell you what," she began, "I do just as much marriage counseling as I do divorces."

I bet you do, you're the type who will do anything for money, I thought to myself. With that bit of homily, we left and went to the storage locker.

Scott wanted me to work and I agreed, not wanting to have to ask him for money, which he had always been reluctant to give me.

He suggested I apply at a truckstop outside of town that he had heard always needed cashiers. He said he didn't want me working in town where I could run into his mother. Geez, could my life get anymore controlled? Well, yes it could and yes it did.

The owner of the truckstop hired me part time, which allowed me to pick up Kali and be with her in the afternoons. I didn't like my job. The owner made no bones about hiring young pretty women to deal with the truckers that came in to eat. He also had a weekly poker game that lasted all weekend and a handful of country singer celebrities, big time and small time, were always coming in and out. I met them all. Some stopped by in their luxurious motorhomes while on concert tours and they all knew the owner.

A few famous ones I met and became friendly with, I wanted to ask, 'Could you possibly help me and my daughter escape this hell-hole of a state? Can you take us on tour with you because I'm living with a powder keg of an abusive husband who's probably going to kill me if I don't get away from him. Can you please save us?'

Of course, I'd just smile and ring up their purchases. I found out a few weeks after working there that the trailers out back housed prostitutes for his clientele to use when they rolled in. The truckstop was actually an incorporated town of which the owner was the mayor. He made his own laws and had a police officer hired to handle any scuffles, either back in the bar area or with one of the prostitutes.

I found out later everyone in Riverton considered the truck-stop town with disdain and were offended by it's ungodly ways. Anyone who worked there got a bad reputation so I looked for another job. Just as I feared, my mother-in-law told the custody judge about the place and claimed I worked there as a prostitute. That's why my husband suggested I work there. Setting me up like that was normal for them.

CHAPTER 47

I eventually got hired by a nonprofit in an office in Riverton's town square. I promised Scott I wouldn't show my face at lunch in case his mother was lurking around downtown.

One thing Scott continued doing was to take Kali to his mothers on Friday nights and not returning until the next day. Those nights were torture for me. I had a very bad feeling about her being there, but if I objected I knew Scott's punishment would be swift and cruel. I just had this overwhelming dread when she was over there.

My new job was boring and the other women who worked there treated me like the outsider I was. They had all grown up together, knew everyone in town and knew everyone's business. I was a traumatized human, no fun, unhappy and scared to death. I knew I was considered a weirdo, being Californian and all. I joined in when their talk was about Jesus and God and church so they would have to accept me into their small flock, but I felt like the black sheep the entire time I worked there.

CHAPTER 48

I had only been working downtown for three months when Scott and I came to blows.

He had been going out by himself on Saturday nights and coming home just in time for me to be leaving for the Sunday church service charade I was doing. I would always take Kali with me so she could have a Sunday school playdate with other kids.

On one of these early Sundays, Scott got home at 6 in the morning, very drunk and smelling of womens perfume and sex secretions. He wanted to have sex, but I refused to even kiss him until he took a shower and washed out his mouth. He was in no shape to do anything but get what he wanted, which was sex, so he thought it would be a good idea to rape me. I rose up on my knees in bed and pushed him onto the floor.

He got up and pulled me toward him and I pushed one arm off mine. With the other, he gave me an uppercut that caused me to almost bite off the end of my tongue. In spite of blood spurting all over us, he socked me in the eye and then knocked me so hard upside the head I went flying into the bedroom door. I scrambled to get up not wanting him towering over me but once up, I realized he wasn't coming after me. He was instead, lying on the floor, passed out. I quickly grabbed my purse with the car keys in it and drove myself to the police station. I told them what happened and asked them to take photos of my injuries. They asked if I wanted to press charges. This was before police automatically pressed charges in spousal abuse cases. I told them I would hold off till later and left for the hospital. I didn't want the police to go arrest him without me being there to take care of Kali. They would have had to turn her over to Child Protective if I wasn't there. I told them I would press charges later but that I needed to get to the hospital.

Ones there I was taken into emergency and was seen by the doctor who had treated me for my burned foot a month before. He put a patch over my very swollen eye and checked to make sure my tongue was still attached. He took pictures of my bruised body and said I needed to have someone come get me, that I was too messed up to drive. He gave me painkillers and tranquilizers, just like the first time.

Killing two birds with one stone, I gave him Bertha's phone number so she could see her son's handywork and also let her know I was back on the scene, ready to take them all on. Her and spider man appeared not long afterward. Bertha drove me in her car while spider man drove mine to their house. She kept asking what I had done to make her son so angry but I was in too much pain to talk. I couldn't think nor speak. Mainly because my tongue was so swollen, it literally filled my mouth, but also her question was asked by a true enabler and didn't deserve an answer.

At their house Bertha marched me up stairs and plopped me on a bed and left. I conked out right after she put a pill in my mouth.

I awoke to voices downstairs. I could hear Kali talking and Scott's voice. I gingerly went downstairs. When they saw me they put me in a chair and gave me some water but only after I asked for it. Everyone was sitting around the dinner table and there were papers that had been handwritten.

Bertha was the spokesperson and she said, "We want to make a deal with you. If Scott signs over custody to you, you have to sign this agreement that you won't press charges against him." The agreement had already been signed by Scott and Bertha's and spider man's signatures as witnesses. There was a line for me to sign my name along with the date. Wait a minute, the date they had on the agreement was the day after the assault. Had I been passed out for that long? Apparently so.

"Scott has agreed to move to Plano and live with his cousin. You will be on your own here because after today, we want nothing more to do with you," Bertha said. Scott got up, hugged Kali, and without a word, walked out the door.

CHAPTER 49

The relief I felt was indescribable. Scott had left in the car that was in my name, but I still had my little Toyota station wagon so I had what I needed to begin again.

I made two phone calls from the payphone at the market. One was to the Welfare Office in Waco, which was the seat of the county Riverton was in, to apply for housing. The other was to the Courthouse in Waco to obtain an attorney the Women's Shelter there said I would be entitled to if I had no money for one. I knew Scott now was going to go through with the divorce and I needed an attorney in Waco. To my dismay, Texas laws are such that whatever county you file for divorce in, that will be your courthouse until the day you die. Even if you move to a different Texas town or out of state, I would always have to return to Waco. The Women's Shelter staff told me they never granted a change of venue no matter what. I won't get into how I feel about Texas lawmakers. Some of their other archaic laws would be to my detriment as well.

After I got an address to go to for housing I got the name of an attorney and called him. He said the paper giving me custody wasn't binding because it hadn't been witnessed by a notary. I somehow knew it was too good to be true.

After hanging up, I drove to the police station and filed an assault complaint against Scott, reminding the sergeant who filled it out that there had been photos of my face that were taken the day before. The cop asked me Scott`s whereabouts and when I told him I didn't know his cousin's name or address in Plano, he looked up at me and said, "Well now how are we going to arrest him if he's not even around?"

"I don't know, his mother lives here and I know her address. She knows where he is," I said, trying to keep anger and anxiety out of my voice. My tongue was still swollen and I had a large cut above my lip, my left eye had a doctor's patch over it but in spite of all that he drawled, "Well, if he's in the Dallas area, it's out of our jurisdiction so you'll have to go there and file," 'Omg,' I wanted to scream, 'HE BEAT ME UP HERE, YOU IDIOT! DON'T YOU PUT OUT APB'S OR WHATEVER TO FIND PEOPLE?' Instead I asked quietly, "So you aren't going to pursue this?" I asked, feeling all the adrenaline I had had earlier sinking down to pass out levels.

"Well, I'll file it but I won't promise you nothin," but before he finished his sentence I was already at the door.

Kali and I went to the welfare office where I got the names and addresses of apartments in town that accepted housing vouchers.

I finally found a five building group of duplexes set in a quiet setting with childrens play equipment and grassed landscaping. I knocked on the manager's door and when she answered she eyed me with suspicion as I'm sure she had dealt with drug addicts, alcoholics and abusive moms. She informed me only moms and their children could stay there, so no overnights with men. I told her I was glad about that so she got some keys off a rack and showed me our new home.

Christmas was coming in a few weeks so Kali and I made decorations and I was given a tree by a young family I had befriended at church.

I had chosen the Church of Christ near the freeway after meeting with the pastor who was much friendlier and helpful than the one Bertha and spider man attended in the downtown square. I soon found out the reason there were two Churches of Christ in town was, according to church members, the youth pastor had a falling out with the old pastor at the downtown church and left to form his own church, along with almost the whole congregation. There had been rumors about illegal activities and secret meetings going on at the downtown church that the young youth pastor objected to but that was all the info I was given about it.

CHAPTER 50

Not long after we had settled in at the welfare duplex, the free attorney from Waco came to interview me and see what my living conditions were in Riverton. His shirt was heavily wrinkled, he was an hour late and his eyes were bloodshot. I hoped he knew what he was doing.

He told me to take photos to present to the judge of Kali's room, all the pictures of her on the walls, the playground and anything else that showed Kali was being well taken care of.

Later in the evening I was sucker punched. It was right after dinner when there was a loud banging on my door and a man said, "Open up, it's the Sheriff." When I opened the door the Sheriff stepped in and handed me an envelope and right behind him were Scott and spider man. "This is an emergency court order to take custody of Kali McConnell," the Sheriff said. Scott brushed past me and picked up Kali. I stood there, stunned. After they all left, I sat down, shaking, both with terror and anger. It was too late to call my lawyer. I went to bed and tried to sleep but the rage, the fear, and the panic I felt kept me agitated and awake all night. The skin on my hands started to peel again.

The next day, I finally got the attorney on the pay phone and he had some bad news for me. He said Scott's lawyer had managed to get our divorce case decided by a Criminal Court judge instead of a Family Court judge. When I asked how that had happened he said that it was a known fact Waco judges are influenced by campaign donors and Scott's attorney was one of this judges most generous donors. She called in a favor and got the venue changed to Criminal Court. He then told me my case and Kali's fate had probably already been decided. He said that because I was from California I would never be given custody.

I managed to make it home without wrecking the car through my tears. When I pulled near the apartment, I saw my car, that Scott had taken, in front of it. I parked and after seeing Scott was nowhere around, I noticed an envelope on the windshield. In the envelope there were the keys and a note. It read, "Here's your car, I bought a new one. See you in court on the 24th." The 24th? That was only a week away. I ran into the house and read again through the court order. Scott and his mother were seeking joint custody of Kali with me only getting supervised visits at Bertha's home at her discretion, for 1 hour a week. The hearing would take place the day before Christmas. Christmas Eve. How could that be? All government offices were closed the day before Christmas. Even the mall was closed the day before Christmas in Texas and on Sundays so everyone could go to church. You couldn't even buy alcohol in dry McLennan County but the courthouse was open?

As I sat there, stunned, a tow truck pulled up in front of my place and proceeded to attach itself to my car. I ran out and found the driver so I could ask him why he was taking my car but I already knew. Scott had not made payments and it was being repossessed. He had told the tow company where they could find my car. My credit would be shot, I soon learned, from that and the fact the American Express charge card in my name hadn't been paid by him. Oh yes, and also, the phone that was in my name when we lived in Waco also was never paid by him so I couldn't get phone service in Texas until it was paid. I got the bill by going into the phone company and it was over $500.00, most of it calls to England.

On top of all that, I would lose my duplex because the contingency for living there was that the moms had to have custody, physically and legally.

Because Scott was living near Dallas, I knew Kali would, in all likelihood, live at Bertha's and spider man's so they would have her there for my visits. Omg. This was bad...really bad. I called my mother collect.

CHAPTER 51

My mother and I weren't especially close, probably because she could never understand why I preferred a life of adventure, instead of settling down and living contentedly as a housewife. However, she was who I naturally turned to in a crisis and she was always there for me.

She listened to all my mounting obstacles getting Kali and I out of Texas but could only offer condolences and a little money. She was having 10 family members for Christmas so couldn't come to the hearing. Her party no doubt consisted of all my siblings and cousins and family friends who did not want to get involved. I said I understood and hung up the pay phone and went back to my duplex. The landlady came over when I returned and had heard from Vince that Kali had been taken from me by the Sheriff, so if I didn't get her back on the 24th, I would have to be out by January 1st. I knew I wouldn't get her. I called my pastor.

I shouldn't have been surprised he wanted to help me because I had learned from other parishioners he didn't like any of the people who still belonged to the church he had been Youth Pastor for. He especially didn't like spider man and Bertha. He had heard rumors about them possibly being involved in illegal activity no one had proof of.

He contacted a young couple with our church who had an empty mother-in-law room I could use. I knew them and on Wednesday night, at church they said I could move in on the 1st of January. That was a relief.

I concentrated on getting a job so I could tell the judge on the 24th that I could support us. I had kept my California. Cosmetology license active and wondered if I could use it in Texas. The pastor let me use his office phone to call the Texas

State Board of Cosmetology in Austin. They told me that it would cost me $50.00 to get my California license transferred. I had just enough and got the address and wrote the request and sent it on that day. They would mail my license to the pastor's home address. The next day I went to the town square and put my application into the two beauty salons on the town square. The second one said I could start work the next day. The owner said I could work as a receptionist and shampooer until my license arrived when I told her I was licensed in California. OK, I thought, at least I'm not done for yet.

CHAPTER 52

The hearing went as I predicted. It was eerily quiet in the courthouse. Being as it was Christmas eve, my case was the only one on the docket. Bertha and Scott were sitting on a bench in the hall when I arrived. I was surprised to see the attorney I was assigned got there right after I did and went straight into the courtroom.

Scott's attorney, the woman Scott and I had gone to see a few months prior, was already inside, no doubt paying off the judge to be there on Christmas Eve.

We were all called in and after sitting down next to my attorney I gave him the pictures I had taken of my duplex along with a picture of my messed up face the police had taken. I also had gotten my military hospital records that reported spousal abuse done to me by Scott. My attorney said the abuse done to me would carry no weight. "Why not?" I asked.

"Just because he hits you doesn't mean he hits his daughter," he said.

"So watching me get choked and beat up isn't considered harmful to her? And if he hits me isn't it only a matter of time he will hit her?" I said in a low voice.

"Children are considered men's property, so no. Now be quiet, the judge is coming in."

After we were sworn in my attorney asked to approach the judge and after nodding, my attorney took the photos and gave them to the judge. The judge completely ignored them, not even looking at them..

The judge allowed Scott and his mother to testify and listened intently about what a bad mother they both thought I was.

When it came my turn to testify, the judge ignored me and began going through a stack of files on his desk.

Scott and Bertha told the judge I was a kidnapper and a California hippie who was probably on drugs. They told the judge about me working at the truck stop near Riverton which raised the judge's eyebrows. I was tempted to stand up and scream at both of them, but I've seen enough court dramas to know not to.

The hearing took no longer than a half an hour with the judge ruling Scott would get Temporary Primary custody with his mom getting Temporary Possessory Co- Custody.

I would get visitation rights of one hour a week at Bertha's house at her discretion and supervised by her and spider man. This game we were playing with my daughter's life and mine was stacked against us. I was too angry to cry.

CHAPTER 53

I spent Christmas alone, except for a holiday church service. I had been sincerely praying, hoping for a miracle. None came that day.

I was told by Scott that I could come over to his mothers the day after Christmas to see Kali and give her a present. I had been given a doll to give her by my pastor. I went after they had finished their lunch at noon.

Scott answered the door when I arrived with Kali in his arms. He wouldn't let me hold her and I had to agree not to cry or talk about her coming home. He said I couldn't hold her but could only hug her while he held onto her. He said I could give her the doll but because there was a large group of people at the house our visit would be on the front porch. That was fine with me, although it was very cold, it was better than being in the house with everyone staring at the woman who I'm sure they were told was so bad that my child was taken from me. "Kali played with her doll, but when Scott said I should leave she began to cry and whimpered, "Mommy, don't leave me."

Scott said, "Well now you've upset her so I'm taking her in." Before I could hug her he took her inside and shut the door on me. I drove back to the stranger's house I was living at, went into the bedroom I had been assigned and cried while praying for the nightmare to end.

CHAPTER 54

I spent the month of January working and going to church with the couple I lived with. They were civil with me but weren't friendly to the point I could hang out with them. When I was at their home, I stayed in the spare bedroom, reading. I'm sure they were skeptical about me, having lost custody.

About the third week after Christmas, my car broke down. I had no extra money to fix it and certainly didn't want to ask the couple I was living with for help.

Scott knew how to fix cars and had worked on mine when we were together so I got up some courage and called him at the number I had been given to contact him if I couldn't visit Kali.

It was a Sunday and he surprised me by telling me he'd be over in an hour. I was both relieved and excited. Just hearing his voice reminded me I wasn't over him yet. In spite of everything he put me through, I still loved him. Or was it something else? He was like a drug and I was addicted.

When Scott arrived the chemistry was still very there between us. I felt all over again the same feelings I had that first time seeing him. 'How is that even possible', I thought? This man had proven over and over he was perfectly capable of destroying me, yet here I was getting weak in the knees in his presence. I found out later what kept drawing me to him, but for now I concentrated on getting my car fixed.

Scott told me I had a cracked block and needed a new engine. He said there was a place he knew of halfway to Dallas where I could get one put in. He said he would pay for it and I readily took him up on it. It was the least he could do for me.

We towed my car behind his. Now that the car that had been in my name was repossessed, he had bought a vintage muscle car with a V8 engìne. He took the back roads to get there and we both rode in silence, stewing in the steaming soup of attraction we still felt towards one another. We both wanted desperately to fix our broken psyches but neither of us knew how. I eventually found out how but by then it was too late. I would have to settle on getting my car fixed for now.

We arrived at what looked like a ranch with a large barn surrounded by cars. The owner came out when we pulled up and Scott got out and talked to him and they looked under the hood while I sat in the car.

Scott finally came around to my side and said the man had an engine he could put in but he needed the car for a week and told me the cost. I nodded in agreement, wondering how I could get back to pick it up. Scott was thinking the same thing and on our half hour drive back to Riverton, he shocked me with his proposal.

He confessed to me that he wanted Kali out of his mom's house as much as I did. He said he didn't like how she treated her and his mom wouldn't let him stay at her house nor see Kali. He said he and his mom had a huge fight over it. He suggested we go to her house together when we got back and demand to see her.

He got no argument from me, mainly because I knew all along what a cold hearted woman she was and was glad he finally realized it too.

I told him that when it was my hour to visit Kali, his mom made me sit on the floor at her feet while Kali sat on her lap. She wouldn't allow me to hold her and could only hug her once while Bertha held her. Every visit Kali would desperately reach for me and when Bertha held her back she would start to cry and whimper. I got angry the first time that happened and Bertha said if I got angry one more time she would discontinue the visits all together.

The second visit only lasted 10 minutes when Kali started crying because Bertha wouldn't let her come to me, Bertha stated that I was upsetting her. She yelled at Kali and told her to go upstairs, threatening to spank her if she wouldn't. She called her attorney and by the second week, I lost all rights to visit. It was all I could do to not beat the crap out of this sadistic, heartless woman. Was she the reason Scott was so abusive?

Scott told me his mom treated him the same way. He wanted both of us to confront her. I asked him if his mom and spider man had any guns. There was no doubt in my mind either one of them would use it on me claiming I attacked them.

CHAPTER 55

Once back in town, I convinced Scott we needed to call her first instead of just showing up. He reluctantly agreed and drove us to the grocery store pay booth. He got out and I rolled the window down to hear what he was saying but all I heard was shouting. He finally hung up the receiver so hard, I wondered if he broke it. He got in and slammed the car door and angrily said, "We're going over there and getting Kali." I told him it wasn't a good idea, but he headed straight for her house.

Once there, he got out and stormed toward the front door with me following behind. He banged on the door and shouted "mom" over and over. Minutes passed and I heard voices inside. Someone said, hush everyone, stop talking. Finally, the door opened a crack and Scott tried to push the door open but when Bertha saw who it was she quickly slammed it shut. Scott kept pounding on the door but I pulled him away and we both went back to his car, a united front in our frustration and anger.

Scott said he was too tired and angry to drive back to Dallas and said we should get a motel room. By then it was 11:00 and the couple I was staying with always went to bed at 9:00. They hadn't given me a key and I didn't want to wake them up so I agreed to a motel room.

We went to a motel near the church I attended along the freeway and Scott got a single queen bed. I didn't think that was such a good idea, but didn't say so. I was too tired and too emotionally jagged and couldn't take anymore unnecessary drama.

I blamed Scott for the mess we were in but was in no position to tell him that's how I felt. If only he would stop hitting me when he was angry, I would love him until the end of our lives. He had trained me not to dig too deep into his behavior that was erratic on a good day and homicidal on a bad one. It takes insight and an ability to self examine to work one's way out of bad behavior. It also takes being responsible for one's actions but as far as he was concerned it was me who was making him abusive. It was always my fault.

We could, on rare occasions, laugh together but those days were long passed. We were now always right on the edge of disaster and both feared acting natural or getting too comfortable with one another because one sentence or word taken the wrong way could hurl us both into the abyss of conflict. It was better if I just kept my mouth shut and turned off my personality. I really did not want to live that way, but for now I had to follow his lead. He was very much like his mother, a cruel taskmaster who expected blind obedience. I thought all this while laying on my side away from him, pretending to sleep so arguments over sex wouldn't get me kicked out into the cold. Disfunction on his part had gotten me thrown out before and I had no doubt it could happen again.

CHAPTER 56

Scott woke us up early and said he had to go to work. I had Mondays off and told him this as I headed for the bathroom. I locked the door out of habit ever since that day in Hawaii when he walked in and beat me up. When I came back out, I could tell he was plotting something. "I think you should move up to Dallas near me where you can get better work. Come back with me and while I'm at work, you can look for work in my car," he continued as I sat there like a small child, "You can't keep living with that couple and after the divorce goes through in February, we'll be close enough together to share custody." Before I could respond he said, "If we're both in Dallas, the judge will remove my mom as co-custodian." All I could do was nod, yes.

"Where will I live up there?" I meekly asked as we got in his car.

"You can stay with me at my cousin's." Oh dear, I thought, now his bad behavior will infect the rest of his family. He went on, "I'll tell mom you moved away and you are giving me custody." I knew from experience that if I agreed to this he could use it against me at the divorce if he once again switched into destruction mode. I didn't trust that he and his mother hadn't planned this whole dramatic ruse to get me completely out of their lives and give my daughter over to them to destroy.

I did move up to a suburb in Dallas but not with him and his cousin. It was actually on the complete opposite side of where he lived. I had made enough money from my hairdressing job that paid for the deposit and first month's rent in a one bedroom apartment. I did use his car to find it and also signed on with a temp agency in a week's time.

There was a Kindercare a block away that I could afford to have Kali at while I worked and I found the largest Church of

Christ I could find so I would have a lot of potential network of friends and Sunday school for Kali.

I didn't feel guilty about my strategies concerning integrating us into a Christian community. At the time, I was really investing myself into the Christian religion in a sincere effort to pray myself free of the horrific marriage I was in. I felt that as long as I was sincere in seeking answers and resolutions, I wouldn't be faulted in the event there really was a god.

The hearing for our divorce was in March, in Waco of course. Scott and his mother appeared before the judge but Scott sided with me and asked that he and I share custody, with his mother eliminated from any rights.

The judge agreed and granted the divorce. However, right away I started having visitation issues with Scott. He believed he could just walk into my apartment whenever he wanted, even on my visitation weeks. I told him to at least call first, but I guess that was too difficult for him because he would just burst in my door. He was drunk during these times and would head straight for my bedroom, saying, 'I know you have some guy back here' and would look under my bed and rifle through the clothes in my closet. On one of these occasions, on Kali's birthday, he followed me in the door from behind when I was coming home from the store and scared the crap out of me. He had been hiding behind a tree.

"It's not your visitation week," I said, "but you can give Kali your gift."

He went into the living room, picked Kali up and headed out the side door where his car was parked. I followed him out shouting, "Where are you going with her?" Without answering he opened his car door and put her in the pàssengers seat. I ran out and when I reached him, he hit me so hard I was knocked out.

I came to on my neighbors couch who had watched the whole horror show unfold. Her husband had carried me into their apartment.

"Do you want to go to the hospital?" she asked.

"No," I said, quitely, "How long have I been out?"

"About 10 minutes," she said.

"I need to call the police," I said and thanked them before stumbling back to my apartment.

CHAPTER 57

Before this latest drama, we had picked up my car, after the custody hearing, on our way back up from Waco. I no longer had to depend on Scott for transportation or the bus system.

The day after he knocked me out, I gathered up all the evidence proving past abuse he had done to me and drove to the police department of the suburb I was in. I told the desk Sergeant I wanted to press charges against my ex and after sitting in their lobby for a half hour, I was finally taken to a room where two officers heard my account of the abuse and looked at past photos and doctors reports. I told them he had taken our daughter on my visitation week

I wanted him arrested, however, the officers convinced me that would just make him more angry and abusive. They also reasoned that if he lost his job going to jail he wouldn't be able to pay child support. When I informed them the judge didn't require him to pay support after he lied and said he wasn't working, they both just stared at me, out of excuses as to why they didn't feel like going after him.

They suggested I get a restraining order against him, but to do that I would need to file in downtown Dallas. Oh, geesh. I was really getting tired of the police passing the buck and enabling abusers by never holding them accountable.

I begrudgingly left after filing a report that I knew they probably filed in the trashcan after I left and headed downtown. I was working as a temp and had not gotten a job that Monday so I had the afternoon to get this all done in time to pick up Kali at Kindercare. Scott had called the evening he drove off with her to tell me his plan to take her there Monday morning.

When I had picked up Kali and we got to our apartment, I first went to the neighbor who had helped me and thanked her and asked if she would be a witness at the restraining order hearing scheduled in two weeks. She agreed and Kali and I went to our apartment for dinner.

Scott's phone calls started shortly after we walked in the door. There were at least 20 that night. He called apologizing, he called crying, he called screaming. My answering machine was soon filled with his messages. By the 10th call, I stopped answering.

Answering machines had just been invented where you could put a cassette tape in and record the messages. I bought one and it was in use that evening. I wanted it for the hearing as proof my ex was a psycho. Unfortunately, the judge refused to listen to it. Scott was at the hearing and told the judge lie after lie about how he had taken Kali because he feared for her life, how I had chased him with a knife and that ol' Texas chestnut about how I was from California and probably on drugs and slept with men....blah, blah, blah. All lies. When it came my turn to tell my side, I was tongue tied and stunned by his lies. If my neighbor hadn't told the judge what she witnessed and how she helped me, I doubt I would have gotten the RO. I found out soon enough though, that RO's are not worth even as much as toilet paper. At least TP serves a purpose.

CHAPTER 58

Having joint custody with Scott was a nightmare. On the weeks he was supposed to bring her to me at a public place, because he wasn't allowed 50 feet from my door, he would always be hours late or not even show up with her.

On my weeks, I always arrived early but when Kali would see me and try to run to me, Scott would hold her back and tap his watch saying, I have one more minute with her. Kali would be crying, at first pushing against him to get away, but eventually just whimpering and sitting, resigned to his control.

On one of these occasions, after I had driven onto the freeway, he soon caught up with me in his car and screamed for me to pull over. When I ignored him he tried to run my car off the road, with Kali in the backseat. I finally pulled over to prevent an accident and he pulled up behind me and came running up and began beating on my closed window screaming for me to unlock my door and roll down my window. I asked him what he wanted and he said, "I don't have your new phone number and by law you need to provide me with it," he screamed.

You may be asking, why didn't you call the police on your cell phone? For the simple reason they hadn't been invented yet, not for another 10 years.

While I sat there waiting for him to go away, I took out my map of Dallas County and found the nearest CHP office. It wasn't far, only two freeway stops away. I was, at this point, not only fed up but also terrified of Scott. With him standing outside my car, I started it and got back on the freeway. He caught up just as I took the off ramp and pulled into the CHP office right after the stop light. Before Scott could figure out what I was doing, I had Kali in my arms and was in the CHP lobby. I breathlessly explained what was going on just as he pulled into the driveway. A CHP Officer went out to confront him but Scott took off when he realized where he was at.

The officer came back saying he didn't get his license number and when asked why he didn't pursue him, he stated, "Oh, they only do that in the movies, I'm not going to go after him." But again, I filled out a complaint after showing them my restraining order and left, knowing it would never see the light of day.

When I got home, I called Scotts cousin's number and gave his wife my new number. Within a matter of minutes my phone was ringing. It was him, screaming at me about having to talk to him by law concerning Kali, according to the restraining order. So I asked him what he needed to say concerning Kali, but he couldn't think of anything.

I said "That's what I thought," and hung up on him. He called again another 10 times, finally quitting long after Kali had been put to sleep.

CHAPTER 59

I was making friends at church and had joined the choir. Kali had fun at Sunday school and we began being invited to parties and BBQ's.

I was trying hard to present myself as a mentally healthy, happy go lucky single woman but inside I felt enormously damaged psychologically and had strong feelings of self doubt and failure. I began beating myself up for being dupped by the handsome, phony man I had stupidly married. I was also very conflicted with mixed feelings of hating him, soon followed by strong feelings of compassion and longing for him. I was, in a word, miserable. I'm convinced he knew this and went out of his way to capitalize on my vulnerability and insecurities.

I had befriended a single man at church who, in another time and headspace I could have fallen for romantically. I knew he was interested in pursuing a relationship with me and on one occasion when I was to pick up Kali he insisted on coming with me. A part of me wanted to know how much of the shit show of a traumatized, divorced woman's life he could handle, and I agreed.

Scott, meanwhile, had moved to Waxahachie and went back to his old job there. I told my new found friend we'd have to go there and we drove to the apartment address Scott had given me. We went to the door together and knocked but no one answered. It was a Sunday so I knew Scott wasn't working. We gave up and sat out in the parking lot waiting but after an hour headed back to Dallas. Before getting on the freeway we stopped at a Burger King for something to drink and we both went inside.

Who should be sitting in the booth next to the front door but Bertha and Kali. Kali immediately rushed over to me. After scooping her up I turned to confront Bertha but she was already out the door, running to her car. Ya, you'd better run, you nasty old woman. On the way back to Dallas my friend suggested that either Bertha was supposed to be at Scott's place and either didn't know what time or forgot the time.

I said, "You're being far too generous giving her the benefit of the doubt, I am sure they planned this and if I took Scott to court about not having her available they would say, '"We had her available at Burger King but she didn't show up.'"

Meanwhile, I was furious that Bertha was back on the scene and now that Scott was now closer to where she lived than to Kindercare in Dallas, he was leaving her at Bertha's while he was at work. I didn't want Kali with either of them.

The whole way home Kali said she never wanted to go back to Bertha's. Once back at Kindercare she was not only telling the staff there the same thing, she was also crying throughout the day, wouldn't eat or play. She also started sucking her thumb again and taking her under pants off.

By the Wednesday after getting her, I was called in to talk to the Kindercare Manager and get Kali. She said they couldn't comfort her or help her. I took her home and held her on my lap until she fell asleep. She woke up an hour later screaming, "Spiders, get them away, no, no, stop," Omg, the first thing I thought of was spider man. Scott, I thought, you have a lot of explaining to do.

CHAPTER 60

When it was time to take Kali to Scott's, I made a decision about what I needed to do to protect Kali.

Instead of taking her to the park where we usually met, I took her to his apartment. I knocked and when he opened the door Kali clung to me. Scott and I looked at each other and without saying a word we hugged. He took us to the couch and began to cry. "Please, please, come back to me. I can't take this anymore." I had to accept because I absolutely did not want Kali with Bertha and spider man. If I lived with Scott she could be kept safe. We had my apartment in Dallas cleared out the next day.

CHAPTER 61

I realized our chances of making it as a couple were slim to none. For my daughter's sake though, I needed to totally commit to the fantasy idea of hearts and flowers that made me feel warm and cozy if we were going to survive. Being the only adult in our marriage it was my responsibility to fix it. Spoken like the true martyr I was at the time.

Thanksgiving was my first test in keeping the fantasy alive but reality will not be ignored and will slap you right up side of your head. For me, that meant literally.

I had bought all the TDay necessities for spending it together and even made his favorite; pecan pie. I was busy preparing the stuffing when he came in from work and dropped a reality bomb at my feet. His mother had called him at work and insisted he and Kali go to her house for TDay. Of course I wasn't invited even though he had told her we were back together. Wait, I thought she was a Christian and knew the Bible. Apparently she had failed to read where it says, 'A man shall leave his birth home and cleave to his wife'. Maybe it was supposed to say 'leave his birth home and take a cleaver to his wife.' I admit, I didn't take this news with graciousness and poise. I remember staring at him in disbelief and saying, "You have got to be kidding me."

He immediately went on a strong defensive and shot back, "No, I'm not and I don't want to talk anymore about it, we'll be leaving at 8 tomorrow." Quick, fairy godmother, sprinkle some fantasy feelings over me so I can get through this without getting beaten. All the fairy dust in the ethers couldn't cover me and blind me into la la land.

It also didn't help that Kali refused to go if I wasn't. It took me an hour reading to her and holding her and telling her I would be home waiting for her when she returned. I thought I had gotten her to sleep but as I got into bed and was setting the alarm clock she rushed into the room to my side of the bed, crying and holding her stuffed dog and saying, "Mommy don't make me go tomorrow, I'm scared." Scott, who was laying with his back towards us, rose up and swiftly came around the bed and shouted in her little face.

"You are going with me, now get back to bed before you get a spanking."

She ran out in terror and cried all the way back to her bedroom. I tried to get up to follow her but Scott took me by the shoulders and pushed me back down and said, "She has to learn to obey me."

I layed down and rolled away from him, shut my eyes and tried not to let panic take over.

CHAPTER 62

I decided to not get up and send them off to grandmother's house so Kali wouldn't get upset and because Scott knew I was a late sleeper it wasn't hard pretending I was asleep when they left.

That Thanksgiving was and still is one of the worst days of my life. I don't watch the Hallmark and Christmas movies or the chefs the networks trot out with instructions on how to cook a turkey, so TV was out. I finally ended up jumping back into fantasy mode so I set about cooking the turkey and all the side dishes, set the table with the fall place settings I had bought and sat and waited, pretending they were at the store.

Around 7 pm, the door opened and Kali ran into my arms. Scott followed with a five ft. Christmas tree. I got up and helped him get it in the house and went to find Kali who had gone into her bathroom. I followed her in and she was crying and trying to get her underwear off. She looked completely disheveled like they had driven through a tornado on the way home

She kept saying, "My pants are all yukky."

Taking them off for her, I realized they were loaded with what looked like semen. They smelled awful, reminding me of a sex orgy party some friends and I had gone to not knowing what kind of party we were walking into. We turned around and left but the smell was seared into my nostrils forever. In hindsight I should have preserved them for forensic testing but the DNA Code hadn't been cracked yet and I couldn't imagine an orgy involving children going on at Scott's moms.

Kali started crying and Scott came in and she ran into a corner saying, "I didn't tell her Daddy."

He grabbed her up and stuffed her through the doorway with her screaming for me and me chasing after them yelling for Scott to put her down. Instead he took her into her closet and shut the door and I could hear him hitting her. She was hysterical.

I opened the door and jumped on his back that was facing me and screamed, "You stop hitting her."

He stood up and I fell back and he turned, his arms outstretched for my neck. That seemed to be his favorite maneuver of abuse. I got up and ran through the apartment to our bathroom but he caught up with me and punched me so hard in the shoulder I thought he had dislocated it. He then punched me in the stomach and slapped me hard upside my head so hard my ear rang for a week afterward. He left me a crumpled heap on the floor and stalked out the front door. I found out later he got a DUI after leaving, his third since I had known him. He called me from jail the next morning to come and get him but I didn't answer the phone. I just sat and listened to his request get recorded on the answering machine.

I instead called the Social Services number listed in the phone book and asked for the number of the Waxahachie Women's Shelter. The woman who answered said the shelter was in Dallas and gave me the number. I called it and was told they had room for us. Next, I called the police and told the dispatcher I needed to report an assault and needed protection to leave for the shelter. I just hoped they would arrive before Scott posted bail and got back to the apartment.

For once, the timing was perfect. The police arrived and I was showing them the huge bruise on my shoulder and the side of my face when Scott walked in the door. In spite of me telling them he hit Kali and myself, the police once again heard him blame me and said he wanted to file an assault report on me. I countered by telling them I had jumped on him because he was hitting our daughter and told them he had called me from jail wanting me to come get him. They asked what he had been picked up for and when I said a DUI they finally had the good sense to detain him, at least until I could get out of the apartment. Seeing him put in handcuffs and taken down to the squad car was such a relief I had to stifle a laugh and handclap.

I quickly got our suitcases out, (by now I should have labeled them Women's Shelter as this would be the third one) and filled them with necessities. Kali helped by joyfully picking out her favorite toys, seemingly as happy as I was that we were getting out of there, without her father.

CHAPTER 63

The laws have changed now concerning charges against spousal abusers. Back when I was being abused it was so common for women to go back with their abusers after dropping charges the laws were eventually changed so that even if the abused dropped the charges, the DA's would not. Also, when a child is involved, now, a female Social Worker accompanies the police and examines the child for bruises and collects samples for DNA analisys if sexual abuse is reported.

It was and is hard for 'normal' people to have compassion for women who always return to their abuser. 'He must not have hurt you that bad if you went back with him'. They just didn't/don't understand the net abused women get caught up in with their abuser. Add to that the fact the police, who are mostly men, don't know squat about psychology. But another equally important reason is; abused women love their abuser, albeit an enmeshed love, a trauma bond, a Stockholm Syndrome bond, a hope bond, but a strong bond nonetheless, as strong as a one inch thick steel cable that takes years to saw through.

Abused women return to their abusers for many reasons, the main reason is income, as it's the men who make the most money. That really hasn't changed. For every dollar a man makes, a woman earns 75 cents doing the same job. Also, because men do have more money, they can afford a better attorney and also keep paying the mortgage or rent. Another reason is the profuse apologies the abuser makes, swearing on a stack of Bibles it will never happen again.

Living at a shelter without the security and comforts of home is not like being at a spa. It's a place of broken promises and often broken bones with children who will be scarred long into adulthood by witnessing but often also being abused as well. I hadn't learned the "cycle of abuse" yet, but eventually would.

None of that was available for us back then and in spite of evidence and repeated abuse, I thought about the uphill battle I would be facing as we made the drive to Dallas. Little did I know that mountain would be Mt. Everest in size, especially in the flat badlands of Texas.

A Women's Shelter is a hospital for the psyche and what the women who go there may or may not know is that their spouse or mate and father of their children is a Sociopath, a Psychopath, most certainly a Narcissist and probably a Pedophile. Back then, the masses weren't aware of the terminology or the pathologies. We just all knew how we were being treated was not right and that we were in danger. All residents there were/are the lucky ones who, in spite of lifelong put downs by fathers, then mates, know they deserve better. The unlucky ones are still living with their abuser, believing they are not worthy of better treatment. They have internalized the outward abuse and aid and abet the abuser with their own self hatred and there they will remain until they die or are killed, by their abuser or often their own hand but will certainly die a prisoner of a madman.

CHAPTER 64

I found the shelter in Dallas that was in the quintessential huge Victorian house that shelters are in. We were taken upstairs to a cozy bedroom with twin beds.

After putting down our suitcases, I took Kali to the playroom that had a young volunteer sitter and unloaded the car then met with the Director to fill out paperwork. She told me she had set Kali up with an appointment to talk to the Child Psychologist who would be coming in at 4 o'clock. It was now 3 pm so I had time to put our meager possessions away and get Kali down for her afternoon nap. I needed one as well so we went to our room and laid down on our beds. It didn't take long to fall asleep but as I drifted off I remembered that Kali had told her father 'I didn't tell her, Daddy'. Tell me what? I looked over but Kali was asleep.

I woke up after feeling Kali's little hand on my arm. When I opened my eyes Kali said almost whispering, "Mommy I need to tell you." I sat up and hugged her and said, "Tell me what sweetie?"

"Mommy," she timidly continued, "Grandma sticks pins up my bottom."

"You mean like diaper pins?" I asked

"No," she continued, "really long pins, and she sticks them in Stormy Gayles and Phillips too." The two children were spider man's grandchildren.

She continued, "There were other people there too, sticking in pins." Oh my god, oh my god.

"I believe you sweetie, but I want you to tell this doctor who wants to talk to you about it. Let's go see if she's here, OK."

"OK, Mommy." I picked her up and took her down to the playroom and breathlessly knocked on the Director's door. After letting me in I told her what Kali said and she told me the Psychologist had just arrived and after bringing Kali to her she said, "You can't be in with us while we interview her so wait in the living room."

I meekly obeyed and sat in a chair facing the door they took her into so I could see when it was over. The Director and the Psychologist were in there for a half hour and while I was sitting and waiting, the front door opened and a woman came in the house and went straight to the room Kali and the staff were in, knocked on the door, then went in. Omg, they were all in with Kali for another hour. I later found out the last woman in was from Child Protective Services. What could Kali be possibly telling them? A part of me dreaded knowing and for good reason.

When the door opened and they all came out, the Shelter Director and the CPS social worker headed for the Directors office and motioned me to follow. The Child Psychologist took Kali into the playroom to stay with her.

I sat down and they both sat, facing me, and Katherine, the CPS Social Worker said, "What we have to tell you will be very upsetting. We ask that you don't scream or cry loud enough for others in the house to hear you."

"I'm prepared to hear," I said, but really wasn't.

"We believe that Kali is the victim of Satanic Ritual abuse, porno sex trafficing and torture done by her paternal grandmother and her husband. There were also numerous adults involved. Do you know of men named Mita and Flighta? This is a picture Kali drew of Mita and Flighta," to which the CPS SW said, "The costumes and symbols on their capes are typical of Satanism. Do you know if any of Kali's fathers relatives are involved in it?"

I sat stunned, trying to take in what they told me. I finally shook my head no, I don't know any men with that name. Katherine then asked, "Kali also said other children were filmed doing sex acts and were tortured as well. Do you know Stormy Gail and Phillip?" I shook my head, yes and said, "Those are spider man's, I mean, Leroy's, grandchildren."

She looked down at her notes and said "Kali said Leroy and the other men put their pee pee's in the girls and white stuff came out." The Director then showed me pictures Kali had drawn for them. The men were wearing black capes and hoods that had symbols on them. As I sat staring at them, I began to quitely cry and was soon heaving with sobs.

Katherine said, "The symbols are used in Satanic rituals but pedophiles and sex traffickers carry out the same ceremonies Satanic groups use to brainwash and frighten children so thy won't talk. Human sacrifices are done in front of the children and they are told the same thing will happen to them if they talk. They are also told that their parents will be killed if they tell their parents."

I looked up and said, "After Kali's father brought her back from her grandmother's house, she started crying when I was getting a bath for her and when her father came in she ran to the corner and said, 'I didn't tell her daddy' and he took her into her closet and I could hear him hitting her. I ran in and jumped on him and he beat me up and that's when we came here."

Kathrine said, "I know this is a lot but tomorrow we are taking you both to Dallas Children's Hospital so she can be examined. You must understand that child pornography, sex trafficking and Satanism are real and tomorrow I will bring you articles and books on the subjects so you can educate yourself. There's also the fact her father is involved as well so we will be driving to Waxahachie tomorrow to talk to the police, then to Riverton to make a police report there also. Tonight, don't talk to her about any of this. She is still very afraid you will be killed if she talks to you about it. Also, we know telling us all about what she went through was hard for her so just act as normal as possible tonight and I will come get you both tomorrow at 9 am." They both stood up and I managed to stand and cross the hall to the playroom.

The following day was spent going to the Dallas Child Protective office where Kali was again interviewed alone by two separate Social Workers trained in Ritual Abuse and torture. After both interviews I was given a certified, Texas sealed stamped copy of each interview with signatures of both the interviewing social workers and the Director. The social workers assessments were written at the bottom.

Both social workers gave opinions that Kali was telling the truth and that she had been severely abused and used in pornographic films. It was all I could do to keep from fainting from shock.

In the afternoon we were driven to Dallas Children's hospital where Kali was examined by a pediatrician who used a new sexual abuse assessment tool he had invented called a Culposcope. His report came back that Kali had significant tears and scars in the vagina and labia and in his opinion she had been penetrated over 10 times by numerous objects including penises. I tried hard to keep my composure.

By 5 o'clock, her and I were both completely emotionally and physically exhausted so the Social Worker who was put in charge of our case took us back to the shelter. She told us she would pick us up in the morning to drive us to the police station in both Waxahachie and Riverton to report the abuse. So my mother's intuition and assessment that Bertha and Leroy were not just creepy people, but also sadistic people were right. I would never doubt my intuition again.

Lying in bed that evening, trying to sleep, I also had an ominous feeling about what could go very wrong with too many good ol' boy Texas cops untrained and just plain ignorant not taking this seriously. I realized there was the real possibility I would be blamed and accused by Scott and his gang. After all, I was a Californian and they were Texans.

CHAPTER 65

Our Social Worker, Katherine, knew the chief of police in Waxahachie. They had met when he worked in Dallas right out of college and had worked on many cases together. That fact calmed my nerves somewhat heading into his office in Waxahachie.

After much flirtation and old friend banter Katherine finally showed him the Social Worker's and the doctor's reports and told him what Kali had told 6 people, (one of whom I found out was the Daycare Director at Kindercare who had called to report that Kali told her as well some of what happened to her), Katherine told the C of P, Derrell, that Kali's story was consistent with all of them and that I had not been present during any of their interviews.

Derrell listened to what she told him, but then said, "Now Kathy, you know if the abuse was done in Waxahachie and Riverton, we can't submit any Social Workers interviews or doctors reports. Kali will have to be examined by a doctor from Waxahachie."

I almost jumped out of my chair I was so angry. Instead, I calmly said, "What do you mean you won't acknowledge those reports? Don't you think she's gone through enough interviews and exams? She's only three years old."

Derrell eyed me suspiciously and said, "Well that's another problem, here in the great state of Texas the Grand Jury doesn't allow into evidence testimony from a child under five."

"Why do you have to present this to a Grand Jury, don't you have a DA here who can bring charges?" I countered. I could tell Katherine was afraid I would jump over his desk and slap his smug Texas face.

"No, the DA doesn't make decisions on Child molestation cases. Incidentally, because Dallas is so far away from Waxahachie we may have to refer this to Riverton, isn't that where the abuse took place?"

Katherine jumped in and said, "Kali reported her father sexually abused her at his apartment here in Waxahachie and in fact, told us he had sexually abused three other little girls who live at the same apartment building."

Derrell sat back and said, "So you're telling me this three year old said she was sexually abused. Who taught her to say those words?" he said, looking at me.

Katherine was beginning to get frustrated as much as I was. "No Darrell, she didn't use that terminology, I'm using it to tell you what happened to her. If you want me to say,`My daddy put his pee pee in me and white stuff came out', then I will, but do I really have to do that?"

I interjected, "Why isn't her father being arrested for child abuse?"

Derrell said, "Well like I said, the Grand Jury decides that on the evidence and because right now you don't have any beins' as how it's out of Dallas, we need to get our doctor to exam her."

Katherine asked, "When will that be?"

Derrell said, "Well, we'll get you one and let you know, but now I'd like for you mame, to step out of the room and I'm going to talk to your daughter with Katherine here."

I got up and headed for the door with the realization this policeman was going to make this harder than it needed to be. When I reached for the door handle, Derrell said, "Oh, and one more thing," I turned to face him, as he continued, "Aren't you and your husband in the middle of a custody fight and you're in a shelter in Dallas for spousal abuse."

"Well no, we have joint custody and we have been divorced as of March," I said, pulling back my hair so he could see my bruises, which were purple by now. "And you're not from here, I can tell by your accent," he went on.

"No, I'm not, I'm from the great state of California." I glanced at Katherine who shot me a look that said, 'don't poke a rattlesnake.'

CHAPTER 66

When Katherine and Kali finally came out she said we would go have lunch, then head to Riverton, about 45 minutes away to go through this same ordeal with the police there.

It hadn't dawned on me until Derrell brought it up that I might be accused of telling her all this because Scott and I were in a custody fight. How did Derrell know that? He must have talked to Scott when he was arrested.

We stopped at McDonalds and I glumly ate while trying my hardest to not just melt into a puddle of raw emotion right there in front of Katherine and Kali.

We drove right past Bertha's and spider man's house on the way to the police station which were both on Main Street. Again, I felt like asking Katherine to pull over so I could go in and beat the shit out of Bertha, but I'm not stupid.

The police sergeant we talked to acted like Katherine and I were creatures from a planet whose language he didn't understand.

Katherine asked to speak with the detective on duty and he said, with a straight face, Oh we don't have no need of a detective ma'am, you can talk to me."

'How can we talk to you, you don't know our language and you clearly are in no way capable of handling our problem', I thought.

I took the lead and said, "Three months ago I came here at 7 in the morning with a black eye, a swollen tongue and facial bruises. A policeman here took photos so I know you have a file on my ex husband. I am in a women's shelter in Dallas and my daughter says she was sexually assaulted by her father, his mother, step grandfather and people in this town." Katherine put her hand up to hush me and said, "This child has told me that she was filmed doing sex acts in the basement of her grandmothers church, her home and at a daycare and at your local cemetary."

The cop's face went blank and I could see the wheels in his brain thinking, 'who could it be, my brother goes to that church. Is it the DA? I always suspected him of something. Or could it be me?? Did I black out one night and have sex with this little girl'?! Instead he said, "Well that's a lot of accusations so let me get someone to help," and he walked as fast as he could with a belt all jiggly with guns and batons and handcuffs, all necessities for arresting Californians.

A big, over the bellied cop came in and took us into a room about the size of a cell. It was probably the interrogation room.

I let Katherine explain everything because my attention was fixed on Kali who needed a nap and wanted me to hold her. The policeman, who said he was the shift Sargeant, was honest and said he knew all the people Kali had accused and said, "These are fine, upstandin' pillars of our community here that y'all are talkin' 'bout. Y'all are saying the pastor of the Southside Church of Christ is involved in some Satanic rituls, herebouts."

Katherine explained to him that Kali's grandmother's husband was a deacon there and had access to the basement for filming child pornography because he had the keys, that the cemetary was used, as well as a daycare.

"You sure. So where is this daycare and you sure it was Riverton cemetery?" He scratched his chin then said, "Well, fill out this form and I'll give it to the DA. But, just sos ya know, he belongs to that church also and he'd know if there was devil's work there. Just hand it over to the desk Sergeant when you leave."

Katherine was just as frustrated as I was, especially after he refused to look at the written statements of Dallas SW's and doctor, telling us, "Oh we don't cotton to what Dallas says, they always make a big deal out of nuthin. Besides, they're over an hour away."

Once in the car, I expressed my fears that none of Kali's abusers would be investigated. She told me Texas counties are very prideful and don't share information with each other. She went on to scare me further by saying the paperwork we filled out had probably hit the wastebasket before we even got to the car.

Once back at the shelter, Kali and I ate with the others, who all looked at me suspiciously. Word must have gotten out about Kali's accusations because one mom sitting next to me said in a whisper loud enough for the whole room to hear, "We don't need any devil worship in here," then turned back to her plate.

I whispered back, "Well if there is any, it won't be by me." She turned to the woman on her right and got busy nosing into her business.

Kali and I went right upstairs after chores. We had another exhausting day and in all likelihood would have another tomorrow.

CHAPTER 67

The next morning, just before group therapy, the Director called me into her office and said an apartment had opened up for Kali and myself and we could move out that afternoon. She said furniture had also been donated, along with kitchen necessities. I was overjoyed, however, the women at the shelter were not. Somehow they all knew that I had gotten a place before any of them did and they let the staff and me know it wasn't fair.

There was also a girl who spoke up during group and said I had stolen her ring and she found it in my closet. Huh!? That same girl later that day was arrested for theft by the cops who came and took her away and took her children and put them in foster care. I'm telling you, I have a Comeuppance angel.

Women's Shelters are no different than any other microcosm of humans forced to be together. What we had in common was our histories of abuse, our mangled bodies and our collective depression. What we didn't have in common was our education, our mental faculties and our instinct for survival. I never seemed to fit in at a women's shelter, maybe because I didn't want to believe I was in one and would be gone soon or maybe because I'm the type who has too much pride to be a victim. Whichever, I hadn't been there long enough to make friends or consider it home, anymore than what it's like leaving roommates behind in a hospital.

Kali and I loved our apartment. It had 2 bedrooms, 2 baths, a large open kitchen with a good sized living room with a fireplace. There was a jungle gym set out front in the circular yard for little children.

Kali quickly made friends with a little girl next door and I was relieved and happy for the first time in three years. The only thing that could ruin it was the Texas judges, CPS, and of course Scott and his family.

The day after we got moved, Katherine called and said we needed to go to a doctor her police friend in Waxahachie had set up to examine her.

On the ride over, Katherine voiced her concerns that this doctor was only a GP, not a pediatrician. Wait, what!!! Turn this car around please.

Once in his exam room, it was only him and me and Kali. Katherine said she needed to make a phone call. The doctor was nice enough but when I asked him about his training he admitted that he had never done a sexual abuse exam on a child. "Have you done one on any aged woman?" to which he replied, "No."

"Then why are you doing this exam?" I asked.

"Well the police gave me this case," he replied. I asked him if he was going to use a Colposcope and after he asked, "What's that?" I was tempted to scoop up Kali off his table and walk out. In hindsight, that's exactly what I should have done..

He put Kali up on the table and pulled her panties down and she immediately started screaming. He persisted and spread her legs apart, peering in with a flashlight. She was squirming and hitting him so he finally said, "OK, all done, you can wait out in the hall while I write my report."

While we waited in the hall Katherine finally came back and asked how the exam went. When I told her about it, she said "Oh this is not good." A few minutes later the doctor came out and gave her his findings. He excused himself and Katherine quickly looked for the results. 'Inconclusive.' We both looked up at each other in disbelief.

The whole way back Katherine raged about the enemic laws and procedures for sexual child abuse in Texas and how frustrated her and her colleagues were with it.

Katherine drove us home and said she would contact me as soon as she found out anything. She called the next day after finding out the Grand Jury would meet in one month to determine if Scott should be charged. I had three weeks to get my ducks in a row.

The first duck was assigned by Katherine. She wanted me to have Kali draw pictures from memory of abuse done to her. She wanted me to keep a notebook and label the bottom of each drawing, explaining what Kali had drawn.

One of the first she drew were children with large cages around them. The cages were drawn as large circular swirls so I had to ask her what they were. She said the cages were from the room of rabbit hutches that were in the back of spider mans and Bertha's house in their shed. I had completely forgotten about those hutches. Scott and I had seen them when we were living in Riverton. She said the cages had spiders in them. The spiders were kept in jars in the house by spider man.

Kali did a total of 15 pictures that she drew herself. There was a picture of her grandmother wearing a lion mask and a black robe. All the pictures were terrifying but the ones that were the most chilling were of three children laying on tables tied up with a cat on their chests who had knives sticking in them and blood dripping down. Kali said they were tied down with kittens strapped to their chests who were stabbed and that the kittens clawed the children trying to get away. The most bone chilling of all though was a picture of her grandmother standing over her, holding a knife in her hand stabbing a baby. A baby named Sam. Kali said Bertha had stabbed the babys mother the day before and then made Kali stab the lady's baby.

By the 2nd week, I took the drawings into Katherine to look at. She was as shocked as I was. She made copies and gave them back and told me the Waxahachie police wanted me to take a lie detector test. What? Was Scott going to have to take one? She said she didn't know but that I needed to drive down there without Kali. That's right, Texas, make it just as hard as you can on the protective parent.

As soon as I got back home, I called an organization in San Antonio who could help battered women get compensation for abuse done to them. The woman I spoke to asked me about my situation and after telling her she said she knew the social worker in California who had headed up the famous McMartin Day Care ritual abuse and child porno ring case. She told me her name and gave me her phone number.

I immediately called and the SW answered. I told her about what Kali and I were going through and she said she would try to help us, that she was going to call a woman in Georgia who she heard about and get back to me. I felt better after talking to her.

The lie detector test was an ordeal. I had the mom of Kali's little friend watch her but she told me to be back by 5. The test was scheduled for 3 o'clock. The test was taken in a building that was part of the Waxahachie city jail. When I arrived I was led to a room that I knew right away was a jail cell. I sat on the concrete bed and waited, and waited for at least an hour. By the time a cop came and got me I was humiliated and angry. I had told them I only had childcare until 5 and needed an hour to drive back to Dallas.

I know lie detector tests aren't allowed into evidence and said as much to the tester so he asked "So you are refusing to take the test?" He continued, "You know that if you refuse it's a good indicator to us you have something to hide."

I wanted to smack him but just said, "just please hurry, I need to get back to Dallas."

He hooked me up and asked me my name, then he asked me if I had ever said things to get my husband into trouble that weren't true. I said "No." Then he unhooked me and said I needed to wait. He took the results into whomever was standing behind the huge one way glass window. When he came back he said I could go. I thought about asking for the results but realized if I did it would look suspicious. Why would I have to ask him if I was truthful when I knew I had been.

CHAPTER 68

I got back a half hour late much to my neighbors chagrin. She told me on the porch that her husband doesn't want her taking care of the kids of all the single moms that lived at the apartment complex. She said he was home and not happy about Kali being there. My thought was, 'Let me by you, I'm gonna go slap the bastard for you', but instead apologized and said thanks again and Kali and I walked home.

I needed to find a job where Kali could go with me. I looked through the Dallas paper want ads and found an ad for a Childcare van driver. The ad said the drivers' children could attend the Daycare free of charge. Perfect! I called and got an interview for the next day and spent the evening looking for my military records and letters of recommendation from my colonel and my Master Sergeant. I also had a perfect driving record, no accidents, dui's or tickets.

I was starting to feel human again as I left the interview with a job starting the next day. Kali would accompany me in the center's van and be with the other children while I helped serve lunches and supervise the half hour of free time the kids had before their parents picked them up at 5 pm.

I also ended up teaching some classes and leading exercises in the afternoon. I would drive some of the children home as well. The pay was horrible of course but the money I was saving on childcare and having Kali with me were priceless.

I had only been working 2 weeks when a very bizarre and inexplicable event occurred.

It was a Sunday and after church I was making sandwiches for us while Kali played outside with her little friend. Kali came into the apartment and after closing the door sat down on the couch. I said, "I'm not done sweetie if you want to go back out and play." What she said stunned me. "I was sitting up on the slide when this big white light came in front of my face and this man dressed in white told me I had to get into the house," she said matter of factly. I put down the mustard jar and ran to the window that looked out on the playground to see if the man was still there. There was no one. The neighbor's daughter was still on the playground so I ran out and asked her if she saw a man talking to Kali. "No, nobody was here, can Kali come back out and play?" I told her we were going to have lunch and went back in.

I was definitely bewildered as I went back to making lunch until a man passing by the kitchen window on the walkway caught my eye. Omg, it was Scott. I quickly ran to the door and locked it just seconds before the doorknob began to turn. Finding it locked Scott began banging on the door shouting, "Let me in. It's my visitation week and you have to let me take her."

Kali ran to her bedroom crying "No mommy, please don't make me go with him."

I didn't answer Scott who was now screaming and banging on the door. I picked up the phone and called Katherine who said she would call the police. After hanging up I ran in and held Kali who was white with fear. Finally the phone rang. It was Katherine who said the Dallas police were on their way, that there was a warrant for Scotts arrest out of Waxahachie. It was a matter of minutes when the two officers rounded the corner and saw Scott banging on the door and threatening me. I saw an officer take out his gun and told Scott to get down on the ground. They handcuffed him, then drug him off. He was yelling that he knew his rights, that it was his visitation week and making a huge scene.

I called Katherine after bringing Kali out of her room and asked her, "How does he know where we live? He's not supposed to have this address?"

"I don't know, did you tell anyone where you live?"

"No, the only people who know are shelter staff." I was shaking. "What if he posts bail?" I asked her. "What if he comes back?"

"I'll call my policeman friend and tell him he needs to get the DA to hold him until the Grand Jury hearing next week." Katherine said.

"OK, let me know if that's going to work." I said and hung up not feeling secure or safe and knew Kali couldn't be alone at all. The next day, I called Katherine who said Waxahachie was keeping him until the Grand Jury hearing.

The daycare only had a half day so I was home the next day when the SW from California called. She told me about a woman who was planning on helping moms with attorney costs in child sex abuse cases and the SW had given her my name and number and she would be calling later that evening.

That evening I sat with the phone in my lap while Kali watched cartoons. When it rang I was ready.

"Hi, I'm a concerned citizen who is helping moms in distress and I hear you're going before a Grand Jury against your husband next week for sexual child abuse," and before I could say anything she continued, "Well let me tell you those Grand Juries are a joke and you will lose your baby if your ex goes and gives his good ol' boy crybaby song and dance to a bunch of Texas farmers and housewives." I almost laughed at the way she voiced exactly how I felt about Texans. Her southern drawl was elegant and genteel, unlike the Texas twang that hurt my ears. "Now, I'm going to give you some instructions before I agree to help you. You need to send me any proof you have and your SS number so I can have my people check and make sure you're not an ex-con or anything. You got that? I also want to let you know that if the mom I'm helping now in Mississippi loses her two chil'ren at her hearing in two days I'm going to be using my money another way to help. But let's not think about that right now. I'll let you know in two days if I'm going to help with your legal fees or help you another way. So I will call you after I get your proof and do a check on you. You got that, but in the meantime I want you to think about what's important and have that all packed and ready to go. Do you have a car or do you need money to fly?" She then laughed this delightful, cheerful laugh and said, "Oh I just got way ahead of myself so I'm gonna hang up now but let me give you the number where you can fax me your proof." I wrote it down and hung up the phone, feeling exhilarated and terrified all at once but my head didn't explode so I went about making dinner for me and my precious little girl.

CHAPTER 69

After dinner I took my copies of abuse, Drs. and SW reports and assessments and Kali and I went to the Western Union office to send the copies. The stack of papers was an inch thick and at 10 cents a fax, it took what little extra money I had.

We returned home and after putting Kali to bed, I called my mom and gave her an update of what was going on with us. She was her usual stoic but unhelpful self so I hung up after 10 minutes. I was emotionally and physically exhausted. One thing about my mom is she never offered advice or her opinion. I could have just as well talked to my face in the mirror. I wanted advice. I wanted her opinion but knew if I asked her for either, she would just say, "Well, whatever you do, I love you." Really? Well if you do get involved, put some skin in the game! Talking to her was a frustrating chore, but periodically I would call her and see if she had any solutions or suggestions for me, but so far, none. Neither her nor my four brothers, nor any family members wanted or offered to help us.

Kali and I went to the childcare center the next day and a truly awful thing occurred. I was taking a group of kids home in the van when I pulled up to a red light. Looking around at traffic I caught the man in the car next to me leaning over to get my attention. Once he had it he sat back up and I saw he was naked from the waist down and was masterbating with his left hand. He kept pointing down to his performance with his free hand and threw his head back laughing. I hoped and prayed the children hadn't seen this disgusting display but I added this to the list of reasons I no longer trusted men and wanted out of Texas.

I was thinking about the pervert when the phone rang as Kali and I came into the apartment. I ran for it and was relieved to hear that sweet as pie voice saying, "Hello, I got your proof and checked you out with my FBI friends. You are an exemplary citizen with a clean record and not one traffic ticket." She laughed and continued, "Ok, this is what's gonna happen. Tomorrow, I'll be in Mississippi to go to court with this mom who is seeking custody of her two children from her pervert husband. If it goes South, pardon the expression, and she loses, I will no longer help moms with their court costs." But before my heart could sink down into my shoes, she said, "But what I will do is pay for moms and their children to get protection another way. I want you to think about whether or not you have the gumption to do this. Now if she wins her case, then I will help you with your court costs. If not, I'm not going to keep throwing money at judges who always favor the abusers, the men. How does that sound?"

I stammered out, "I'll do whatever I have to to protect my daughter from her father and his family."

"Good," she said, "That's what I like to hear. Now when is the Grand Jury meeting on your ex-husband's case?"

"It's set for two days from now."

"Ok, call me when you find out if there's a conviction. If there isn't one and you need to leave there I will have a man call you at 8 am the day after. If you want me to help you say yes and he will give you an address to go to. Do you need money or plane tickets?"

I said no again, that I had a car. She said, "Ok, tonight and tomorrow night pack your car with expensive appliances and stuff that's hard to replace. You can always get clothes on the road so don't just take clothes." At this, she laughed and said, "Look at this like a grand adventure. Ok, now I'll know tomorrow how the mom's case in Mississippi turns out and if she wins, I'll help you with attorneys fees, but if she loses, I'll help you get the hell out of Dodge. Oh, and one more thing, you do have custody, right?" She said this laughing like she was really enjoying all this. I trusted her because she was a woman whose steel had been forged in the hottest of fires and she had not only survived it but came out laughing her head off. I loved this woman.

CHAPTER 70

We met Katherine at her office the next day early in the morning to drive us to the hearing. We stopped at the police station before heading to the courthouse. Katherine went in and talked to her friend about our case while Kali and I sat in the hall. They were in his office for almost an hour and my mind wandered to what they could be doing in there. According to Katherine they had dated but after school they both married other people, only now they were both divorced. They finally both came out and he went down the hall while Katherine came and sat next to me. She had a worried look on her face. She told me why. The doctor who had examined Kali reported his findings as inconclusive.

"Well we have the Dallas doctors report," I said, but she shook her head.

"That evidence won't be permitted because Dallas is too far away. That goes for the SW's reports as well." I jumped up and looked down on her.

"Well what about Kali's testimony?"

Again she shook her head no and said, "In Texas, children under the age of five are considered too young to tell the truth."

"Well, who is going to go before the Grand Jury?" to which she replied, "Well it will be me and Derrell." She had more bad news. "He also got the lie detector report back and that was also determined to be inconclusive."

By now I was beginning to panic. She stood up and said, "Let's head over there now, we'll be called soon." As we were walking towards the Courthouse, Scott was being led by two police officers towards the back of the building. He was wearing a suit, ready to give his lying testimony.

The hallway for the Grand Jury chambers was very small. There were only two benches facing the courtroom so Scott was escorted to one bench while Katherine, Kali and I sat on the other. I was trying hard not to hyperventilate with him being so close.

Scott leaned over and said, “Hi Kali, as soon as this is over, I'll take you to McDonalds.” She didn't respond but turned her head and buried her face into my shoulder. After he was told to not talk by his lawyer, Katherine whispered, “This is his visitation week so if the Grand Jury declines to charge him he will be free to go and legally take her. I am not going to let him, I will put her in Protective Custody through the Dallas system but we will have to leave before he insists on taking her because visitation is set by McLennan County in Waco, he can legally take her.”

OMG. Just then a bailiff came out and called Katherine, Kali and the Police Captain, her friend, into the courtroom. They would not allow me in there so I had to sit, not 10 feet away from Scott. He kept looking over and grinning like this was all just a game.

Ten minutes later, the doors swung open and Kali ran to me, Katherine's friend headed for the stairs and Katherine came and sat down next to me. Just then the bailiff called Scott and his lawyer in. After the doors closed Katherine said, “Follow me,” and we all headed for the staircase. She said, “Hurry and get Kali into her car seat,” when we reached her car. Once we were all in she started her car and within minutes we were on the freeway back to Dallas.

I just sat speechless while she told me Scott was going to walk. “The Grand Jury refused to hear my testimony because I don't represent their jurisdiction.” she explained.

“What!” I finally blurted out, “but you are a Texas Social Worker.”

She clarified, saying, “I'm a Dallas Social Worker. So this is what I'm going to do. I'm going to put Kali into protective custody and he won't have access to her until the custody judge can hear the case in Waco.”

“That judge in Waco will not give me custody and if he refuses your testimony and the Dallas doctors Scott will retain visitation and may possibly get full custody." I said, my voice rising to panic pitch. She said, "It's the best I can do."

"Don't you have housing for a protective parent so an abused child doesn't have to go into foster care?"

She shook her head no.

"Well, when will I be able to be with her?" I was fairly hysterical at this point.

"Well Texas law says one hour a week is supervised. You will have to attend parenting classes and a psychological evaluation and after six months of completing all your courses and passing the psych test, you can petition Dallas County for custody."

"Why am I being punished, why is my baby being punished for what other people did to her, this is an outrage!" I wailed.

"Because you've gone back to him on numerous occasions and he was able to find out where you lived, so clearly you can't protect her."

By the time we got to Dallas it was dark and everyone was gone at the Social Services office. We went to Katherine's office and she made a phone call while Kali and I sat in front of her.

After hanging up she said, "There aren't any emergency vacancies until tomorrow so I'll sleep here with Kali."

"Wait, what?" I stammered, " Where, on the floor?"

"You can't legally stay here so you'll have to leave now, I'm putting her in emergency custody because he knows where you live and will come for her. Being at home with you would be putting her in danger," she said.

"Katherine, let me take her to my friend Linda's where we can spend the night. I'll have her back at 8 tomorrow." Katherine thought and finally said, "Call your friend and I'll talk to her to make sure she understands the situation."

I gave her my friend Linda's number and after they talked she said, "Alright, you can take Kali over there but you have to be back here at 8 sharp tomorrow."

"I will, thank you Katherine." I picked up Kali and headed for my car in the parking lot.

I drove us to Linda's and left Kali with her while I went home, called Angelica and left her a message that I needed her help, then started packing my car with clothes and appliances like Angelica instructed. The phone rang while I was collecting Kalis toys and it was Angelica. “What happened at court?” After telling her the situation, she said, “Ok, tomorrow morning at 8 am sharp you will get that phone call from a man who will give you an address.”

I said, “Have him call me at my work number. I need to go pick up my paycheck so I can buy gas and hand over the keys to the bus at the daycare where I work. I go to work at 6:30 and don’t want the kids and moms stranded without a ride to the daycare,” I explained.

“Ok, pick up the kids but be there at 8 am to get that phone call.”

“I will, I’ll get back at 7:45 so I can tell my boss I have an emergency and have to leave,” I told her.

After hanging up I finished packing the car, left a note on the managers door, turned off the heat and the lights, and left a note with the keys in an envelope in the managers mailbox outside his door telling him I had to leave and to give my furniture to the Dallas Women’s Shelter or just rent it out furnished.

I stopped and got food at KFC for Kali, Linda and myself and drove to her duplex to begin my life on the run.

Part 3

CHAPTER 71

In the morning, Kali and I drove to the daycare where I did the morning pickups. After that I went into the office and got my two weeks paycheck and as I was walking out the door the office phone rang. It was 8 am. The secretary answered, said, "Just a minute, Kif, it's for you."

"Hello," I said. "Are you Kiftin O'Tool?"

"Yes," I said, my adrenaline shooting throughout my body.

"What's your answer?" a man's voice asked. Without hesitation I said, "Yes," already feeling like the fugitive I was about to become.

"Write down this address," he said. I took a pen out of the secretary's craft made container and wrote the address he gave me on my paycheck envelope. Without formalities we hung up and I told the secretary I had a family emergency and had to leave.

She was used to the high turnover rate so she just kept typing and said, "Ok, I'll tell the Director."

I thanked her then quickly went into the toddler room and scooped up Kali and her toys and was out to my car in five minutes.

In the driver's seat, I told myself to calm down as I sat staring at the address. It was in Mississippi. Out of state. I knew that wasn't good. I was hoping it would be in Texas. It meant the FBI could get involved. I knew Katherine would wait a little while for me to show up with Kali, then she would call the daycare and ask for me. I had to get on the road before she sent a posse after me.

I went to my bank and cashed my paycheck and took out all the money I had in there and closed it out. By 8:30 we were on the freeway headed for the border.

I had to keep reminding myself that it could take weeks before the FBI would get involved. They would first have to be convinced I had fled the state. Besides that, I had custody so it wasn't like I was kidnapping her, I reasoned. He would have to go to court to get custody before the FBI would do anything. I tried to relax and talk calmly to Kali about the fun trip we were on, but until we were out of Texas, I kept nervously looking at my rearview mirrors for troopers eager to pull someone over. My car was packed to the ceiling except for a small opening so I could see out the back window, making it legal. It reminded me of the alcoholic landlady's car and how Kali and I were now homeless, just like her.

It would take us 16 hours to get to Shreveport, LA, on Highway 80 and I hoped I could stay awake that long. My adrenaline alone might get us there.

It didn't. We made it as far as Tyler, Tx. where I went to a Sonic for food, then a Motel 6 on the outskirts of town. Back then you didn't need to show ID so I gave my middle and my previous marriages last name, which Scott didn't know, and a made up license plate number. I brought some of Kali's toys into our room and turned on the TV for distraction from worry and then we went to sleep fairly confident we were safe.

Kali woke me up just before the sun was coming up and after washing up we got back in the car and got back on the highway towards Shreveport, another 8 hours away. At least we'd be out of Texas once we got there.

My little car was 11 years old but had a new engine and tires and good gas mileage. I just hoped nothing major would happen because we'd be stuck in the middle of nowhere with no money to fix it.

We finally made it out of Texas by dark and I found another Motel 6 in Shreveport. After checking in I felt safe enough to go into a McDonalds that had a playground for children. Kali joyfully played on all the equipment oblivious to our situation, unaware she could have been in a foster home right this minute instead of with her mom if I hadn't taken her. I picked her up and hugged her so long she squirmed out of my arms and ran for the slide.

CHAPTER 72

It took three days to get to Gulfport. Both of us were road weary by the time I pulled into the circular drive of the mansion on the bay. We were greeted by a woman maybe 10 years older than me who had a very warm and kind demeanor. She called for her teenage boys to help with our luggage and brought me into the living room to meet her mother and husband. There were twin little girls a year older than Kali who took her by the hand and took her into their toy stocked bedroom to play.

My host said her mother lived in a small house outback and she said both her and her husband were doctors. Her name was Betty and she was a PhD professor at the college and he was Robert, a Pediatrician. They had met Anjelica, my millionairess, at a consortium for sexually abused children a year before. Betty told me Anjelica was in town and would be over later. They were all going to a meeting that night where Robert and Anjelica were going to speak to Social Workers about the ravages of sexual child abuse. I told her I would like to go and she said, "No way, you are in hiding right now and we don't want you on the cover of a newspaper or magazine." Betty then said she was picking Anjelica up at the courthouse and asked her mom to get everyone fed. Robert went upstairs to change for the meeting.

When Angelica walked in the door it was like sunshine with angel wings and a sparkly movie star all encasing this tall, slender, very well dressed southern belle. She was appropriately named. She positively oozed charm and mirth but made spitfire, street smart wisecracks punctuated with a contagious little girl laugh. She was used to being the center of attention and she could work the crowd with her huge personality and down home wisdom.

I felt lost in the crowd and self conscious of the reality of why I was there. These all were wealthy and educated people while I was a refugee from a battered women's shelter who had run out of money just before showing up, like a beggar at their door.

All attention was given to their presentation that night and the three of them huddled in the family room to go over their meeting that evening. Betty asked if I would help her mom with dinner for the kids, and cleanup. I felt more like a maid than a torture victim who needed their wounds looked after.

Once in the kitchen with Betty's mom, Sherry, I changed gears and concentrated on not breaking any dishes or giving away too much about myself. I wasn't sure Sherry knew about my situation or why I was there. For all I knew she may have thought I was the new live in maid. To my relief she did know why I was there but when she began questioning me I told her it was best she not know too much in the event I was arrested. I didn't want her to be an accessory.

In fact I marveled at how Angelica, Robert and Betty were so nonchalant about having a fugitive in their home, putting them in danger of being arrested right along with me.

The next morning I spent making additional copies of all my records and in the afternoon I repacked my car after being told Kali and I would have to continue on to a new safehouse. Angelica, Betty and Bob planned on going public with their plans of hiding moms and after Easter would be inviting reporters and national magazines to report on the plight of protective parents.

Monday, the next day Angelica and Betty went to Court to support the mom who was facing losing her children to her abuser. They came back very upset. The mom not only lost custody but had her parental rights taken away. She had a heart attack right there in the courtroom and died. She was only 25. Angelica was especially upset because the same ruling had been given to her by a judge in Florida 14 years prior. She had walked in on her husband who had his penis laying on the high chair table and had their one year old daughter's hand on it. Angelica went hysterical and called the police but her husband accused her of being crazy and had her committed to a mental hospital. Husbands were allowed to legally do that in the 60's and 70's. In the hospital Angelica met a millionaire who was dying of cancer. He married her and when he died she inherited his fortune and ended up marrying the man's doctor who was also wealthy. Anjelica swore she would use her wealth to help moms who were going through what she had. She read about the case of the mom in Mississippi and paid for the woman's lawyer, but to no avail. That was when she decided to put moms in hiding.

Her first husband got his comeuppance 14 years later when the daughter Anjelica lost told Children's Services her father had raped her and another girl in Florida for years. He went on the run and was finally caught in Nevada where he had also been charged with raping two girls there. Angelica went to his trial with her daughter and they cheered when he was given a long sentence.

CHAPTER 73

The following day Kali and I went with Angelica and Betty to New Orleans. Anjelica wanted us to meet with the well known attorney Gloria Allred, who was a Women's Advocate in California. She had been on the McMartin case there.

In the meeting Kali got under the large office conference table and stayed there the entire meeting. Gloria had tried to question Kali, but Kali refused so Anjelica and I filled Gloria in on what had happened. When I brought out the pictures Kali had drawn of ritual abuse done to her and the Dallas SW's interviews and assessments she had been abused during rituals and porn films, Anjelica was shocked but Gloria wasn't so she explained to her that more and more ritual abuse cases were coming to her attention. I was the first to go into hiding because of ritual abuse but I wouldn't be the last. Within three years, 80% of Angelica's cases were ritual abuse.

Gloria said she would take on my case for $7k. I knew my family wouldn't help me and Anjelica decided to continue on with helping me. We went to a nice restaurant and had lobster and drove back to Gulfport.

We stayed with Betty and Robert for the remaining week while Anjelica returned to Atlanta to be with her family.

On the Sunday before we were scheduled to keep traveling our host family made a surprise birthday and Easter party for Kali. That Sunday was Easter and also Kali's 4th birthday. She was showered with gifts and chocolate bunnies. Way too many to take with us.

The next safehouse was in Alabama, another state I never wanted to be in. The couple Anjelica had us stay with were very young and they really didn't have the room or resources to take us in. They were arguing when we arrived and I wasn't sure if we should stay. I didn't know if they were fighting over us being there. The wife went upstairs after meeting us and the husband assured me they weren't arguing over us. He said we could sleep on the pull out couch in the living room and stay for two days. He said they both worked and would be gone early in the morning. He told me to help ourselves to food in the refrigerator, then went upstairs.

The first thing we did the next day was find a bookstore were I bought a book that was written for men to get a new identity when they wanted to skip out on paying alimony and child support or get out of paying taxes they owed.

It recommended going to a cemetery and finding someone born before Social Security numbers were mandatory for ages 18 and up. They should also be around the same age.

Kali and I drove around the next day until I found a cemetary. I had Kali stay in the car while I walked around looking for a tombstone with the right gender and birthdate. It didn't take long to find one of a girl born 2 years after me who died at age 8. I wrote down her name and birth and death dates.

I said a prayer and thanked her for helping me save my baby.

Our next stop was Alabama State College. We went down to the basement where the microfiche records were and requested the date of the deceased girls newspaper obituary would be reported in. I put it in the reading machine and scrolled to the date and found the article about her death. I needed it to get her parents' names so I could write to the Alabama State Capitol and request her birth certificate. I needed it to obtain a Social Security number and identification for a drivers license.

The article made me cry. She had been camping with her family, a sister and two brothers and her mom and dad and grandparents. She was wearing a summer dress and got too close to the campfire. Her dress caught on fire and soon her long blond hair and before anyone could reach her she was engulfed in flames. 90% of her body was burned and she died in the hospital the next day. There was a picture of her sweet face before she died.

I quickly wrote down all the information I needed and used a typewriter at the college library to write a letter requesting a copy of her birth certificate giving the mothers name from the article. Macabre, I know, but I had to protect my daughter and this little girl was going to help me.

I gave the return address Vicki had given me for our next safehouse which was Vicki's sister's motel in N. Carolina. She said her sister would give us a motel room and I would work at the motel.

We went back to the couples house and only the husband was there. He said he and his wife were getting a divorce and she had gone to her mothers. I couldn't fathom why they had agreed to help us when they were in the heated throes of a separation. He left to go see his friends at a bar and Kali and I ate sandwiches then went to sleep. No one was there the next day when we left for N. Carolina.

CHAPTER 74

It would take us 11 hours to drive to N. Carolina and I didn't have a safehouse for us to stay at so I just had to power through until we got there.

Kali slept most of the way and when she was awake we would sing songs and talk about the scenery. Occasionally she would spontaneously tell me about abuse done to her at Berthas and spider mans. One of her memories was of a night she was taken out of the storage space below the staircase where they kept her in a rabbit cage to be part of a ritual ceremony. She said her father was there and was sitting at the bottom of the stairs with his hands covering his face and when he found out the ritual he objected and attempted to take her from spider man. She said they all jumped on him, tied him up and took both her and Scott to the backyard where they were tied together against a tetherball pole with ropes and chains and left out in the cold.

I had read the books the Dallas SWer's had given me about cults and child pornographers that said the cult will set up a scene wherein a child is "saved" by a member. They do this so the child will put their trust in that person who reports back to the cult members if the child has told anyone or if the child attempts to run away.

I would like to think Scott was actually trying to protect her but he was such a master manipulator I would never know for sure. I also remembered the magazine I had found that depicted women and children being tortured. Was he reading it for pleasure or was it a souvenir of his training? Or was our daughter one of the toddlers in the pictures?

A ritual she also talked about was when she was clothed in a long white dress and married to Satan. The books said they only do this if a child is exceptionally smart and beautiful, which Kali was both and it was a ceremony wherein the child gives their soul to Satan. Kali told us Bertha demanded she give her soul to Satan to which Kali said, "No, I won't!" She said Bertha slapped her hard across the face and that Scott's sister brought her ice in a bag so she wouldn't have a bruise. The books also said the more intelligent a child is the easier it is to get their personalities to split.

This was a technique used by Hitler's henchman doctor who did experiments on children in the concentration camps. When the war was over, he was actually brought to the U.S. to teach the CIA how to make master spies who would have multiple personalities before moving to Brazil where he died while swimming. This was the MkUltra project that began programming children from birth. They would strap them to gyrating chairs, zap them with electricity and using flashing lights and hypnosis that altered the child's realities until they promised not to tell anyone. Making them watch as people and animals were skinned alive or dipped into acid, warning them this would happen to them made their personalities split into fragments of reality. The project consisted of doctors who were trained by the Nazi Dr. Josef Mengele, called the 'Angel of Death'. An Illuminati Satanic survivor, a descendant of the Rothschild family, actually met Mengele in New York when he himself was trained from birth to become a trainer. People with this condition go into a fugue state when a personality is presenting where the other personalities don't know what's going on. They were trying to train the children from birth as spies to not talk if they were captured by the enemy by switching out the one who had the secrets with a personality who didn't know them. This would be done by triggers such as color codes, numbers, words, colors or bells. It never worked, both because it was unsustainable and unreliable. MkUltra was discontinued in 1974 by the U.S. government, however some children who went through this torture went on to become Satanists who continued these practices into the 1980's when the world became aware of Satanism and mind control. It was called the 'Satanic Panic' and as a result, many non cult or non family related people (mostly mom's) had to hide their children because they believed what their children were telling them about what was happening to them while with the parent practicing Satanism and mind control; on their own child(ren). The protective parent faced a reality that no one believed them when their child did tell. The public just couldn't believe there are evil people who torture and even kill children for personal power. It was easier to blame the protecting parent.

The pornographers and cultists both use splitting to keep victims and children from talking. It obviously didn't work with Kali. She didn't tell me however, because they told her they would kill me if she told me so she told the staff at the Dallas shelter. My sweet little girl is going through all this. I hoped and prayed she would come through unscathed. Only time would tell.

CHAPTER 75

We finally reached Raleigh, N. Carolina and Vicki's sister Alice's motel a little after midnight. The night clerk was waiting for us and showed us our room, which was thankfully on the bottom floor. We didn't even unpack, just laid down and slept.

Early the next morning before the sun was up, someone knocked on the door. I jumped awake, already afraid the FBI were on to me. I was exhausted but Alice wanted me to start working for her right away. I really wanted a day to sleep and unpack but she said she was short staffed and needed me.

"I can't just leave Kali in here by herself," I said.

"Well sure you can, just let her watch TV and check on her every so often." she replied.

"You mean lock her in here by herself, she just turned 4 a few days ago," I said, a little shocked at her insensitivity. I needed to call Vicki because this wasn't going to work out, I thought. "We're not unpacked and I need to change our clothes." She had the advantage but I wanted her to know I wasn't her servant. But then again, she could turn me in if she felt like it. Oh crap lady, just be a little more compassionate and accommodating and I'll clean out your grease trap if I have to.

I splashed water on my face and brought Kali into the kitchen with me. I would rather have cleaned the motel rooms. I had done that as a student when going to college in Redding. I could have Kali with me in the rooms and we would be out of eyesight. I wasn't given the option however. Alice wanted me waiting tables and cooking, both jobs I was especially bad at. It was impossible. Kali was in a strange place and wanted to be near me but Alice wouldn't take no for an answer. By noon, I called Anjelica collect in my motel room and told her my predicament. She said she would talk to Vicki about her sister. Shortly after, Alice knocked on the door and said I could stay at her house and do maid work. She gave me the address and said she would meet us there in an hour. Thank god, or whomever. However, Vicki's sister was a personality I found hard to warm up to. I don't know what I was expecting. I really needed someone I could talk to about what had happened in Texas and maybe have a good cry while getting sympathy from a kind soul. Instead, I felt like a reject, a lesser than human who had no right to happiness or comfort. I didn't get it from the courts, from the men who had power over me and now I didn't get it from this woman who saw me as little more than a servant.

At Alice's home we were shown the basement bedroom that was nicely furnished and had its own bathroom. Alice met us there and she immediately took me upstairs to her huge walk-in closet that was piled high with clothes and shoes and a huge mound of tangled belts. She wanted me to clean her closet and left right after giving me more instructions, going back to the motel. She didn't say so but I knew she wanted it cleaned by the time she came home. Kali was bored and cranky and I couldn't play with her. I tried to make a game of putting clothes of the same color into piles but she didn't find that fun at all. Neither did I. Once I got everything hung up I went downstairs to see if I could find something to feed Kali. I had poured her some milk when a black car pulled up to the house and two men in suits came up the walkway. One of them told the other to go around back while he tried the front door. He pulled his suit coat back and unbuttoned a gun strapped to his chest. Omg, it's the FBI, I thought, Vicki's sister reported me.

I got down on the floor and told Kali to crawl with me down to the basement. We made it down there while the man with the gun knocked on the door and I could hear the backdoor handle being turned. I hoped Alice had locked the doors. There was a phone in the room in the basement and a window just low enough for me to see the mens legs. I called Anjelica and whispered, telling her what was happening. She said to just wait for the men to leave and she would have her younger sister pick us up and take us to the airport. She said she had another safe house for us. We would be flying to Washington D.C. It occured to me as we drove that my car with Texas license plates was still at Alices in front of the house. If it was the FBI looking for me, they had my license number. I would feel helpless and destitute without my car; without freedom and at the mercy of others for transportation. I was nervous for the first time and hoped my car would still be at Alices when and if I returned for it. For now, I concentrated on getting through the airport ticket counter. There were no TSA Agents back then to throw your water bottle in the trash, make you walk barefoot through the scanner or X-ray your sandwich baggie filled with soaps and other liquids. It was before the hijackings that made flying no longer fun.

I decided to not think about my car and there were tickets waiting for us at the counter just like Anjelica said there would be.

CHAPTER 76

We arrived in Washington at 11:05 pm. Kali was groggy and fussy from being woken up when we landed.

Anjelica told me a man would have a sign with my new name on it that I wasn't used to using. I saw him and introduced myself and all he said was, "Follow me." I had only brought Kali's small carry-on bag so we went directly to his car. When we pulled out of the parking garage the rain was so loud we couldn't hear each other talk, which was good. The less we knew about each other, the better. I did find out later from Anjelica that he was a PBS Executive and it had been him who called me that morning in Dallas to ask if my answer was yes.

It didn't take long for us to get to his mansion. I took note that the car we had been picked up in was a vintage Rolls Royce. This was a world away from our time in Alabama. There was a party going on at his home but I had to turn down his invitation to have a drink and some food. Kali needed to be put to sleep and I was weary from worry and the days scare and plane ride.

We were taken upstairs by a maid once we got inside. The man went into his guests who I'm sure had no idea what he was involved in. Kali and I were taken to a bedroom where we both went right to sleep.

The next day, there was a knock on the door. It was a different maid who handed me an envelope and after taking it she brought in a tray with eggs and English muffins and orange juice, milk and coffee for us.

I read the note while Kali ate. It said we were going to be picked up by the husband of a couple who lived in New Jersey which would be our safe house until Anjelica could figure out who the men were at Alice's. We had an hour before his arrival so I ate and then we changed into the only other outfits I had brought for us both.

The man who came and got us made it clear he was not happy his wife had gotten them involved in hiding moms and their children. He told me on the long ride all about their struggles to get custody of her daughter from her first marriage. He said his wife had lost custody a year before and was only granted visitation on the weekends which, he said, made her a bit crazy. He told me the hearings and fights with his wife's ex had put a big strain on their marriage and how taking me and another woman who his wife invited to stay with them was adding to the strain. I apologized for being a burden and realized again people were risking being arrested themselves. He thanked me but said that if they were caught housing fugitives she would lose her daughter permanently.

When we arrived at their house, there was a woman he said was his wife walking around in the driveway yelling at someone on the phone. He got out of the car and approached her trying to get her to quiet down but she pushed him away and kept yelling. He took me and Kali into the house and we followed him up the stairs to an attic that had some beds and cots set up. He said he had to go to work and would be gone until the next evening. Before he left he said, "Tell her you're Mormon even if you aren't one." He saw the bewildered look on my face and said, "You'll know why soon enough."

The little girl who was his wife's daughter shyly came into the room right after we did and she offered a stuffed dog to Kali. She was a little older than Kali, maybe six months or a year and I was glad Kali finally had a playmate. "Let's all go back downstairs, it's almost dinner time," he said. On the way down we heard Tina coming in the front door still talking loudly on the phone.

The woman who Anjelica placed us with was starting an organization that would help moms retain custody. The woman's name was Tina and right from the get go I knew she spelled trouble. Her first question was, "Are you Mormon, because if you aren't and you want to stay here you have to study it and agree to convert to it." Before I could say anything her doorbell rang and she brushed past me to answer it. "Who is it?" she said angrily.

"It's me, Gloria, Peggy's sister. We spoke yesterday."

Tina opened the door and with agitation said, "Hurry up and get in here before anyone sees you." The young woman came in with a child about Kali's age. She had a look of panic on her face and an aura of desolation, kinda like the aura I had.

"Are you Mormon, Peggy assured me you are?"

Gloria averted her eyes and stammered, "Ah, yes."

"Good, because I only help Mormons who will be going to heaven," said Tina. Without asking me my name Tina said, "Come upstairs and I'll show you your room." I thought better of telling her I had already been up there and just meekly followed along. I checked to make sure the three girls were all right and I tentatively wound my way up the staircase and followed the sound of Tina's voice which was high and screechy and accusatory. I caught up with them while Tina was demanding to know if Gloria had any liquor or cigarettes with her and looking now at both of us said, "And I don't allow no coffee drinking in my home either." Before either of us could respond she pushed past Gloria and pointed out who would sleep where and said, "I have to get back to the kitchen so unpack and come downstairs."

I wanted to look at Gloria for any signs of her realizing we were in a possible hostile environment but didn't want to take a chance because of her might thinking Tina was the perfect hostess. I didn't want to piss Tina off by forming a united front against her. After all, she had taken us in and was helping so we needed to be...grateful?

I had gotten used to saying grace before eating with the friends I had made at the Church of Christ in Dallas. Tina asked me to say it but I didn't know if the Mormon grace was different or had special hand gestures like the Catholics so I just used my most sanctimonious, fervent voice and asked God to bless the food, while secretly praying she hadn't poisoned it.

After dinner, Tina said she had phone and prayer work to do and went upstairs leaving Gloria and myself to do the dishes. We acted like the fugitives we were, not really trusting each other or sharing our decidedly harrowing stories.

We finished the dishes and I told Kali to follow me upstairs to get ready for bed. Gloria and her daughter, Grace, soon followed and she and I went about making beds out of the sheets and blankets Tina had left on the cots for us. I told Gloria to take the pullout couch for her and her daughter.

I tried to think of something to say to Gloria to break the ice, but every question I thought of was either too nosy or asked for too much information. As moms in hiding, if we were all caught together, each other could also be arrested.

Gloria broke the ice finally by saying, "Kali has the most beautiful blond hair and green eyes." Genius, we could talk about our girls.

"Oh thank you," I said. "Grace is so cute. Did you make her dress?" There, that was a safe question. She said she hadn't but it led to more small talk discussions about our daughters. She did confide that Anjelica had helped her too. I decided not to ask her if her case was ritual abuse related in the event it wasn't.

I wanted to talk more about being in hiding but just then Tina came bursting into our room with lessons we were to study on Mormonism. She sat down on the pull out couch Gloria hadn't finished making and began proselytizing and pontificating on her religion. We sat on the cots and stared at her, the captive audience we truly were. I looked over at the girls who were playing on the floor and noticed Kali was rubbing her eyes. It was her bedtime so I took a chance of Tina thinking I was ignoring her and finished making up her cot. Tina kept talking, louder now to make sure I heard her, but I sat on my cot and put Kali on my lap and she soon fell asleep. *Can you take a hint lady, the kids need to sleep. Can you just please leave.* I sat for another half hour before I put Kali on her cot and layed down on mine and closed my eyes. I know I snore but I knew even that wouldn't get a religious zealot to shut up.

The next day, Tina put Gloria and I to work. We each had to take a shift watching the children and reading Mormon stories to them. While one of us watched the girls, the other had to clean the house and help Tina make phone calls to get support for her organization. Tina had a list of rich Mormons who she called to ask for money. When it was my turn to make the calls, I wanted to tell her that Mormon men do not believe women have rights, that they belong in the kitchen, pregnant. I thought everyone knew that about the Mormon religion but maybe Tina had been a recent convert and had no idea what their beliefs were. The chances a Mormon woman had money or time to give to a women's organization that wanted to take children away from men was absurd and doomed for failure. It could quite possibly even get her kicked out of the church. However, I dutifully made calls and read a script Tina had written up in order to appease her and earn my keep. I wasn't a bit surprised that literally every number I called either hung up or said, 'No, absolutely not!!'

I volunteered to make dinner at around 4 pm just to keep from having to make phone calls. Tina told me to cook the chicken in the fridge and potatoes in the pantry. Kali woke up from her nap and came and sat on a bar stool while I cooked. We sang songs and I showed her how to shake salt on the chicken which amused her for a few seconds. I put it all in the oven then scooped up Kali and we went into the living room where Gloria was sitting with Grace watching TV. Tina came downstairs while we were watching Sesame Street on PBS and went immediately to the TV and turned it off and turned and said, "Cartoons are not permitted in my home." She then marched into the kitchen to make sure I had cooked dinner to her satisfaction.

Gloria and I looked at each other and I said, "Do you want to go for a walk or do you think we would need to get her permission?"

"I think we had better ask." Gloria said, "but I doubt she'll let us."

"I guess we shouldn't," I said, "dinner will be done soon, I'm going to go in and talk to her."

"Ok, but I'm going upstairs."

Just as Gloria reached the top of the staircase, Ken, Tina's husband came in the front door. He looked like a man who really didn't want to be home. Instead of letting Tina know he was home, he went upstairs. All was obviously not well in the land of Mormon.

I went in with Kali to help Tina, who looked up from washing dishes and said, "Set the table please. I have all the dishes on the table." I was tempted to tell Tina her husband was home but decided that was their drama.

Kali helped me put the silverware next to the plates like she had been taught and when we were done we sat at the table in the middle, between where I figured Ken and Tina would be.

Ken came down and sat at the end of the table and asked Tina when dinner would be ready. She turned to him and said "It'll be ready when I serve it." Ok, no 'Hi, how was your day?' or sweet kisses or anything resembling a loving couple.

Gloria and Grace finally came down and sat across from me and Kali. I know she was feeling the same as me. Like strangers who were sitting watching this marriage scene like spectators at a movie.

Gloria finally spoke, "Tina, do you need help, I can get water for everyone?"

"No," was all Tina said as if to say, 'No, and I really don't want any of you here.'

Dinner conversation was stilted at best. Shouldn't we all be talking about how screwed up the system is that put us all here, strangers that needed to somehow all survive?

I barely ate but thankfully Kali finished her plate. Tina announced after dinner that we would all go upstairs to read the Bible and the Book of Mormon before bedtime so after the dishes were done we all trooped up the stairs and sat on our respective beds. Tina brought in a huge Bible and Joseph Smith's book of fantasy and made us take turns reading. The girls all went to the other side of the room and played.

About a half hour later, Gloria got up and went to check on the girls. Tina stopped talking when Gloria said loudly, "What are you doing?" I could hear Kali and Grace talking but couldn't make out what they were saying. Gloria brought Kali and Grace over to us and asked Kali to tell us what they were playing.

Kali said, "We were playing doctor," to which Grace said, "Yah, we were taught this game."

Gloria sat down visibly shaken and said, "When I went over, Grace's panties were off and Kali was putting her finger in her."

"What?" shouted Tina.

Grace said, "That's how they did it to us."

"Who are they?" Tina shrieked.

"The men in capes," said Grace.

Gloria and I looked at each other. OMG, was Grace a victim of ritual/pornographic abuse as well? Tina was hysterical. She jumped up and pointed a finger at me,

"You, you have brought evil and Satan into my home. Get out, get out now."

Ken came running down the hall shouting, "What's happening?"

Tina pointed at me and said "Get her and her demon child out of my house, now."

Ken tried to calm her down. "It's raining Tina and I'm not going to put a mother and her child out in the street." But Tina was throwing our clothes over the banister to the ground floor.

I grabbed Kali and her things and ran down the stairs. I could hear Ken shouting, "You can't throw them out, it's raining outside and she doesn't have a car."

"I don't care," Tina screeched, "I want them out."

Ken came down the stairs and told me to get in the car and he would take us to the airport. He went back in the house for a long time while Kali and I listened to the rain. Ken finally came out and got in the car.

"I called Anjelica and she is flying you back to N. Carolina. I'm taking you to La Guardia and there are tickets there waiting for you." Thank god, I was finally going to wake up from this New Jersey nightmare.

When we landed, Anjelica's youngest sister picked us up. She said the men who came to Alice's house were looking for her ex, not us. "I'm taking you back to Alice's house," Connie, the sister said. "Tomorrow you may be going to live in the apartment above the motel office that is vacant."

"Oh my, thank you," I said, "Thank your whole family."

The next day I drove to the motel and talked to Alice about the apartment. I told her I was waiting for my income tax check and the birth certificate of the deceased child who's name I was going to take on, Linda Wallace. I needed to get used to being called that. She said I could stay until I got them.

Alice told me I didn't have to work and after two days I got my income tax check, enough to buy a better car and one that couldn't be traced. Now all I needed was the birth certificate. I got that after five days. I went to the SS office and presented it, telling the curious clerk that I was a missionary's daughter who had just moved back to the U.S. and that's why I didn't have one. She really didn't care so I got my card.

Getting a driver's license was a whole different set of roadblocks. Most states have their DMV connected to a Sheriff's Department so there are sheriffs watching over the clerks for possible crooks or DUI probation breakers or people like me. I went in to get mine but quickly turned around after I saw the Sheriffs. I didn't know if my face was already on their bulletins so I didn't take the chance and gave up temporarily.

With money for a car, I drove around looking for one. We stopped at a gas station to get a Car Trader. At the register was a People magazine with a mom on the cover who had gone into hiding with Anjelica. I bought it and quickly went back to the car to read it. She was in hiding with her new husband who she only knew a short time after leaving her ex and her daughters father. I believe she was the second mom Anjelica put into hiding only a month after hiding us. I was shocked that both she and Anjelica chose to expose themselves and let the public know why she was protecting her daughter. Omg, she was so brave. I could never do that. I wondered if she had a good support system, something I didn't have. My mother didn't have the money to help me and my four brothers had abandoned me long ago, invoking the demeaning attitude toward me that my father had left behind after his death. I was the blacksheep. I was scorned for my sensitivity and kindness to all. I hated my fathers hatred of people of a different color or people who struggled financially or from the adversities of life. I was called many names by my family; a hippie, a weirdo, and a communist. No, none of them would come to my aid and to be honest, I wanted nothing to do with any of them and had felt that way long before leaving home.

CHAPTER 77

While living above the motel, I continued driving around looking for a car. I finally found a small used car lot that had decent looking cars and pulled in to look around. The man who came out to talk to me up was very kind and jovial. He started up a few cars for me and after looking over my car as a trade-in, I decided on a navy blue station wagon, much bigger and years newer than my little Toyota. I knew that doing the paperwork and title in my name could be my undoing but I had to take the chance. I needed a station wagon big enough for Kali and I to sleep in if it came to that and a car I could rely on. My little Toyota had served us well but the tires were bald and the brakes were bad. The owner could tell I was nervous about the whole transaction. I had the feeling he knew I was hiding something because he lowered his price without me asking to 'keep a few bucks in my pocket'. We went back to the motel and on the way I made a decision.

When we got back to the hotel, Alice told me Anjelica had called and would be calling me from a pay phone that evening. She called at 8 and said I should come over to her place in Atlanta to her home where I would meet Vicki, a grandmother whose daughter and grandchildren Anjelica had put into hiding. She said Vicki would be my contact from now on.

I told Anjelica I had seen the article in People and wasn't she afraid of being caught? "Listen, I'm friends with the Governor. We all belong to the same Country Club so don't you worry," she said laughing the whole time. "You'll be leaving tomorrow and if you get too tired to make it all the way you can stop at my momma and daddy's in S. Carolina. You can get directions from Alice. OK, I've got to go interview another kid, I've got 10 moms and 18 kids needing help and get 20 phone calls a day." She had a good laugh then said, "and you're not the only one talkin' bout ritual abuse. Gotta go now," and hung up. Omg, was this the start of a national crisis?

The next day we pulled into Anjelica's around dinner. Her children, all 4 under the age of 12 seemed unfazed by all the comings and goings of strangers in their home. The house was a stately Colonial and the walls and floors were covered with antiques. Anjelica was a very successful Art Dealer and she was famous in Buckhead, the wealthiest suburb of Atlanta for lavish cocktail parties at night and garden parties during the day. Anjelica kept Kali and I relegated to the kitchen where her children came in and out getting snacks and beverages. They would say hello then bound off like deer playing in the meadow. She had a large accordian folder with my paperwork and photos in it and took them all out where we could go over them. She said she wanted to interview Kali, alone and video tape it. She explained that if she or any of us were arrested she would have proof the children weren't coerced or told what to say. She said Vicki would be over soon to meet me and said Vicki was also a Christian and was going around to pastors to get prayers and support from the churches for helping moms.

Vicki came over and we had an immediate connection. She was in a living hell, same as me and we had much to talk about. That night Kali and I stayed at Anjelica's in one of her guest wing suites, replete with a jacuzzi tub and four poster bed. I felt safe and secure for the first time since running.

The next day Vicki came to pick me up to go to some pastor interviews she had set up. Vicki also lived in the exclusive Buckhead community and knew many pastors there. Kali stayed behind at Anjelica's where Anjelica's husband was taking them all on an excursion while Anjelica interviewed more moms and children at home.

Most of the pastors we spoke to said the only way they could help was prayer work because taking in families who were breaking the law was too risky for their congregations. Vicki was getting frustrated so I suggested we call it a day and return to Anjelica's.

Kali was happy and laughing when we returned and I was grateful she got a break from the stress I was under. Sadly, the next day I told Anjelica I needed to go to a state where I could get a driver's license in my new name.

Anjelica said there was a safehouse in Alabama and maybe I could get my license there. I really didn't want to go back there but I had no choice. I had a little money left but didn't want to spend it on a motel. We made the drive back to Birmingham.

When we arrived I called the number Anjelica had given me for the safehouse on a payphone. The woman who answered gave me her address and we got there as the sun was going down. It was a small apartment complex similar to a refurbished motel. We went up to a second floor apartment and knocked. We were let in by a young woman in her 20's. There was another young woman in the tiny living room that was only big enough for a loveseat couch and 2 bean bag chairs. I introduced myself and Kali and thanked them for helping. Mary, who let us in, told us to follow her into the kitchen that was only big enough for a cafe sized table and two chairs. I couldn't recall ever seeing an apartment so small. I asked Mary if she was sure she had room and she said that there were 2 small bedrooms but that Kali and I would have to sleep on the living room floor because two additional roommates lived there and they would be home from school shortly. I told her I'd get our sleeping bags out of the car and while we were in the car Kali began to cry softly.

"I'm hungry mommy," she whimpered.

"I know sweetie, we're going to go to McDonalds after we take our sleeping bags upstairs."

"OK, can I have a toy there?" she asked.

"Yes, now let's get these upstairs." I said, but said under my breath, "let's get this night over with."

When we got back after eating, the two roommates had gotten home. One was a girl named Sue who told me she was a Social Work major and it was her who suggested they all take us in. She said she had seen Anjelica on a talk show and called Anjelica to offer help. I thanked her and asked her if there was a homeless shelter she could recommend for us to stay at. Surprisingly she did. We all agreed Kali and I would spend the night there but go to the shelter the next day.

CHAPTER 78

The next day I drove us to the Good News Christian Shelter that had rooms for families as well as a men's building. The Shelter also had a thrift store residents could work at and a church where attendance was required for staying there.

In the family building there was a small office in the front and seats where clients could sit and wait for an interview. There was a mom and her daughter who looked around seven and a little baby, still wrapped in a blanket. Kali loved little babies and quickly made friends with the mom and little girl but all her attention was on that baby.

When the mom went in for her interview I told her I would watch her children. She thanked me and said she would keep the baby with her but her daughter could stay with us. The interview was over within minutes and the mom came out and they were led up a staircase.

I let Kali sit outside the office reading her little book during my interview. I planned on giving the interviewer phony information and didn't want Kali to say 'That's not your name mommy'. The name I gave was Sally Nelson and I prayed I wouldn't be asked for ID. I wasn't. I also said we were victims of spousal abuse and that the women's shelter was full. The interviewer said, "Well you are in luck because we have 1 bedroom left. Also, if you have a car you can work doing house cleaning instead of working in the thrift store that only pays $1.00 an hour. If you work outside you get $5.00 an hour that is paid daily in cash. Church services are at 6:30 and everyone attends. Lunch will be served at 12:00 everyday. If you work outside you can pick up a sandwich to eat at your job during the breakfast hour between 7 and 8. It's 11:30 so I'll take you up to your room and then you can line up for lunch."

"I do have a car," I said, "and I would like to work outside. Is there a daycare or do I take my daughter with me?"

"There is no daycare, the mom's all help each other out. That mom who I checked in before you has an infant and can't work so maybe you can ask her to watch your daughter. You can pay her and that way she can make money too. OK, sign here and I'll take you upstairs."

We went upstairs and walked down a long hall.

"There's only two bathrooms on this floor and we ask that you only spend 15 minutes in the morning so everyone can wash up."

We stopped almost at the end of the hall where the woman turned and pointed to the last room and said, "The mom and her two children are in the room next to you. Tomorrow at 8 am be at the office to get your work assignment. Read those rules I gave you because if you break one you will be turned out."

Kali and I opened the door to a drab, dark room with a stained bedspread on the double bed but to us it was an oasis. Kali and I laughed and jumped up and down on the bed. Sleeping on the floor had been brutal for both of us and we both needed a nap.

We went down to lunch before having a nap. If you missed a meal, you didn't eat. There were long tables and I saw the mom with her children at one of them. There were spaces across from her so after getting our food we hurried over so I could talk to her. She was glad to see us and introduced herself as Michelle. Her children were Jennifer and baby Caleb. I introduced myself, quickly searching my brain for the name I had given the intake worker.

I told Michelle I got a job working off site and she agreed to watch Kali for $2.00 an hour. That left me $3.00 an hour. I had made more than that as a babysitter in my teens but it was money for gas.

The next morning after taking Kali next door I went downstairs and was given the directions to my first job.

I finally found the house and the woman let me in and brought me into her dining room. There was a huge chandelier on the table and she said my first chore would be to wash all the crystals on it. She said my doing a good job would bring me back the next day but if I broke any or didn't finish she wouldn't have me back. I really needed the $40.00 a day so I had it cleaned by lunchtime. She then wanted me to shampoo all her carpets and that chore took me up to 5:00. Before I left she said she would hire me back the next day to scrape the paint off the walls of the little house out back so she could make an office out of it. I was so exhausted I almost said, "No way," but of course I said yes and returned back to the shelter.

After dinner everyone was required to go over to the chapel. I almost fell asleep just as a woman next to me asked if we could talk afterwards. After the service she handed me her card and said that she and her husband had a Christian TV station and she wanted to interview me about the shelter. That meant taping it so I leveled with her and told her my situation and why I shouldn't be seen. She got very excited and started talking about spiritual warfare and that she and her husband wanted my story about how Kali had been the victim of ritual abuse. She said she would be back to get us the next night to take us to their tv station. I figured only Christians would be watching and because their viewers were only in the thousands we wouldn't be caught. She also assured me our faces would be blacked out.

After work the next day, Kali and I drove to the station where I met her husband. The taping was done by the couple and took forever so we got back late at the shelter. I got a lecture from the guard but he let us upstairs after I told him I was interviewed by a Christian TV station.

When I saw Michelle at breakfast she said there had been a report of a scandal about the shelter on TV. I panicked thinking it was my interview but Michelle said the pastor was being investigated for only paying the thrift store workers $1.00 an hour but using all the profits to buy himself a mansion in Birmingham's richest suburb without paying taxes. There were also rumors he was having an affair with one of the thrift store workers. Michelle told me reporters had been there the day before trying to interview the pastor and his wife and anyone else they could get to talk.

I was sent to a different house after breakfast to work at and this house was huge. The woman who hired me wanted me to help her set up a spare room into a gift wrapping room. How many gifts do you give that you had to have a room dedicated to gift wrapping? Apparently rich people do. She was very nice and when she saw me eating the moldy sandwich I had she made me soup and grilled cheese.

When I got back and after dinner, I was headed down the hall with Kali when the intake worker and guard yelled up, “Everybody out, the police are raiding us.” We all panicked and I ran back to our room and grabbed as much of our things as I could and made it to my car just as two squad cars drove up with their lights flashing. Why did we have to vacate? I found out the next day, the federal agents closed the whole place down and everyone was put out on the street.

I called the couple with the TV station and told them what happened. She told us to come to her house but after talking to her husband she said he would only put us up for 1 night. I didn’t get paid for that day’s work but at least I didn’t have to go through an interrogation.

The next day we got in the car and I drove to a payphone. I called Vicki, Anjelica’s right hand woman. She said there were no safehouses available but she did have a friend at a church in Atlanta who might help. I gave her the number of the payphone and she called me back and said I should go to the woman’s church for Wednesday’s service, that evening, and look for a woman with a red hat and purple scarf. So we set out back to Atlanta. I found the church and Kali and I sat through the whole service in the back so I could look for the hat and scarf. No one was wearing either. After the service everyone filed out and it was just us there. I saw a bulletin board and went over to it and found a handwritten note saying a woman needed a roommate in Snellville, wherever that was. A janitor began cleaning the church and I asked him if he knew of anyone wearing a red hat and purple scarf. “No,” he said and went back to cleaning. We went out the door and were walking to our car when the janitor came out and caught up with me and asked “Do you need a place to stay? I belong to this church and the lord is telling me you have nowhere to go.” When he told me his wife would welcome us I felt it was safe to follow him.

His wife was very kind and made up the couch bed for us. She had some dinner leftover that she gave us. It was only 9pm but they said goodnight and everyone went to sleep.

In the morning after we talked for a while the wife said, "I have a friend who runs a women's shelter. Let me get you her number." She called the number for me and told whoever answered that we had driven in from Birmingham after getting away from an abuser and did she have room. She then handed the phone to me and the lady gave me directions. I was relieved beyond words.

CHAPTER 79

The shelter was in the South end of Atlanta. It was a Victorian like they all seem to be, lots of rooms and a large white porch. It was on a large piece of property and neighbors on either side were far down the road. There was a big manicured yard with play equipment and an actual treehouse that had a large rec room filled with children sized chairs for sitting on and all manner of learning items. It was so big it also had an office off the rec room where paid childcare workers did the children's lessons and paperwork. It was like hitting the women's shelter dream house lottery.

Kali wanted to play with the children in the yard but we first had to meet the Director and the other residents. Kali did find some children watching cartoons in the main house and she quickly made herself at home among the children.

The Director took me into her small office and asked my name and our situation. I gave her the new name I had adopted that was on my new Social Security number, Linda Wallace. I told her we had been living in Birmingham at a shelter that got shut down for suspected fraud and there were no other shelters open. I told her we made the drive to Atlanta on the promise we would have a place to stay, but it had fallen through. The Director, Marie, kept nodding and writing on her form like this was a story she had heard hundreds of times.

When we were finished with the interview she took me into the kitchen and said our chores would rotate everyday. She said my chore that night would be to wash the dishes. That I knew how to do. She then took me upstairs to our room. We would be sharing it with a young woman, in her early 20's and her son.

I hadn't paid attention to the fact there were railroad tracks across the street until the train went by late that night. Both Kali and I jumped out of bed when it went by blasting it's horn. There was a crossing right in front of the house and when it passed by the whole house shook like it was going to crumble into dust. The young girl and her son slept right through it but the month we were in that room, the same thing happened every night with Kali and I jumping out of our skins.

Kali loved this shelter, she had lots of playmates and everyone loved how smart and friendly she was. She was a very beautiful child who was even tempered and so loving and sweet. I prayed all during our time hiding that she wouldn't be permanently damaged by our travels or by the abuse from her father and his family. It certainly taught her to adjust to new surroundings and I honestly didn't know if that was a good or bad thing.

I really wanted to make money so I drove to a nearby mall and applied at the Dillards Department store. It was getting near Christmas so I was hired on the spot. I would be working in the jewelry department selling Swatches, a new, very popular and mid priced watch line. I tried to act normal but I couldn't shake the fact I was hiding a huge secret and I wasn't the confident, outgoing person I tried to portray. I kept thinking at any moment my boss would approach me with officers behind her to arrest me and every time she approached our department I practically jumped out of my clothes.

Like all sales jobs at malls, my job was only part time. Out of my pay the shelter wanted 10% of my pay along with a dollar an hour for childcare so saving money was hard.

My goal was to get a driver's license under my new name and the Director told me there was a DMV satellite office 4 miles down the road we were on. I knew I would have to take a drivers test because you always have to when you move to a different state. My dilemma was I didn't have an out of state license to show them with my new name. I used my missionaries daughter's ruse once again and again, it worked.

Unlike most DMV's there was only 1 other person in the waiting area. I was set up for a driving test immediately and a big, bored looking man came out of an office and he followed me out to my car. Now, in every other state I have taken a drivers test in which you drive all over, on the freeway, downtown where you have to parallel park while the proctor is watching every move you make. This test though, was on a black top out back of the office with cones set up like a maze. If you made it through without knocking over any cones, you got the golden ticket, a driver's license. They actually made it for me right there and I drove home legally with an illegal name.

One evening at the shelter a group of young women from a sorority came to the house with used clothing and accessories. All the shelter women were in the living room so there were 5 of us. Instead of us all just plowing through the clothes the spokeswoman of the group would hold up a garment and announce the size and if one of us showed interest in it they could raise their hand and then stand to have the item put in front of them to check for fit. They wanted everyone to get some clothes. The only problem with that was three of the sorority sisters were my size and none of their clothes fit anyone but me. There was resentment towards me but I couldn't help it, I was the only one who could get into those clothes. And they were nice clothes, good quality, current styles and I really needed them for my job. I explained to the women that my boss at work had commented on my wardrobe telling me my clothes were not really in keeping with their high end goods. I ended up with eight beautiful dresses and there suits that night and felt like a queen for a day. My plan was to get a full time job in an office or sales job.

As our time was nearing the end of the two months we were allowed to live there I had to concentrate on where we could live.

I decided, since Anjelica was now in the national news, it was safest if I went out on my own and didn't depend on her for safehouses. Calling her was almost impossible to do because she told me the FBI had all her three phone lines tapped and there was a permanent agent sitting in an unmarked police car a few houses down, watching her. Also, Vicki's phone was tapped because the FBI were looking for her daughter and grandchildren. Vicki and I also stopped visiting pastors so neither they nor us could get arrested.

The shelter got the Atlanta Constitution and also a small paper called the Dekalb News. Everyday I looked at the roommate ads.

There were more in the smaller paper and I found some ads in the Dekalb area. I also saw a want ad for an advertising salesperson for the paper itself. My plan was to get a roommate first then the job. I used the shelter typewriter to make a resume. Among my important papers, I had my military service papers and two letters of recommendation from my Colonel and my Master Sergeant. They were both glowing, plus my Colonel had made me a Sergeant for staying in until he retired, an extra six months. For sales experience I listed my time selling in a jewelry store after high school and AT&T for 2 years in my early 20's. I had been a long distance operator for them and put in my resume I could handle myself on the phone.

The first roommate ad I called was a Korean woman who said she had two twin girls Kali's age. She owned a house with a big backyard and lots of play equipment for children. It sounded perfect. I drove over immediately and met her and rented the room that day. The next day I went to the newspaper to get an application and while there the head of advertising came into the receptionist area and told me she would interview me after I filled out the application. When I finished she gave me a verbal and written test to make sure I could write because I would be making up my own ads, artwork and all. She said I would be contacted within the week. She called me the next day and offered me the job with a monthly salary plus commission. The only thing missing was someone to share my joy with. She said I could start the following Monday so I had three days to get moved and spend time with Kali, getting her adjusted to our new home.

CHAPTER 80

It was obvious the woman we moved in with really didn't want a roommate but had to have one to help her pay her mortgage. She only spoke broken English so a lot of miscommunication went on between us. She demanded that all electric appliances be unplugged after use which meant getting down under tables to reach the plugs or in back of the stove. I had a very hard time remembering in spite of her signs everywhere to unplug the appliances. She also had signs up about not using the dishwasher or garbage disposal.

But what got us kicked out was something far more serious. Both her twins and Kali were in a pre-k across the street from the house. After living there for a month, the pre-k owner had my roommate call me at work, and she needed to talk to me about Kali. I panicked, thinking maybe Kali told her we were in hiding. What she did tell me was just as bad. Kali had taken off all her clothes and asked the other children to touch her sexually. I almost fainted. When we went home, my roommate was at the top of the stairs and said, "You can't live here, you go now." I told her I understood and packed up our clothes and went to a hotel near my work.

After eating some fast food and letting Kali watch Rugrats, I sat near the phone and looked for another roommate ad. As I looked, I remembered the name and number I had gotten off the church bulletin board three months before. I found it in my coat pocket and dialed the number and spoke with a woman named Joy. She said she had a daughter one year older than Kali but she worked at home and was looking for someone with a child she could babysit and who would be a companion for her daughter. She said she had a basement apartment in her house and lived in Snellville, a town

I found on the map that was 45 minutes from downtown Atlanta, where my job was. I asked if we could drive out the next day.

Kali and I made the long drive out of Atlanta to a town that was just a lot of strip malls along the interstate and a lot of fast food restaurants. It definitely lacked Southern charm and really had no downtown. Joy's house was in a cul de sac sitting alongside other ranch style homes. The basement apartment was really just a basement, an unfinished one at that. The upstairs part of the house, however, was cozy and had a large kitchen. There was another roommate who lived in the second bedroom who Joy told me was visiting her native country for the next four months. Kali and Brandy, her daughter, acted like long lost sisters and went into Brandy's room to play. I hoped and prayed Kali wouldn't take her clothes off again and ask Brandy to touch her. Joy was, well, a joy. She was sweet and kind and even though I didn't like either the long distance from work or the basement, I had childcare and rent that was $100.00 cheaper than the previous place and I felt Joy would be a good friend, which I sorely needed. I did warn her about Kali's problem with taking off her clothes and explained why she was doing it. Joy said it was perfectly understandable and she wouldn't ask us to leave if Kali attempted it. I felt great relief and trusted Joy so much I confessed to her that we were in hiding. She said she wasn't afraid and as a Christian, she prayed God would surround all of us with protection and peace.

CHAPTER 81

Joy belonged to a 'faith' church in the town of Dunwoody. She took us there and introduced us to a few members of the congregation. It was a large church with a few hundred parishioners. It was large enough to have a choir, a wing for childcare and two pastors. It was a Christian church that wasn't denominational. The pastor was not sent the sermon by higher ups in a corporate church, but rather wrote his weekly sermon after reflection and prayer. There were many sermons where the pastor would start out by saying 'I had planned on speaking about greed today, however the holy spirit has pressed upon me to speak about listening to the still voice in our minds when addressing a life dilemma.' The pastor wasn't fire and brimstone' nor was he 'preachy', he was mostly common sense and really good at explaining scriptures. I really liked the church and we quickly became members. I soon joined the choir and Kali and I were attending twice on Sunday and Wednesday evenings. Our pastor was always inviting very colorful and popular guest pastors to visit and bring their bands and backup singers. He even invited a woman pastor who gave prophecies and 'spoke in tongues' and could 'slay in the spirit'. That pastor was nearing the end of her sermon but hadn't called out a prophecy when all of a sudden she came over to the side I was sitting in and looked straight at me pointing out the zirconia cross I was wearing and said "God wants you to know you are safe and you will be coming into money in your future." I almost fainted with relief. I was the only one she prophesied for that night and after her sermon asked me to come to the front of the church along with five others she pointed out. She lined us up in a row and walked in front of us putting her hand on our heads and when she did, everyone of us fainted and were caught by her male assistant who, unbeknownst to me, was standing in back of me to catch me before I hit the ground.

Now I don't know why or how this church worked but there were definitely strong feelings on my part and I felt like I had jumped on the highway to heaven at that church. I was on the slip stream of spiritual power and felt very in tune with a higher power. Like I said, it was a 'faith' church and for the first time after going into hiding I felt that if I listened to my inner voice, Kali and I would be OK.

At work, I needed to change Kali's birth certificate to Wallace. Every fourth Saturday, I had to work by myself. I took advantage of my breaktime using the company copy machine and stock art to change her certificate, even making a state seal in case some-one looked for one.

After working for a year and attending church for that long, I began feeling pressure from my conscience to tell my pastors that I was hiding in the event I was caught and arrested. I felt closer to the Associate Pastor who was also more accessible and told him. I knew I was taking a chance but I thought it only fair to let them decide if I was too much of a risk for them. Much to my relief, he told me they would protect me.

At around this time, the house Joy was renting was being sold so all of us had to move. I decided to move closer to work so I called one of the For Rent ads in our paper for another room-mate situation. The woman who answered was at least 10 years younger than me. I could tell by her voice and inflections. She sounded very shy and unsure of herself.

I went to meet her on the weekend in Stone Mountain, which was closer to my work and my church. She was single and had two daughters, one a year younger and one a year older than Kali. Her apartment was too small for all of us, but she said there was a three bedroom apartment available in 10 days at the end of the month. The rent was cheaper than Joy's and she said I could have Kali in childcare where her girls were. Joan worked for a rental agency and was from Louisiana. She confessed she was shy because her father had molested her from the time she was a child and in fact her oldest daughter was his. OK, that's shocking. I did not feel I could tell her we were in hiding.

Joan was a nervous, high strung thing. She never played or talked to her children and in fact, all three girls were in my bed at night where I read a bedtime story to them and talked to them about life and laughed with them. Then they would go in with their mom who would be asleep. She preferred to be alone to read and every night she went to the gym after work sometimes taking the girls and putting them into childcare there, which they told me they hated. I was taking them and my daughter so often on weekends to museums, putt putt golf, roller skating that I offered to take care of them full time in exchange for her paying all our rent. During the summer, her childcare was more than what I gave her in rent.

The reason I wanted to leave my job and spend all my time with Kali is that she was beginning to have night terrors and was acting out more and more about the torture she had endured. I was very worried she would tell a caretaker, who are mandated reporters, what happened to her or take her clothes off again and attempt to act out the abuse with other children. My boss was allowing her to stay with me in my tiny cubicle at work when she was sick, which was very frequent, but there was nowhere for her to sit and it affected my work. I needed a job where she could be with me.

Joan at first agreed to my offer so I gave notice at work. On the weekend before I was to begin staying at home with all the girls, Joan changed her mind and said she was sending the girls to live with their grandfather and step grandmother in New Orleans. I was angry, both about her pulling the carpet out from under me but also angry she wanted to hand her daughters over to a man she told me had molested her from the time she was eight until age 16 when she had her 1st child. She had married a young boy of 17 but that marriage only lasted six months and he had been out of their lives by the time she turned 17. I asked her what she was going to do and she said she was moving to Decateur with a man she met at the gym who didn't want children. She said she was moving out at the end of the month, only a week away. Great.

I called my Associate Pastor and asked him if he knew of any parishioners who would take us in until I got another job. During the week up until I had to vacate, I put Kali back into child care and applied at the Atlanta Constitution Newspaper and Parenting Magazine. I also applied at a new company that sold souvenirs to sports teams and schools.

My pastor called me mid week and said a young mom from our church named Cindy was looking for a roommate. She owned her house which she had inherited and ran a very successful infant care business out of her basement which had been converted into a nursery. She had a son Kali's age she also took care of and would watch Kali for nothing after school. Her house had a custom designed backyard replete with every kind of play toy imaginable. Kali and I moved in on the weekend.

I did get a job offer from the souvenir company and was to start on Monday. So far, I was able to keep us afloat. But not for long

I had begun thinking that if I went back to Texas, I couldn't be arrested by the FBI. However, every time I thought about doing so the possible scenarios of that decision played out in my mind.

If I went back to Dallas and sought to get protection for her by CPS, she would be relegated to a foster home and only allowed one hour a week with her, maybe less because I had not shown up with her as instructed. Also, because any decisions about custody and visitation would be in Waco under the jurisdiction of the criminal judge who had everytime refused into evidence anything I or an out of county social worker or doctor presented as evidence. I was furious that her and I would be punished like her father who would have the same visitation as me. Because he seemed to be able to track me down they considered her being with me put her in danger. Why didn't the states have safe homes for moms and children in our situation? As long as she was with me, Texas would consider her in danger all because of her abusive father who the state refused to incarcerate.

While living with Cindy, I began having dreams of being arrested. I had Kali enrolled in the closest elementary school where Cindy had her son. A few weeks after we moved in, we all went to Open House at the school.

While walking down the hall towards Kali's room I saw three figures a few people ahead of us that were unmistakably familiar. As if she could feel my eyes on the back of her head Joan turned to take her girls into the classroom she was in front of. But, before doing so she turned her head and looked straight at me. Without greeting me or coming over to us she scowled and entered the girls classroom. I turned to Cindy to voice my concern about seeing her, in the event the FBI had tracked me to her address, I chided myself for being paranoid.

I put my fears aside until later in the week. As I was outside washing my car a city bus drove by and stopped on the corner to let off a passenger and who did I see sitting next to a window looking straight at me. Oh no, it was Joan and now she knew where Kali went to school and where we lived. I couldn't believe how bad the odds were against me. If the FBI had already questioned her, I had no doubt she would notify them where we lived.

That night I woke up at 11 after having a dream being told to go back to Texas. I was so stressed out, I called the Associate Pastor and asked him to pray with me, that I needed clarity about what to do. I got out my big 16"x12" Bible and made sure my large packet of proof was in it. It was. In Georgia, if you are arrested you can take your Bible with you into jail. It's all that's allowed to be taken and it's against the law for law enforcement to deny you your Bible.

I tried to sleep but had dreams all night about Kali and I being separated and her calling for me.

CHAPTER 82

The next day after putting Kali on the school bus, I went into the house and got my purse and coat and went to my car parked in the driveway. I got behind the wheel and as I was looking down to buckle my seatbelt there was a tapping on my window. I thought it was Cindy but when I sat up and looked, there was a gun barrel pointed at me. At first I thought it was Scott, but on closer look it was a woman. Soon my car was swarmed with plain clothes men and women. A helicopter was circling overhead and unmarked cars were parking on all sides of my car.

My door was opened and a man yelled, “Get out of the car, turn around and put your hands behind your back.” He was talking while walking towards me. “Are you Kiftin O'Tool McConnell?” he asked.

“Yes, are you the officer in charge,” I responded.

He said “Yes, my name is Hugh Mitchell and I'm with the FBI”. He showed me his badge.

“Well, Mr. Mitchell, I would like to get my Bible, it's in the house so if I can get an escort I can get it.” He smiled then, seemingly impressed that I knew that law.

I was escorted into my bedroom and picked up my Bible I had put on the bed that morning as if in anticipation of all this. On the way out, I called down to Cindy that I was being detained. She quickly came upstairs and watched as I was put in the backseat of an unmarked sedan.

Hugh got in the backseat with me and he complimented me on my calm demeanor and went on to say that most people scream and yell and try to run away. He thanked me for not kicking or spitting on anyone. I had to laugh at that but quickly turned the subject to my arrest. I asked about Kali and he said she was picked up at school and was in the custody of Child Protective.

I told him I wanted my boss to know I wouldn't be showing up to work. He said, "If he owes you any money you can claim it in spite of your false identity. Give me his number and I'll call him and tell him that." I really liked this man.

I asked, "Can you call a friend, Anjelica Wilson for me and call the Atlanta Constitution as well, oh, and my pastor?" On the drive downtown I told him both my daughter and I had been victims of severe abuse by her father and that I had proof in my Bible.

He asked to see it and when I nodded yes, he opened the Bible on the seat between us and took out the packet I told him it was in. He quietly looked at the Dallas Social Workers state stamped sealed reports, the Dallas doctors reports, pictures of abuse to her and me and said, "Jesus, we have arrested the wrong person."

As we drove down into the Federal Building underground parking lot he said, "I know the Head of Atlanta's Social Work Department very well and I'm going to make copies of all this and have her come down to look at these. While that's being done you will have to be in a holding cell here until we can decide what to do here."

"Thank you so much for being kind to me," I said.

"Well thank you for being honest and trying to protect your daughter," he replied.

He walked me to the elevator and after exiting escorted me on a perp walk through a big office of people sitting at desks who all cheered when they saw my handcuffs.

"Calm down you bloodhounds," he said, "we may have a victim here." He took me into his private office at the end of the room where I was fingerprinted and had a mugshot taken. He took my handcuffs off after I reassured him I wouldn't try to escape and he poured me a cup of coffee and pointed to a chair for me to sit on. He sat down and made a phone call to the Social Services Director and was soon telling her about my case.

He said to her, "Those idiots in Texas really did a number on this mom and in my opinion it's her ex and his family who need to be arrested. Oh, and this is a possible Anjelica Wilson case." Then after listening he said, "She has pages and pages of proof," then laughed and said, "Yeah, she had it in her Bible." After listening he said "OK, I'll fax these over to you." He then called Anjelica. Was she on his speed dial? My my, I thought. I didn't hear their conversation because a woman came in and escorted me to a long corridor that led to a room with cells. It was a holding cell without walls but I was the only one in there.

By now, it was noon so a PB&J was brought in to me shortly after the door locked behind me. I began to pray in earnest that Kali would be safe.

After a half an hour I was escorted down to the parking floor where there was a van waiting to take me somewhere else. The woman who escorted me also gave me my packet of proof and said, "Be sure and hang onto that". I peppered her with questions before we reached the van about if Anjelica had been called, if my daughter was alright but she said she had no information.

The van pulled into a courtyard that had walls topped with barbed wire. County Jail was on a sign at the entrance to a courthouse across from the jail. I was led in and put at the back of the hearing room. A row of prisoners, all linked together and handcuffed, were escorted in and seated in front of me. Soon, we were all told to rise for the judge.

My case was called first and a bailiff took me in front of the judge. After reading the charges of Interference of Child Custody the judge asked me questions about how I was pleading, if I waived my rights and if I waived bail and not having an attorney I said yes to everything. Big mistake. I basically threw all my rights out the window unknowingly. I should have told the judge I hadn't spoken to an attorney. Once the judge was through with me I was escorted outside where Anjelica was waiting for me in the hall along with her attorney, and reporters who were both in the hall and outside waiting. I was asked questions by reporters but concentrated on Anjelica and asked her how I could get an attorney. I told her my credit card in my phony name was taken by the FBI and I didn't have cash. I was hoping she would pay for an attorney for me but remembered her saying that once we were caught we were on our own. I gave her the name of my pastor and asked her to call him and let him know. Anjelica"s attorney introduced himself and when I told him I was already before a judge who I told I couldn't post bond he said, "Oh that's bad, you need to get that reversed."

"How?" I asked, as the van door was closed on my question, with no answers or opportunity to talk to Anjelica. The van drove over to the building across from the courthouse and I was taken out and put in a holding cell.

CHAPTER 83

I sat in the holding cell for a half hour with two other women. None of us talked. They probably felt like I did...in shock. We were still in our street clothes and if I was being judged for mine I was probably taken for committing a white collar crime. One woman was dressed in jeans and a sleeveless t-shirt that showed off her tattoos. I had nothing else better to do so I speculated on her arrest; petty shoplifting, drug possession? The other was dressed in a flaming red body suit that showed off her breasts. More importantly, neither looked dangerous or intimidating. No one spoke.

I was the first one brought out where my personal items were pawed through and bagged. They took my paperwork packet with the evidence. There were copies out that Anjelica and my pastor had but these were the originals and when I asked to keep them, it fell on deaf ears. Once my mugshot was taken and I was fingerprinted, I was escorted down a very long hall and at the end was taken into a room where I was given a night shirt and pants set. No stripes, no numbers, just County Jail stamped on every square inch. After my beautiful suit and high heels were scrunched up and waded into a baggie along with my bra, which I was told could be used to strangle someone or hang myself with, I was escorted down another long hall.

I was taken to a huge room the size of a basketball court but instead of bleachers, the walls were four high bunk beds. There were also cots on the floor with only enough room to stand up next to each other. I asked for a toothbrush and soap and the guard said, "This ain't no Beverly Hills hotel, all you get is a washcloth and one sheet." After plopping them on my bed she turned and went out the door that looked like the door to a meat locker.

The noise was literally deafening. The one TV suspended from the ceiling was on full blast and there were at least three poker games going on at the only three tables in the room, all near the door. There were at least 500 women crammed in this place. I surmised the women at the tables were the self proclaimed leaders who you knew would smash your face if you dared sit in one of those seats at those tables. I asked the young woman next to me, laying down, where the bathroom was and she just flipped her arm out and pointed. Soon after she started talking to herself, arguing really. I guess my question brought her back to a reality she had been avoiding.

I got up and went to where she pointed and it was worse than what I had imagined. Only two scummy metal basins for toilets and two equally scummy showers with no doors. Each shower had a bar of lye soap attached to a short chain. No shampoo, hair conditioner, razors or sinks. Now I knew why all the women's hair looked like dollar store Halloween wigs.

When I came out of the bathroom everyone was gathered around the TV and when I came out to see what they were looking at one of them yelled, "Hey that's you on the news." We watched what the local news crew recorded as I was led out of the courthouse. Anjelica was talking to a reporter telling all of Atlanta that my daughter and I had been viciously abused by my ex who was at that minute flying out to Atlanta to get my daughter. Omg.

"Wow, ain't you lucky getting your case on TV," someone at one of the tables commented.

There were four women who came up and told me they were in there for either killing or fighting off their boyfriend or husband.

I was listening to them when a guard came in and said I had a phone call and could take it on the phone on the wall next to the door. It was the Atlanta Constitution. The reporter told me she was a member of my church but we hadn't met but she had seen me there. I gave her my story and she said it would be printed the next day.

About a half hour later I got another call from a TV reporter who told me Scott was in town and she had interviewed him. He had told her I was a kidnapper and he was taking Kali back the next day. She recorded my statement that he and his family had involved our daughter in kiddie porn and sexual child abuse. That night on the news her interview with Scott was televised. I watched it with the rest of the inmates who all booed him. Thank you ladies.

I was terrified of hearings with him. He lied with impunity and so damn handsome everyone believed him. He had honed his acting abilities since a boy and was very good at coming off with righteous indignation as the victim in situations where he was the perpetrator. I did not feel confident. I was so rattled that when my Associate Pastor called I asked him to come meet with me at the jail as I was limited to only 15 minutes on the only phone in our cell block. He agreed but his hesitation in saying yes indicated he was not looking forward to it.

The next day I was called to the door and escorted to see my pastor. Before seeing him, I was forced to stand and wait in a 2ft x 2ft cubicle with nowhere to sit. There was only a 3in. X 5in. window on the door too high to see out of. It absolutely reeked of urine and cigarettes and the floor was ankle high in cigarette butts. I had told the guard who escorted me to this coffin that I had to use the bathroom before she crammed me into it, but it fell on deaf ears. I had to stand there for 45 minutes before I was finally let out and escorted to a cell that looked like a wild animal cage. My pastor was in it waiting for me and he told me he had been waiting two hours to see me. The warden wanted to make sure getting visitors was torture for everyone so you would think twice about having them and made the visitors suffer so they would be reluctant to come. The cage we were in had nothing to sit on and was exposed on all four sides with bars and a guard sitting a few feet away listening to everything. I broke down sobbing. After my pastor hugged me he had a message from Anjelica that there was going to be a hearing the next day to determine if Scott would get permission to take Kali back to Texas. Anjelica also told him that she had talked with the Governor of Georgia about my case and he had considered having it moved to Georgia. He had told Anjelica that it was apparent Texas could not, would not protect my daughter. She also told my pastor she was coming to the hearing and bringing all my records and would testify that she had interviewed Kali without me present and Kali had told her the same things she had said all along to the SW's and doctors. That gave me valuable relief along with my pastor's soothing prayers. He told me the congregation was holding a benefit and fundraiser for me that Anjelica was going to speak at as soon as I was released.

While being escorted back to my cell block, the female guard slipped me a piece of paper and said in a low voice, "The women on the floor below you are on your side you, don't let anyone know about the note." When I was back on my bunk I picked up my Bible and placed the note so it was hidden and read it. It said "The floor you are on is hell, we are sorry about you being in there with serious felons and mentally ill inmates. We saw you on tv and we support you." Thank you ladies. It truly was hell and as I had no attorney or money for one and had waived my rights to get out on my own recognizance, I was stuck in there for 13 days.

While I was incarcerated a mom who was nine months pregnant went into labor the fourth night I was there. Of course she was screaming in pain. All the women at the tables, who always stayed up late, banged on the door and yelled for a guard for a good 20 minutes. Finally the door opened and three guards came in screaming for everyone to shut up and turned all the lights on and said they were staying on for the entire week as punishment for causing a disturbance. They were told about the woman in labor and after one guard looked over at her, said, "She's faking it," after yelling at her, "if you don't stop screaming you're going to solitary." About that time her contraction subsided so all the guards turned and left while being told she was in labor.

Some of the women went over to help her give birth but I quickly fell asleep, emotionally spent. The next day when I woke up EMT's were putting the woman on a stretcher and also carried the baby out, who wasn't crying. One of the women who's bunk was below the mom said she had died during the night but that the baby had been born alive but now she thought it was dead as well. It's umbilical cord was still attached because there hadn't been anything sharp enough to cut it and it hadn't cried for at least an hour.

I was horrified. I also found there was no outdoor or fresh air access. The women were caged 24/7. The women in there were tortured with nonstop overhead lights, loud talking that never ceased, no access to sunshine and the bread was moldy, the milk was warm and curdled, the hot dogs they served everyday looked like 7-11 rejects. We were forced to eat on our cots so there was no dining area that would at least give us a change in atmosphere and feel halfway human sitting at a table. You could literally die in that place. Many had been in there for a year, like the troubled young mom who's bunk was next to mine. The only reason you could get a break was if you either went to an AA meeting or if you went to Bible study. I chose the latter because I didn't drink.

CHAPTER 84

I was worried sick about Kali. By then she had just turned six and I missed her so badly. I was terrified the judge would allow Scott to take her.

The next morning, I was called to the door and was escorted out to the van that drove me to a courthouse in downtown Atlanta. Once we had arrived I was taken to a holding cell with other prisoners. When I was finally let out and taken before the judge I felt some relief that it was a female judge. As soon as I sat down I was put on the stand and was told all parties involved would convene in a large conference room. On my way into the room I had to walk behind Scott and he and I were seated across from one another much to my dismay.

Scott started right in demanding to be heard first as this had always worked for him in Texas. However, this was not criminal court like in Texas, this was family court and the judge was having none of his bullying or bluster. Anjelica was there along with her lawyer in case she got arrested for being involved. She could stand up to a Grizzly bear and she and Scott went toe to toe. He told her in a rapid and loud voice that he was going to sue her and have her arrested. The judge called a bailiff over and said something to him and the bailiff went over and tapped Scott on the shoulder and did the finger wave for him to follow him. Anjelica laughed and winked at me. A few minutes later the bailiff came in with Scott and told him to sit down and stood behind him.

The judge looked at him and said, "Are you clear now on the fact I don't want anymore outbursts from you?" Scott sullenly said, "Yes."

My FBI agent, Hugh, was in the room along with his friend, the head of Child Protective Services of Atlanta. She was seated next to the judge and gave her my proof, telling the judge that in her opinion Scott should not be handed over a child he had clearly abused. Scott's head almost exploded as he whined out, "I wasn't convicted on those charges," to which the Head of CPS said, "We've been informed of the very incompetent job performed by the Texas judicial system pertaining to child protection." She put her hand up and gave him the 1 inch sign with her fingers, saying, "The Governor and I came this close to taking over this case because of Texas laws." This was disappointing because I so had wanted Georgia to take over from Texas.

The judge said, "I'm going to go over this paperwork while both parents have a 1 hour visitation with Kali. I'll make my decision and will give my ruling tomorrow."

I was escorted to a room that had a one way mirror so we could be observed and Kali was brought in by a SW who of course stayed in with us. Kali and I hugged for a full minute and she wanted to sit on my lap the whole visit. I couldn't cry or act upset so she wouldn't get upset. She showed me her doll her foster mom gave her. She had been placed with a single mom who had two little girls so at least she had playmates.

Our visit was over way too soon. I managed holding in my tears until she was walked out by the SW. A guard was standing by ready to take me back to jail. I walked back shell shocked. I didn't dare think about the future or what I would do if he was allowed to take her back to Texas. I was taken back to jail. That night I could barely sleep. I was so anxious.

The next day I was summoned to the door and was put in the van and driven downtown again to the courthouse I had been at the previous day. I was immediately taken in front of the judge and after being sworn in, I was escorted to the witness stand. I saw Anjelica in the audience but also saw Scott seated at a table for the other party.

The judge asked me why I felt I had to run with my daughter and I told her about the events that led up to that decision. She said she understood and I was dismissed.

When Scott was brought to the stand he conjured up his crocodile tears and began begging the judge to let him have his daughter.

He pointed a finger at Anjelica and blurted out, "I want to make a citizen's arrest of that woman. She's behind all of this."

Anjelica just sat stifling a laugh. The judge listened to him rage on for a few minutes and then said, "We will convene for an hour while I make my decision," and with that she brought down her gavel on Scott's performance.

I really wanted to talk to Anjelica but was taken to a jail cell at the back of the courtroom. It was noon by then and I was given a mystery meat sandwich but was much too nervous to eat.

An hour later, I was escorted back to the courtroom and was seated, handcuffed off to the side. The judge came in and I could see my packet of proof in her hand that she placed before her. With no explanation she said, "Mr. McConnell, you will not be allowed to take your daughter back with you. She will remain in foster care and as soon as the Texas courts are notified, she will be flown to Waco where she will be placed in foster care by the Mclennan County CPS that has jurisdiction over custody."

I was only half happy. I was apathetically happy from steeling myself, that he wasn't getting her, but crumpled like a rag doll at the thought of having to go back to Waco before the criminal judge whose court ruling I had defied. I was right back in the dilemma I faced before running with the laws of Texas stacked against me, only now I was a felon and had no home for Kali there. Having to always return to Waco for judgment from a judge who had clearly been paid off by Scott's family and his attorney who put our case into criminal court instead of family court, I still couldn't win. Texas, 'good 'ol boy' prejudice against everyone who wasn't a Texan and their county infighting and jealousies and arcane laws that refused to honor expert findings and decisions from neighboring counties are what made me make the decisions I had to protect my daughter and hide her. not only from her father and his family but also from the state of Texas.

I was able to relax for the first time in ten days while in the cell block. It also helped that when I returned and told women

I had befriended what happened, word spread about my case and the whole cell block cheered and the Christians among them gathered in a circle and gave thanks to god. Two of them began singing a gospel song and soon everyone was singing. I was pulled into the group and sang along, really grateful.

Two days later I was once again called to the door and was led to the room where my clothes and personal effects had been stored. I was scheduled to go before the judge and would be allowed to wear my street clothes. In spite of my suit having been crammed into a large baggie, it was surprisingly unwrinkled. I was taken to the courthouse around the corner and when called before the judge he said someone had posted bail for me and waived extradition. Omg, I was so relieved. He said the kidnapping charges were out of Waxahachie, TX, and I had to give my word I would return to Texas to face the courts there. When I gave my word he said he would waive extradition.

Not knowing what all that meant, Anjelica, who was waiting outside for me with her attorney, said that meant I could be free in Georgia. I was very relieved, to say the least. My friend Gail from church said I could stay with her and her sister. Angelica and her attorney drove me to Gail's house and Gail said she had started a fund to pay for attorneys fees in Texas. There was also a benefit to be held at the church where Anjelica and various Women's Group's would speak. My Associate Pastor also spoke and he thanked the anonymous donor who had put up my $1,000.00 dollar bail. There had also been a documentary done on ritual abuse which was running rampant in the 1980's and money would be collected for me there as well. I spoke also and cried thanking all in attendance which numbered over 200.

At the benefit, I was approached by another friend who said she was giving me her frequent flier miles to fly back to Texas.

Also coincidentally, there was a sister church to the one I attended in Dunwoody and a couple there had already volunteered to let me stay with them when I got to Waco.

Part 4

CHAPTER 85

I found out from Georgia CPS that Kali would be flown back to Texas in three weeks. I wanted to fly back immediately to rent a home so that when a custody hearing went back to court I would have that ready. I also needed a job to prove I could support us. The couple who offered to take me in, however, needed two weeks to clear out a bedroom so I stayed at Gails without a car as mine had been repossessed. At least I would get another visit with Kali before we both flew back.

I had totally lost my appetite and decided to do a spiritual fast up until I had to return. I knew my hosts, Gail and her sister, were eager to get their living room back as were the two huge Ridgeback dogs that normally had the coach all to themselves.

I was finally able to call my mother during this time and tell her all about our time in hiding. We hadn't been able to talk for fear the FBI were listening in. She didn't offer to help me financially and I was too nervous to ask her for help. I was afraid if she said no, I would be devastated. She told me my brothers were not happy about what I did because of the stress it put her under so I knew they wouldn't help me either.

I apologized for making her worry and the possible shame I had brought to her. However, she was noncommittal, as usual, about her true emotions concerning me and Kali. I didn't find out until a year before she died how angry she had been. She had changed her number and had it unlisted so the only way I could communicate was by snail mail. She never responded to any of my letters and when she died, I only found out by my oldest brother three days afterward. He called and said, "Mom's dead and it's your fault," he shouted. "Oh, and both you and Kali were written out of her will." He hung up without giving me a chance to ask questions or reply.

I sat stunned. Four days prior I had gotten a phone call from a woman who spoke in a phony English accent, saying, "Your mother's dying." then hung up. My first clue was that she used the word "mother" instead of the British "mum". I deduced it was my brother's wife who had called. I called back numerous times that evening and the next day but it always went to voicemail. I thought about driving the six hours it would take to see her but I had a final the next day and my job at Sears plus Kali's class were going on a field trip the next day. Besides, my youngest brother told me in front of Kali that he had no intention of being an uncle I could count on for help. He also had attempted to beat me up in front of Kali after getting drunk at my brother Clark's house when Kali was only two. My other brothers had to hold him back. I knew they would all be there with my mother and I was frankly afraid of all of them. So much for a supportive family. My mother always made no bones about not wanting girls. Her sons were her life and I knew I was not wanted when I overheard her tell a friend when I was a freshman in high school that if abortions had been legal when she was pregnant with me she would have gotten one. Growing up I always felt like she was always competing with me. Her insecurities were evident and contagious. I felt all along that she encouraged my fathers dismissal of me and enabled and encouraged him to make fun of me, treat me harshly and play down my talents and achievements. It didn't help me letting him know I had great disdain for his derogatory remarks about blacks, browns and every other skin color that wasn't white. He left a legacy of prejudice and intolerance behind for my brothers to shoulder, which they all gladly did. I was the black sheep, always championing the underdog and the downtrodden. I was called a communist, a nigger lover and a hippie and I disliked them just as much, if not more, than they disliked me.

Thoughts of my birth family were soon replaced by thoughts of my current family; my daughter and my friends. After two weeks, I flew into Waco where I was picked up by the family from the sister church.

I wasn't sure why they had offered their home for me to stay at. They weren't particularly friendly or curious about my situation. There was a tension between them and they barely spoke to each other. I was very disappointed when we arrived at their home. It was way out in the country, far from Waco. Without a car, I had to rely on them if I wanted to look for work or a place of my own. I also found out that phone calls into Waco were long distance and they really didn't want me using their phone and running up charges. I got a strong impression that they were poor and thought I would be giving them money. They also didn't invite me to eat with them and had indicated early on I was not to be in their kitchen without one of them OKing what I ate. I decided to continue with my fast.

The second day there they said they were going to church and I had to ask them if they would take me. They reluctantly agreed complaining about their car being too small. I felt like I had landed in the Twilight Zone with them. I hadn't unpacked at their home so brought my suitcase with me to the church and the first thing I did when we got there was to find the pastor. I introduced myself and asked him to ask the congregation if anyone could offer me a place to stay in town. He waited to the end of his sermon then called me to the stage and without introducing me gave me the microphone. I told my story and began to cry. I felt so lost and adrift and depressed. I couldn't finish and handed the pastor the mike and sat in the front row.

Thank goodness a young woman told me I could stay with her and her adopted son in the downtown area. She said she lived near the bus line and within walking distance to shops and grocery stores. The couple who brought me left before saying goodbye to me or before I could thank them. Weird.

Janet lived in a duplex that had two bedrooms. She said I could stay in her son's bedroom and he would sleep with her. He was only four and she said he slept with her alot anyway. On the way to her place I asked if it would be possible to use her phone number when applying for work and she said, "Of course you can help yourself to food and anything else you need. The only thing is you'll have to use the bus system to look for work." "No problem," I said, "it shouldn't take me long to get out of your hair and be able to give you some money."

"You don't owe me anything," she said. Omg, what a relief.

The next day I used her typewriter and made up a new resume, using her address and phone number as my residence. I listed my experience at the newspaper and my two years working at a temp agency in Dallas and Waco along with accounting and phone experience while working for a major life insurance and telephone companies. I also called Waco CPS and gave them Janet's number to reach me at, as well as Anjelica.

While staying at Janets, I was called by a Waco CPS SW who said they had set up an appointment for me to see a Psychiatrist to determine my sanity. She gave me his information and the time and date of the appointment. I was angry about it. Why did I need to be evaluated? Why not Scott. I knew I would have to jump through hoops to get Kali back but I was tired of jumping. She also said I had an appointment to see the Director of CPS. It was on the same day as the mental evaluation, both in offices near the courthouse downtown.

I also got a call from Anjelica who asked if I could go help a mom in Ft. Worth who had been caught. The judge was going to give his ruling within the week and she needed support. I told Anjelica I needed support myself and got her caught up on my situation. I told Anjelica to give me her number and I would call her. "You can't," Anjelica said, "she's in jail. She can only call you collect."

"I can't do that," I said, "this isn't my phone, but call me and let me know what happens." Later that week Anjelica called and told me the mom in Ft. Worth had been given 20 years and had her parental rights stripped. Her pedophile husband was getting sole custody of their two children.

"That could very well happen to me," I told her, "I'm facing kidnapping charges in Waxahachie and a custody hearing here in Waco before a criminal judge."

The bus was only a half block away so the next day by 8 am I was on one riding to the temp agency I knew about. They had me take a typing test and after passing it said they would call me the next day if a job became available.

The agency paid weekly so by the first week back in Waco, I had enough money for a deposit on a place. I had money my Associate Pastor had given me collected at the benefit held for me for rent so I stood in a phone booth and called the first rental ad in the free paper I had gotten at the gas station behind the phone booth. The man who answered said he could meet me there in a half an hour.

The house was on a street right off the one I was standing on which was a major thoroughfare in town. My lucky day. I hopped on a bus that stopped in front of the gas station and rode it 6 blocks and got out at the street the rental house was on. The house was an old Victorian with stained glass windows and a freshly mowed lawn and trees in the front yard. The owner was there when I arrived and ushered me into my new home.

It had a master bedroom with French doors and a huge bay window that was off the well furnished living room. The kitchen was tiny but workable and there was a second bedroom as big as the master. All the rooms, including the living room, had fireplaces that were in working order. It had a clawfoot tub and hardwood floors and a walk in closet in the bathroom. It was fully furnished and even had kitchen dishes, silverware and pots and pans.

"Where do I sign?" I asked and after filling out the short application and giving him first and last month's rent he gave me the skeleton key for the front door. Just in time for Kali to fly into Waco. "If you want to buy this house, I can sell it to you for 12 thousand." he said before getting in his car.

"No, I would love to but I'm not there yet," I said.

As soon as the landlord left, I took out the little mail-in camera I had bought and took pictures of the house and Kali's bedroom and the living room and walked down to the mall a block away to get them developed. I wanted CPS and the judge to see I could care for her.

However, when I used a payphone near my new house to order a home phone, I was told by AT&T that there was an outstanding $500.00 bill in my name that would have to be paid before I could get service. It still hadn't been paid by Scott. He had screwed me over once again. His credit had been very bad when we married, so literally everything: utilities, the car, rental agreements had all been in my name. Destroying my credit was just one of the ways he used to bring me down.

Not tonight, however. Tonight I will be sleeping in my own home. While at the mall I bought sheets for both beds and an electric blanket for each. My landlord said he would keep the electricity on if I would pay him for it along with my rent payment.

I actually felt enormous relief that I could use my real name and no longer had fear of getting arrested. I felt safe knowing Scott didn't know where I was but had a hunch he would know soon enough.

CHAPTER 86

The good thing about temp agencies is that you can choose the days you want to work. I called the agency I was listed with on Monday morning that was set up for the two appointments I had. When I told the agency scheduler I could only work four days that week, she said, “Well you got such glowing recommendations at the bank you worked at last week, we want you back as soon as you can get here,” she said with a thick Southern drawl. “Yes, ma’am,” I said happily, feeling good about myself.

The day of the appointments I was very nervous. I knew instinctively getting any of these Texas good ‘ol boys on my side was going to be very hard.

Right on cue, the shrink had an attitude towards me that can only be described as hostile. He hurried me into a small room and shoved tests on the desk he sat me at.

“You will be timed on the first one so don’t sit and think too hard on any one question,” the psychiatrist said. Having said that he tossed a pencil on the desk and turned and said, “The test starts now.”

The test was ridiculous. “Have you ever gotten so angry you have hit someone?" Even if I had of I wasn’t stupid enough to say yes to that question. Yes, I had hit Scott but only in self defense. The test didn’t ask about that aspect of hitting someone.

The two tests I was forced to take, including a Rorchach, took up the whole morning. By noon, I was hungry and mentally spent. I left the shrinks office and stopped at a food truck on the way to the Director’s office which was down the street from the shrinks.

After eating at a picnic table next to the truck, I stood up, tucked my blouse into my skirt and walked into the CPS building.

I had brought the beautiful briefcase my friend Joy from Atlanta had given me filled with the packet of proof that had been with me for the 3 years I had started this journey for justice; along with the photos of abuse done to me and pictures of my newly rented house in Waco.

When called into the Directors office I sensed right away I was facing Yosemite Sam in the flesh. I put my briefcase down and walked toward the seated Director and another man standing next to him. I put out my hand to introduce myself and the Director barked, “Go sit down.” No hi, hello, my name is bla bla bla and this here is bla bla bla.

I went back to my seat and sat, spittin' mad, but smiling. After sitting they both just glared at me like they were facing a tiger in a circus pen.

I reached down to pick up my briefcase, opened it and held up the proof packet and said, “I would like to show you what's in this packet.” Again, they just sat there until finally the Director said, “I don't think we're interested in anything a kidnapper has to say.”

“May I ask who this man is standing next to you and what your name is?" I asked.

Now they both frowned as if to say ‘We don't cotton to no woman making' demands on us.’

The Director finally said, “This here's your daughter's Guardian Ad Litem, Don Desantis, so he'll be speaking on behalf of her when this case goes to court.”

The man reminded me of Lurch in the Addams Family series. He was very tall and gaunt with a stooped over posture and a sour expression. He looked old, like 90 old.

“My name is Ed Cruz,” the Director growled.

“Well nice to meet you, now as I said, I have two certified Dallas SW evaluations along with the Head of Pediatrics at Dallas Children's Hospital who all state my daughter has been raped by her father, her father's family and other strangers and that's why I put her in hiding. To save her life.”

The Director leaned forward and said, “Oh really now. Well this here is McLennan County, not Dallas County and we will be the judge about abuse being' done. As far as you are concerned you will attend mandatory parenting classes every week, psychiatric evaluations and meetins' with your SW once a week. You will pay the county child support and you will only get 1 hour a week supervised with your daughter and let me tell you if you are late or miss any appointments to any thing I'm requirin' of you, we will take away your parental rights. We have already petitioned the court for emergency custody of her for the next six months so we can figure out if you can become a good mother. Do I make myself clear?"

"Perfectly, I only have two questions. Is my daughter here in Waco and are you going to demand the same tasks for her father, Mr. McConnell?"

The Director looked up at Lurch, who nodded and with a grimace said, "Your daughter flew in last night and is with a foster family. Her father will not have access to her either. There will be a custody hearing in six months so I suggest you keep your nose clean until then. And if I hear from my SW that you make that little girl cry or go all hysterical or harm my SW during your visits I will shut them down so fast you won't know what hit you." Lurch just stood there scowling and nodding.

"Well, nice meeting you both and my hope is that we can all keep my daughter from being abused," I said as I approached his desk and put down copies I had made of my proof.

"Well I call kidnapping abuse, don't you," the Director said. I looked at him and said, smiling, "Well I had custody so how can you call it kidnapping?"

I kept my cool until I reached the bathroom stall in the bathroom in the lobby. If I had had a gun, I would have shot both of them, I thought.

Once the door was latched, I let my tense body go limp and said under my ragged breath, "Those assholes will not break me." I knew I would be tested in a very hot fire in Texas, but I didn't think it would be branding iron hot. However, a seed had been planted in my raked over brain and everytime I thought about all the assholes I had encountered and would still encounter, the little seed kept getting bigger and bigger. What would I do if the seed came to fruition?

I put on lipstick in the mirror and as I wiped some off my teeth with a kleenex, I suddenly remembered my storage unit I had rented before going on the run. I had rented it the first time Kali and I escaped to CA.

While Scott was at work and three hours before our flight, I had put furniture, lamps, toys, Kali's music box collection and anything small I could cram in the small Honda and took it to a rental facility. I had to pay a small deposit and $5.00 a month and because I never knew when I'd be back, I paid three years worth to avoid having to send checks every month. I was reassured I could get a refund if I came back early.

It was worth it because a safe in that storage unit contained a small .22 I had purchased after one of our fights. It wasn't hard to buy what with Texas 'no application or background checks' laws and their 'everyone packs heat' attitudes.

Scott didn't know about it and I had the key to the lock right on my key ring. By my calculations I had another month on my rental tab. Perfect. I would go get my storage as soon as I got a car.

Back out in the lobby I asked the receptionist how I could find out when I could see Kali. She gave me a card with a number on it and said, "If you don't have a phone, there is a phone bank against that back wall for you to use." I thanked her then hurried over to where she pointed.

A woman's voice answered and I explained who I was and asked her when I could see Kali. Just a minute she said and put me on hold.

She came back on and said "Well she just got in last night but we want her to bond with her foster family so it will be a week before you can see her. After the 1st visit goes alright, you will be able to call her foster parents and schedule phone calls with them. You are allowed an additional half hour each week on the telephone but your calls will be monitored by the foster parents so you will have to coordinate and cooperate with them."

"Are you her SW?" I asked.

"No, I was the intake worker and placed her last night in emergency housing. She doesn't have an assigned worker yet.

You will have to call back. Do you want the number for the Foster Care SW?"

"Yes, thank you," I said. I called the number but it went to voicemail. Not having a phone was going to really suck. I left my new address and my name and asked the SW to drive over to talk to me because I had no phone. I also wanted her to see that I already had a house Kali could come home to

CHAPTER 87

I realized I needed to get a job where I could be reached by the SW and where I could make calls. Working at the temp agency didn't give me that ability, so I looked for a permanent job.

I saw a newspaper someone had left behind on a chair near the phone bank so I sat down and looked at the job listings. There was a job listing at a Christian Publishing Co. for a phone sales rep. Perfect. I stood and called their number and got an appointment the next day. It wouldn't hurt that the company had the word Christian in it.

My resume needed updating, however, but I didn't have access to a typewriter. When I asked the receptionist if I could use a typewriter there she said no, but the County Library had typewriters people could use. She gave me the address and said it was within walking distance so I power walked the three blocks hoping it was open.

Luckily, the library had paper available for people like me and two typewriters available for public use. There was even white out for typos. I had my new address and experience making phone sales from the Atlanta newspaper I had worked at for almost two years. The only thing missing was a phone number I could be reached at.

I would just have to sell myself well enough that I would be hired immediately.

The next day I made my appointment on time and was soon brought in to talk to personnel. I had brought along my nice briefcase that housed my new resume and the ads listings from the paper I had worked at. I showed the interviewer all the ads that were my accounts, emphasizing that I had chosen the artwork and the wording placement for the ads. Most of the accounts I had gotten by cold calling the companies and had gotten them to run ads in our newspaper.

"This is the best resume I've ever seen. I want you to meet the head of sales who needs someone right away. Could you start work tomorrow?" he asked.

"Absolutely," I replied.

He called and spoke to someone and after hanging up, said, "Bob will be right down."

When Bob entered, after we met, the interviewer handed him my resume and the newspaper ads where I had circled my accounts.

Bob said, after looking over my resume and the ad page from the newspaper, asked, "Can you start tomorrow at 8:00?"

"Yes," I said, and he said, "Great, welcome aboard." and left.

The interviewer had me sign all the necessary IRS and other paperwork, gave me the salary and a security card for getting into the sales office, showed me the timeclock and said, "You made my job easy today, we will see you tomorrow." He walked with me to the entrance, shook my hand and opened the door that would be my future for at least the coming year.

My next project that day was getting a car. There was still a few hours daylight so I caught a bus and got off at a row of used car lots I had seen on the way to my job interview.

I test drove a station wagon and it sounded ok. It was six years old with 60,000 miles on it but was only $350.00. I bought it and drove it home. Now all I needed was a church to go to.

I decided to steer clear of the Church of Christ. The C of C we belonged to in Dallas, before going into hiding, had turned me off by it's ridiculous rule of no musical instruments. There had been a faction, almost half of the church, who decided to boycott the service one Sunday because the new director tried to lead us in singing Christmas carols, which the old members considered blasphemous. When we began singing Silent Night, the militants, who were sitting all together on the left side of the church, got up and walked out chanting "No Christmas Carols" loud enough to drown out the choir.

The pastor came up on stage and announced services were over for the day and told everyone to leave. The new Choir Director became the old Choir Director that day.

Oh well, I would try to find a faith church like the one I belonged to in Atlanta. The sister church I had been taken to upon my arrival in Waco was too far away for my liking and I didn't like the pastor's sermons at the four services I had attended while living with Janet. I reminded myself to call Janet and thank her again for taking me in. She lived too far away to become friends with and I could sense she was apprehensive about a mom who put her child into hiding as she kept questioning why I 'broke the law.'

CHAPTER 88

Right after I bought the car I went to the DMV and spent the next two hours sitting and waiting to be called.

I wanted to get as much done as I could before my job started. We only got a half hour for lunch and I wouldn't have time to take care of personal business in that amount of time.

Once I was done at the DMV, I went to pick up my final paycheck at the temp agency, then went to the closest Bank of America that I had an account with since I was eight years old. I opened a new account with my paycheck and $300.00 I had to get an attorney with, from the benefit concert fundraiser for me in Atlanta.

CPS tried their hardest to make keeping a job almost impossible. When the SW assigned to my case came to my house while I was at work, she left me her card and a list of appointments I was mandated to attend, taped on my door.

My first week on my new job there were 2 daytime appointments. One was to see a Psychiatrist and the other was a parenting class, both on different days in mid afternoon. I had no choice but to go in and talk to my boss and ask if I could take my lunch break during the times I had the appointments. I also asked if I could have an hour lunch on those days and I would make up the hour I would be missing by staying late or coming in earlier. He was surprisingly accommodating. Probably because he was desperate for help.

I proved I was an asset by making more sales the first day than people who had been there a long time made in a week. I sold like my daughter's life depended on it; because it was.

The small room 12 of us were in, elbow to elbow proved to be a hindrance because with everyone talking it was hard to concentrate. There were four of us who were top sellers so after much requesting we were given our own room, only one person to a wall. We all liked each other and spent a good deal of time talking and making each other laugh. A month into the job I confided to them about my situation and they all agreed I was a victim. Well ya, what else would they say?

I took a chance alienating them but my anxiety was so high sometimes I could barely breathe. I needed comforting. The first three months I was there, I got top performer of the quarter with a prize of a weekend in San Antonio. I asked my boss if I could have the monetary value instead of the trip and to my surprise he agreed and gave me a check for $100.00.

I called the SW and told her I wanted to take my daughter shopping for clothes with the $100.00. It was an opportunity to spend time with her away from the crappy cubicle at the CPS building with the lumpy love seat and metal office chair where the SW sat scrutinizing every word and facial expression.

By then I had visited Kali supervised at the CPS building every week and on Sundays, I would walk 2 blocks to a phone booth on the corner from my house and call her. Rain or shine, cold or hot. It was always the father who answered and he let me know first thing that if I said something he didn't like I would be hung up on. It was so damn hard to keep from crying when Kali would whimper about how much she missed me and wanted to come to my house. Her foster father treated me like I was a serial killer and made it clear he was not happy about spending his time listening to a little girl cry for her mother. I knew his report to CPS was important for the court so it took all the patience and emotional control I could muster to keep from breaking down. Twice he hung up after Kali told me she wasn't happy living there and for me to come get her.

I wondered what damage this trauma to her would be in her later years. I knew instinctively it wouldn't be good. I would find out years later, how damaging it is for children to be sexually abused by aduts they knew and trusted and to see their mother beat up on a weekly basis, only to be ripped away from the only person who wasn't hell bent on abusing them further. Not to mention being separated by the incompetence of the courts and social services. And I would never forget the sadistic abuse done to her by her father and his family

Thinking about all this I went to the storage facility. The clerk let me into the locked units and I went to mine and voila, I unlocked it and saw my things.

The little safe was in the top drawer of a small dresser I had in the guest bathroom at our house in Waco. I kept it there because it had a little key that locked it. I had kept the little key under the bottom of the top drawer, secured there with masking tape. Ahhh, I sighed after finding it still there. I peeled the key off the tape and opened the safe. The pistol was there, never used, by me anyway.

CHAPTER 89

On Sunday mornings I went church shopping. I stayed out of the mega Baptist churches. I was familiar with their fire and brimstone style of preaching and didn't like it. I also didn't want one too small where it would have been too easy for everyone to know my business.

In November I attended a church that seemed just right. It was a spirit led church and the pastor actually made sense. It also had a singles group. I certainly qualified.

We met an hour before the Sunday morning service and went around the circle telling each other how God helped us in our lives. There were lots of activities and get-togethers planned. There was a party if it was a member's birthday and the two leaders opened their homes for those occasions. There were also picnics at the Brazos River park, lunches after church services and even weekend trips to a members family cabin an hour out of Waco.

It was in this group that I met Wayne. He was tall and good looking and had a cheery disposition. His sense of humor was a bit goofy and he seemed just a bit off, but he liked me and I felt safe with him. He owned a house next to his mothers but his job was in Glen Haven at the nuclear power plant there. He was gone all week but came back on the weekends to be with his mom who was in her late 80's.

Our sexual attraction wasn't especially strong so we started out as friends. As we got to know each other on Sundays I soon found out why he wasn't making any moves on me or the other women in our group.

Turns out he had a wife from Sweden. They had a son together and she tried to like the U.S. but she missed her close knit family and hated that there were no social services like healthcare and childcare that were available in Sweden, so she went back with their son. Wayne followed her to Sweden to be with her and their son but couldn't find work, mainly because he didn't know Swedish. His mother was also an issue because of her age. Being her only living son he was her caretaker. After only a few months in Sweden, he told her he had to go back to the States but she refused to come back with him.

Being Lutheran, which is the Swedish national religion, she refused to agree to a divorce. He had been back in the U.S. for a little over a year when I met him.

He was still married, mainly because she refused to give him a divorce. He had tried unsuccessfully to get her to move back to the U.S. so he was in a no-win situation, like I was.

He missed his son like I missed Kali. We had an unspoken agreement to help each other cope. I think we knew instinctively we both had too much psyche stank on us for normal people to want to connect with us.

On weekends, we would spend most of our time together going to second hand stores, garage sales and estates sales. He would usually spend $100 on random items, much of it unusable like the golf clubs he bought.

Me, "Oh, you like to golf?"

Him, "No, I just know these are good clubs."

Me, "Ok, what about the box of rusted tools?"

Him, "If I clean them up they could be worth something."

Me, "Oh, so you can sell them?"

Him, "No, I just want them, ok."

The first time he shut me up about what he was buying I decided to mind my own business and let him do whatever he wanted with his money.

Visiting his mother was not pleasant. I really liked her but her house was wall to wall stuff. The entire living room was packed with boxes almost to the top of the door jam. There was a narrow path that led to the kitchen where his mom sat all day because there was no room for furniture in the living room. I don't know where she slept because both bedrooms were also piled high with boxes and tools and golf clubs, of which there were at least ten sets.

When I used the bathroom, there was a huge hole in the ceiling covered by a tarp and the toilet was falling through the floor on one side. The whole room was rotting away and green and black mold were on every wall and the ceiling. Looking out the small window at the back yard, I saw four broken down campers, the front end of a car and possibly 10 lawn mowers, all rusted and broken. Whew.

Wayne's house next door was pristine. It was the same floor plan as his moms only reversed but it had furniture and was clean. Was his mom a hoarder, I wondered or was he the hoarder? Oh well, I really wanted to suggest his nearly 90 year old mom move into his place but as a friend it was NOMB.

During the week, while Wayne was gone, the weight of my circumstances was often too much and I would break down in tears and end up wailing as I paced around the house, angry about all the injustices, incompetent and unbelieving bureaocracies I was forced to deal with. I also was terrified about an upcoming hearing in Waxahachie I had been summoned to.

Waxahachie was the court Scott had filed for sole custody in after he was exonerated by the Grand Jury there for sexual child abuse. He didn't get it. He had lied to get the FBI involved. I was charged with Interference of Child Custody and a charge of Fleeing to Avoid Prosecution on a phony ruling.

I had to go to Waxahachie to find an attorney to talk to and my only channel of redemption; the press. I got a day off work and drove the hour to Waxahachie and found the library where I could look through the city phone book.

I used the payphone in the library lobby to call the first divorce lawyer listed. Hal answered immediately and said his office was right next to the courthouse and for me to come over immediately, that he had a few minutes to talk. I rushed over and walked in to face a true Texan, pointy boots and all. After listening he said, "I'll help you young lady, now let's go talk to my bail bondsman."

I followed him across the street and we went in and talked to the middle aged man at a desk. "This here's Billybob and he'll charge you a $50.00 retainer fee in the event you need to post bail, ain't that right, Billybob?"

"That's right, give me your name and the case number and $50.00 cash and I'll set you right up," says BB. OK, I thought, this is going better than I had anticipated. It was a Friday and my hearing was scheduled for the coming Monday. After I paid the fee and showed him my summons I asked where the newspaper office was. I did so in front of Hal in case he wanted to warn me that wasn't a good idea. Instead he chuckled and pointed to the cross street and said, "Just foller this road on down and just before the freeway overpass, you'll see it on the right." "What do I owe you to represent me at my hearing Hal," I asked, bracing myself for a charge I couldn't afford. "Well, nothing now but if this goes to trial we will work something out." Perfect. I felt like hugging both men. I got to the paper around 2 pm, hopefully in time to meet the printing deadline.

When I arrived at the newspaper, I asked the receptionist if I could talk to a reporter. I told her it was about a child sex abuse case and she quickly got up and disappeared inside a room. A few minutes later she came out followed by a 30 something reporter who didn't have the prerequisite high poofy hair with a big bow Texas women wore. I hoped she was from New York or a metro paper instead of a sleepy-slow small town like Waxahachie.

Her accent was definitely Northern as she introduced herself then told me to follow her to a room that looked soundproofed.

"Ok," she started, "You have a story to tell?" She turned on her recorder.

I told her about the Waxahachie DA not accepting the proof from the Dallas SW's and Children's Doctor, but had turned it over to the Grand Jury knowing full well children under five couldn't testify against their abusers. I also told her emphatically that it wasn't me who reported the abuse, that it was my daughter who told a Child Psychologist and a SW. The reporter asked why, if I was living with my ex in Waxahachie I had gone to a Dallas shelter. I sat back surprised?

"Don't you know," I asked, "Waxahachie doesn't have a shelter. I was sent to Dallas, the closest one."

"No, I'm new here," and after seeing my worried look, said "Oh, don't worry, I will get this printed."

"Can you get it out to the public by Monday?" I asked, "That's the day I go to court for kidnapping."

"Yes, either Saturday or Sunday and I will try for the front page," she said, then added "I'm so sorry you have gone through hell.".

"Thank you," I said and drove back to Waxahachie feeling hopeful.

CHAPTER 90

The next day, Saturday, I was sitting up in my bed. My bedroom faced the street and had a huge bay window with stained glass on the top sections. The bed fit right into the rounded window well. There were sheers and curtains tied back. The far right window circled around to expose the front porch.

I hadn't gotten out of bed yet when I heard a car pull up in front of my house. I turned to look to see if it was Wayne, but it wasn't. It was Scott.

I froze. He would be able to see me through the windows and my car was in the driveway. He was half way up the walk so I slid off the bed to the right and reached up to get my .22 that was in the small table from Waco I had next to my bed.

Scott began pounding on the door. "Kiftin, Kif, open the door. Let's talk. This has gotten out of control. We need to get back together to get Kali out of foster care."

I stayed low so he couldn't see me and crawled carrying the gun in my right hand through the French doors into the living room and stood up to face the front door. I couldn't remember if I had locked it and was relieved when he tried to turn the door handle and couldn't.

"I know you're in there and I can sit out here on the porch all day until you come out," he said in a threatening voice.

How had he found where I lived again? There was only one way; he was stalking me. I wanted so badly to just open the door and put a bullet between his eyes. No wait, he would have to actually be in the house attacking me for me not to be charged with murder. What were the Texas laws for killing someone who came into your house uninvited? I hadn't considered this scenario when I toyed with the idea of killing him. I hadn't thought through possible outcomes. What if I was sentenced for murder? What would happen to Kali? Would she stay in foster care? Would she be handed over to Bertha and spider man? What if I only wounded him? I was no match for his assertiveness with judges and lawyers. I was too beaten down. I hadn't found my voice. The truth was; I wasn't over him yet. He was broken and I still found self worth in taking on damaged people, even though I was damaged and needed to be put back together myself. The trauma bond that attached me to him like a dog leash was too strong and too complicated for me to get unhooked from around my neck.

With my heart beating out of my chest and a voice that didn't sound anything like the hard ass woman that I wanted to portray, I said, quivering, "You'd better leave or I'm calling the police." I was not good at lying and hoped I didn't sound like someone who really didn't have a phone. I really wanted to scream at him for ruining my ability to get a phone but that would tell him I was vulnerable. He knew how weak in the knees I got around him and he was such a scheming liar that if I agreed to talk to him he would tell CPS I couldn't be afraid of him if I allowed him into my house. And if I told my SW he found me they wouldn't allow Kali to live with me because that would put her in danger of him. They hadn't figured out yet if he was a child molester but they must have because they weren't allowing him to have unsupervised visits with her. He knew that if I told CPS he found me that would work in his favor, not mine.

Oh shit, please come home Wayne, this is torture. This man at my door terrified me with the depths of evil he was capable of.

Scott's voice brought me back to reality when he whined, "Come on, open the door, Kif, I love you, I drove all the way here from Riverton to see you. We need to save Kali, don't you want to save her, don't you care?"

"Kali's SW told me you were living here in Waco with your girlfriend," I said, remembering that although he was a liar, he was a stupid liar who got caught many times. I was feeling braver now. "Does your girlfriend know you're over here?" I asked.

"If you'll take me back, I'll move out tonight," he lied.

"I'll count to 3 and if you're not headed to your car, I'm calling the cops. One, two…", I began,

"Allright, I'm going," he said like a little boy. I moved back where I could see him going down the walk to his car. I sat on my bed and shook until Wayne pulled up just as Scott's car went around the corner.

By the time Wayne got to the door, I had calmed down. We were too new in our relationship for me to go full on drama or throw my arms around him like he was my savior. My situation was bazaar enough without scaring him with panic emotions. After all he was only a friend at this stage.

Wayne said he was going to go check on his mom and then we'd go somewhere for dinner. I followed him out to his car and checked the street for Scott's car in case he was stalking Wayne.

My anger and hatred were finally beginning to emerge. Up to then, my baseline emotion had been terror and survival. I wondered if I could take my hatred all the way, how far I could go in ridding myself of this monster and father of my daughter. I began imagining scenarios and opportunities for doing just that.

When Wayne returned he asked if after dinner, I would be with him when he called his son on his house phone. I agreed and we went to eat.

Wayne's wife answered and their conversation soon turned into an argument. She wouldn't let him talk to her son unless he agreed to return to Sweden. He put the phone down and put his head in his hands and began to cry. I asked if I could talk to her and he nodded.

I picked up the receiver and told his wife that I was Wayne's friend and asked if there was any way I could help. His wife was crying as well and wailed, "No, there is no solution."

"What if you come over with your son and visit Wayne in Glen Haven or Waco. Wayne said you had been living in Ft. Worth and hated it because it was a large city. Waco and Glen Haven are small towns. I would help you and be a friend. I'm sure Wayne would fly you over."

Wayne looked up when I said this and took the phone from me. “Will you come visit, please.” He listened then said “Alright,” and hung up.

“Did she agree to come,” I asked, hoping I had helped them.
“She said she’ll think about it.”

“Marriages can get so messy,” I offered.

CHAPTER 91

My next project was to find an attorney who would take my case. I had been using my work phone to call attorneys on my breaks and lunch and it was very discouraging. None of them were interested as soon as kidnapping, ritual abuse or the fact I was from California were mentioned. Many actually hung up on me.

I finally got a referral from a co-worker and got an appointment the next day after work.

I was nervous seeing this attorney for many reasons, the first being his first name was Steve, the name of my oldest brother, a bully and a man I had despised all my life! Just hearing that name paralyzed me with terror. Another reason was by the time I met him, I practically apologized for bothering him. I had gotten so discouraged trying to find one.

He took me upstairs to his office and I did my usual spiel and set out all my proof and records. He sat up straight when I told him who Scott's attorney was and the judge who seemed to jump to her tune. He shook his head and said, "I hate to tell you this but you are up against the most corrupt judge in Waco and your ex's attorney is one of his top contributors to his reelection funds. I would love to get one over on both of them, so, hellya, I'll take your case." he gave out a good ol'boy, "Wahoo," and slapped his leg.

I was so glad to finally get an attorney but I also wanted him to fight for me and not just to stick it to those two. I asked his fee, and he asked for a $100.00 retainer and we got down to the business of justice.

The first thing he had me do was to be video taped so I could see how others saw me. I was shocked. I knew I was beaten down but I almost didn't recognize the woman I had become. My expressions were minimal, my voice was flat and I could barely hear myself talk. I was a mess! I was a raging lion on the inside but outside I acted like a mouse. The disconnect was astonishing. When it was over my face burned red with humiliation. He commented, "We are going to work on that everytime you come in here." I nodded, ashamed, and gave him a check for $100.00.

Steve and I met three times a week after work. I would practice speaking into a camera while he called the 30 names I had given him who could possibly testify on my behalf.

He called Joy and Gail and told them we would fly them out to testify that I have been a good mother and church goer while in hiding. They can stay at your house, he said. Next, he wanted to talk to Kali's Guardian Ad Litem, (Lurch). After hanging up from that call he said "That man despises you and told me that Kali belongs with your ex's mother."

"OMG NO!!" I shouted. "Call Anjelica, she will come and bring the press."

"Oh no, that would be a disaster, that judge does not like bad publicity and in the event he decides custody down the line, you would be tarred and feathered by him," he warned.

"I hate this judge," I yelled.

"That's right, get angry," he prompted me. "You need to let the jury know you will fight tooth and nail for your daughter."

"Wait, what?! You mean the judge who hates me won't decide my fate. We can ask for a jury trial? Are you telling me I could have done that all along?"

"Normally no, not in family court, but your ex's attorney filed this in Criminal Court so he's going to have to suffer the consequences of doing that. Now go home because tomorrow morning, Scott's attorney and I are going to depose both of you here in my office. Don't worry, I won't charge extra for working on a Saturday morning." he said jubilantly.

"Wait, what, Scott is going to come here tomorrow?" I squeeked.

"Yes, so put on your game face," he said.

I went home and tried to keep from jumping out of my skin. Being in the same room as Scott both paralyzed me and made me breathless.

I still ached to my core that I had failed to cure him, or save him or help him. I knew intuitively that he was a broken man who lived in a state that would always favor a good looking good ol' boy but that's not what he needed. He needed to be held accountable but that would never happen in the state of Texas. My first attorney had discovered he had acquired another DUI while I was in hiding. I added to that the one he got in Hawaii plus the DUI just before I ran. The judge refused that evidence along with my medical records proving he had abused me so severely I had to be taken to the hospital. The judge said that just because he abused me didn't mean he had abused Kali so he refused to accept that as evidence.

I thought back on the kiddie porn magazine I had found in the linen closet and regretted not taking it and handing it over as evidence to my attorney, along with the syringes and the rubber hose along with his cocaine. I was living in a state where ignorance and corruption were a given and I was reaching my breaking point.

I couldn't sleep the night before the deposition. I had no phone to talk to my mom or my friends and Wayne had stayed in Glen Haven to work the late shift. He wouldn't get off until midnight and the hour and a half drive to Waco would be too hard so I was alone. I absolutely did not want to sit in a room with Scott.

CHAPTER 92

When I arrived at my attorneys, Scott was sitting next to a man. His female attorney was not there. I found out later that she dropped out of the case because Scott had never paid her for the first hearing.

My heart was racing and the lack of sleep made my eyes red and sunken into my head. I was having a hard time focusing and staying awake.

Scott was joking with the two attorneys like this was some thoroughly entertaining event. He had the kind of joy people had while watching a hanging in the town square.

After introductions, my attorney stood and said, "Me and Barney here are going upstairs to talk in private. Help yourself to coffee and donuts."

Wait..what? No, no you can't leave me with him!

As soon as they disappeared Scott came around the table and sat next to me and tried to take my hand. I jumped up, almost knocking the chair over and headed for the nearest door. It was a small room and had a lock on the doorknob, so I locked it and sat, praying.

I fell asleep but woke up when there was a knock on the door. "Leave me alone," I said. "It's me, Steve, come on out." When I came out all three men were laughing about something. Probably me. I felt total betrayal by Steve but I had paid him and he was who I had to work with.

By noon it was over and I was the first one out the door, crying while beating on the steering wheel the whole way home. Wayne was there waiting for me and stood up as I approached.

"My sister's in the hospital. I'm going to go there and relieve mom who's been there all night. I'll try to come over but I'll probably be there all day." "You look sick," he said.

"I'm just worn out and sleep deprived," I said. "I hope your sister is ok, is it her diabetes?" I asked.

"Yes, she may lose her right foot," he said. "I'll try to get back tonight." He drove off and I went into my sad house and sat alone with my sad self.

I layed on my bed and slept but woke up in the dark from a bad dream. I remembered what Steve had said about Lurch earlier in the week. He said Lurch had final say in these cases and word was he was going to recommend I lose custody and possibly parental rights at the jury trial Scott had set for February, a month away.

Lurch had to go. How could I make him go, how could I get rid of him and Ed Cruz, the CPS Director who I was sure would side with Lurch. It was dark but I walked to the phone booth I called Kali on so I could use the Waco phone book. I scanned the white pages and found them both. I didn't want their numbers. I wanted their addresses. I wrote them down in my address book and went home to look at the street map to find where they lived. I got my gun. I sat with my gun. I prayed with my gun. Could I do this? If I did I would lose Kali for sure. I would also go to jail for the rest of my life.

Steve had also told me that because I wasn't from Texas I might lose no matter what Scott had done. He said that because Scott had full custody he had gotten when I ran, a judge would never agree to me moving back to Cali. or any other state, especially not after running with her. He also reminded me that Texas never agrees to change of venue when it comes to custody. I would be shackled to this gd state and Waco until Kali reached adulthood. I wasn't in jail but I truly was a prisoner of the state of Texas.

The depression, hopelessness and helplessness I felt were crushing me like a ton of concrete from all sides. The skin on my hands was peeling off in big sheets, layers thick. I wanted to scream. I was drowning and gasping for air. I walked through the house ranting and cursing to blow off steam.

There was a knock at the door. I looked up and a man's voice said, "Police, open the door," I looked down at the gun on the bed. Had they read my mind about offing Lurch and Cruz? Why were the police there? I put the gun under my pillow and went to the door. I opened it. The cop in front said, "Is everything alright in there? Is someone with you?"

"No, why are you here?" I asked. "We got a call from your neighbor who said you were crying and screaming," he said.

"Oh, no, I was just talking loud."

"Ok, well take care now." They left and I went back to my bed and sat crying as quiet as I could until I finally went to sleep.

The next day I was again awoken by someone knocking at my door. I became alert, thinking it was Scott. It was Wayne and he looked exhausted.

After hugging, I led him to my bed and gently pushed him down and said,

"Get some sleep," I said. He nodded and layed down and was soon snoring quitely.

I got up and made coffee and scrambled some eggs and made toast. I was hungry from not eating the day before. Both Wayne and I were wiped out from family and me from my murder contemplation. I sat at the little cafe table next to the alcove in the living room, next to a bay window and looking out at the roses, and considered my options.

CHAPTER 93

It was almost Christmas. I dreaded facing it without my Kali. Making it through December I knew would be tough, especially with the custody trial only a month away. I bought Kali warm winter clothes and boots and planned on giving them to her on our next visit. With the help of Wayne I got a small tree and decorated it with all our traditional ornaments Kali and I had collected and made since she was a baby.

The week before Christmas, I got a call at work from Kali's Social Worker. She said Kali's foster parents had gotten permission to take her with the family to Disneyworld so I would not have a visit with her the week before Christmas. I was crushed. How could I give her the gifts I had for her?

I got my answer the next day. A van had pulled up in front of my house and as I watched, a woman I didn't know got out and came around to the sliding door and before I knew it Kali and the woman were at my door. Omg!

After Kali and I hugged, the woman told me she was Kali's foster mom and that she felt bad about me not getting to see her. She said neither CPS nor her husband knew about this visit and that I needed to not tell anyone. While Kali opened the presents I had for her under my tree, Maria told me that Kali would cry everytime she was forced to visit her father and their last visit had only lasted 10 minutes before it was stopped. She said Kali was telling her things Scott and his mother and spider man had done to her and although she wanted to tell Kali's SW what she was saying, her husband didn't want her to. When I asked her why she said he felt sorry for Scott, but that she sided with me.

She also told me Scott had missed two parenting classes and that a supervised visit with the CPS contracted Child Psychiatrist had ended when Kali refused to go into the room with her father, so that was also stopped.

I was gobsmacked and for the first time felt hope. After telling me she was going to testify for me, she said her husband didn't want to lose the income from fostering Kali. We gave each other a look only soul sisters can give each other.

"Men can be so selfish," she said, "But I did get him to not take the stand. He does have to work anyway so he won't be at the trial." Good, I thought.

"I have given your attorney statements Kali made about the abuse done to her and will testify to that."

Kali meanwhile, finished opening her presents and looking at all our ornaments, many she had made, so I suggested we go see her room. The room had twin beds, a beautiful marble fire-place and plenty of room. I showed her the dresses I had hanging in the closet waiting for her return and the bicycle I had bought for her.

"We've got to get back home before my husband get's home from work. You know how angry they can get if dinner isn't ready." she said, giving me another look that told me all was not rosy at this foster home. Kali didn't need another male abuser. I found out from her later just how abusive he could be.

Watching my daughter drive away in a strangers van was so unnatural, such a mind fuck. I went back into my empty house and curled into a ball on my bed, suffering from withdrawal symptoms. Love withdrawal. Even the turn of events on this day couldn't calm the dread I had for the upcoming trial.

CHAPTER 94

The next day, Monday, I called Steve's office to give him the news about the visit and what the foster mom had told me. He wouldn't tell anyone, Attorney-Client privilege. I left him a message on his answering machine.

Steve called me at work the next day and I filled him in on Kali's and her foster moms visit. He said he would question her about it on the stand and get her to talk about anything Kali had told her about the abuse done to her by her father. I also told him the foster mom told me that Scott had missed two supervised visits with Kali at CPS, had not called three times to talk to Kali on the phone and had missed all the mandatory parenting classes.

He, in turn, said he had spoken with Anjelica and wanted her to come testify but she told him she couldn't because she had been arrested and charged with kidnapping. She also told him she was being sued by one of the fathers whose kids she had put in hiding. He was a multi millionaire and she and her husband had to concentrate on her upcoming trials.

He had also talked to my mother who said she wouldn't be coming to help me. She said her sons, my four brothers had talked her out of it. They were all afraid she could be arrested for aiding and abetting on account of talking to me while in hiding. I said I understood but it hurt me deeply that not one of my siblings had offered to help me after my arrest. It took an anonymous stranger to bail me out of jail and a church friend who helped me get to Waco. I wasn't surprised none of them would help me financially or emotionally. I had never been close to any of them because, like my father, they were all immature bullies who were prejudiced against others races, people who were gay or crippled or poor or deformed. Their cruelty to me growing up was extreme and abusive, taking my parents' lead of rejecting me because I refused to glorify in our white heritage. Indeed, I was the black-sheep in my family, so different from all the rest.

Wayne returned on Wednesday night and after visiting his mom and sister, who was in recovery at her home, came to see me. Our relationship was slowly going from friendship to a deeper connection, evolving because of our common bond; missing our children. The night he returned, we went out to eat and he brought up what his future looked like.

"I'm not going to be able to go on like this with her," he lamented. "She won't agree to a divorce, she won't come here, I can't go there. I need to move on, but how?"

Trying to be helpful, I reached out and took his hand and as our eyes met, a bubble formed around us like a protective shield and we both knew our relationship was headed in a new direction. That night, returning to my house, he didn't sleep in the single bed in Kali's room. He slept with me. We actually didn't do any more than kiss.

Our possibility of becoming a couple had entered his thinking and getting a divorce became pressing on him, emotionally as well as physically. Neither of us had had sex for years and being in our 30's, that condition was just not sustainable. From then on, our conversations centered on what our future together would look like.

"Annulment?" I asked over breakfast. Looking up from his Texas toast he gave me a puzzled look.

"If you married here and she took off, you can file for an annulment," I explained. "At least you can in Cali. If the Lutheran church is similar to the Catholic church, annulments are permitted."

He sat back and said, "Let's call her tonight and I'll ask her if she can give me an annulment."

"Actually, you don't need her permission, you can just file where you last lived together. Did you live here in Waco?" I asked.

"Well, part of the time, she left after we bought a house in Ft. Worth." he said.

" You own your house here. Did she live here with you in it," I asked.

"She did for about six months but hated my mom's house next door and refused to go over there." he said. 'I feel ya girl,' I thought.

"Ok, you need to talk to an attorney and find out your options." I suggested.

"After Christmas?" he questioned.

"After Christmas," I answered.

That weekend he drove me to Glen Haven where he had a rental home. The town was nestled in a hilly, wooded area, a welcome change from the tumbleweed infested flat lands that was Texas. There was a picturesque river flowing through town and the downtown square had antique shops and country kitchen restaurants. There was only one grocery store slash general goods store, a small library and a dinosaur museum, of all things. We drove past the new elementary school that Kali would attend if we lived there and past the high school that had the requisite football stadium that the Dallas Cowboys would be proud to play in.

His rental house was small but had 2 bedrooms and a large kitchen. He took me inside and got the sweetened ice tea out of the frig that all Texans love and adore. After we sat down he looked at me grinning.

"What?" I said.

"Oh, I'm just happy to have you here. I've lived here alone for a year and it has really been lonely."

I took his hand and smiling, said, "I think I could actually live in this little town," I said, "anywhere but Waco. Nothing but bad memories and that damn courthouse are there for me."

Wayne nodded and took both my hands and said, "My fantasy is to have you and our children living here. Of course, we'd get a bigger house. They're building new ones up on the ridge that I've looked at."

There was a knock on the door and we both went to see who it was.

It was a small woman wearing a kitten emblassened T-shirt with the fashion of the day owl necklace. She was holding a plate of cookies. "Hi y'all, I see you got company," she said looking at Wayne, eager for some juicy gossip but disguising her lust for wanting to know who I was with being neighborly.

"Hi Shirley, this here's Kiftin, I'm showing her around town. Would you like to come in and let go of those heavy cookies." he said, opening the screen door for her.

"Why, I don't want to impose so you just enjoy them and I'll be going home," she said, not budging. "Where y'all from," she drawled looking at me.

"Waco, unfortunately," I said, regretting it because that gave her the opportunity to tell us some horror stories about Waco. Well I could add my horror story to her list I thought, then realized Shirley was telling me she lived two doors down and if I was ever back in town to come visit.

"Thank you," I said, "nice to meet you and thanks for the cookies."

After Wayne shut the door we looked at each other and burst out laughing. "Let's go eat," he said, "food, not the cookies."

"Be sure and check underneath the plate for a microphone, that woman wants details," I said.

We ended up back at the house after dark and sat in the living room talking and getting each other frustrated with a pretty heavy makeout session.

"I'm calling an attorney on Monday," he said as he headed down the hall to the second bedroom, letting me have the master.

CHAPTER 95

When I returned to work on Monday, I was so supercharged with adrenaline I made so many sales I was given my own office by midweek. I needed to be sequestered because I was having a nervous breakdown. The anger I felt was explosive. I continued making calls and getting sales, but between calls and waiting for the person called to get on the phone, I was cursing out all the people who had failed me and who wanted me dead. I would be crying in the morning and ranting in the afternoon. I looked and felt like a lunatic because I had ominous feelings of doom ahead of me

No getting around it, the charges against me in Waxahachie were looming large in my future and my fate was in the hands of a Texas judge. That was just one of the huge roadblocks in the way of getting my daughter back.

By the time I got home on Tuesday night I knew what I wanted to do but shouldn't do but knew I would do it. Katherine, the SW in Dallas, had given me a copy of the Satanic holidays and had asked me to try to remember the dates Scott had taken Kali to his mothers without me. The ritual days had matched up but she cautioned me that it would probably be impossible to prove anything. I still had the calendar and on this day, Dec 22 there was to be a kidnapping and a human and animal sacrifice. I drove to Riverton to sit outside Bertha's and spider man's house to see if they were up to something they needed to be killed for. Or at least arrested for. I didn't take my gun with me on this visit. I was testing my nerves on this first trip. I was nervous just sitting in my car across from their house.

After an hour while I sat in the passenger's seat gnawing on my Sonic french fries a car pulled up into the driveway. It was Scott and he was with a young woman who looked no older than 18.

She was slender and dainty and I wondered where he had found her. They went into the house without knocking and I could see Bertha's pinched face greeting them. There were the shadow outlines of others behind her but spider man's car and big-rig weren't parked in their spaces so I didn't think any of them were him.

I was tempted to sneak around to a side window that I would be just tall enough to look into but knew if I was caught they would have me arrested for trespassing, or stalking. Either that or kill me. Besides, more people were showing up now and I was sure someone would see me lurking around.

All the people arriving were carrying some kind of bag with them. One man was wearing what looked like a graduation gown. Was that spider man's kid and they were celebrating his graduation? Not in December, I reasoned. Then I remembered the black capes Kali had talked about. Could this be Meta or Flita?

It was getting late and I decided to leave when the front door opened and about 15 people poured out onto the front lawn. The girl Scott had brought with him was now between two men who were on either side of her steering her towards a large pickup. They were walking away from where I was so I couldn't see their faces. The men put her in the truck and they got in next to her, and started driving towards the town square. Scott got in his car along with a woman dressed in black while Bertha and a man and woman got in her car. Soon there was a parade of cars headed downtown.

Where are you going at this hour of night'? I wondered. After the last car left, I started my car, did a uey and headed after them.

I could see the lead car, the truck the young woman was in, turn left down the same street the Church of Christ was on. The train of cars all followed. It was a Tuesday. Why would they be going to church on a Tuesday? Maybe they were rehearsing a play for Christmas in a few days, I thought. Then I remembered. Three years earlier Kali had told the police when Katherine and I had driven her to Riverton to report abuse done to her there that they had filmed her and her cousins in a church basement. She said they had made them lie down on a table while people stuck pins in them and put their peepees in them while a man with a big camera took pictures of them. She had told the police her daddy and gramma and spider man and family had been there. OMG.

I pulled into the parking lot of a plumbing company next to the church. There was a wall of oleanders blocking a view of my car from the church. I could hear car doors shutting and people talking as they headed for the church. I sat waiting for it to bè quiet in the street. I waited another 15 minutes then got out of my car and walked around the oleander and headed for the back of the church. I was hoping there would be some way I could see what was going on in the basement but there were no windows. I did see an air vent that was located at ground level that may have gone into the basement so I sat down to see if I could hear anything.

There were definitely sounds coming from the basement so people were down there. I strained to hear voices. I heard a man's voice say, "Set the camera up over here." After about fifteen minutes, I heard comments like, "Put her on the table" and "The lightings too bright...ok, that's good." Then it got very quiet and after a few minutes I heard what sounded like chanting. It was definitely not a hymn. It sounded like Latin. The sounds made my skin crawl and I felt an incredible sense of evil and darkness. What should I do? The police station wasn't far away. Should I run over there and tell an officer there was a sacrifice being done at the church? It was probably that young girl Scott had brought to B&s's house. I bet she was picked up out at the truckstop outside of town where all the prostitutes hung out. Where I used to work

I stood up and walked around the church to go tell the police but as I came around the corner I stopped dead in my tracks. There was a cop car parked in the street just 10 feet away. Omg, were the cops in on this too?

I backed up around the building and crouched down again. The chanting had stopped but now there was a woman's voice babbling loudly in words I didn't know. There was silence, then a muffled scream that sounded like a woman's voice. Then silence. Then a chorus of voices all saying in unison words I didn't know, loudly erupted. I sat paralyzed. What now? After the chanting stopped there was silence for maybe 15 minutes, then an eruption of clapping and laughter. I could hear people talking, then the sounds of people coming out of the church. I crawled to the corner of the building and watched as people got in their cars and drove away. The cop got in his cruiser and drove past me. I was hidden by shadows and my black clothing.

I saw Scott's car parked up near the front of the church and waited for him to get in, turn around in the street and turn right on Main St. in the direction of his mom's house. Not long after the two men who had put the young girl in their truck came out carrying a very large container between them. They headed for the truck that had been parked behind Scott's and put the container in the truck bed. They got in the truck and headed out to Main St. I waited to see which way they were going then got up and ran to my car to follow. I was shaking as I started the car, the whole time asking myself what I thought I could accomplish by following them. I hated this position I was in. Why was I thrown into being involved in all of this? I had no time to figure that out, I just knew I had to follow those men.

I kept well behind them and soon they turned off onto a county road. I pulled over and watched their tail lights. It was an open prairie so I could follow visually. About seven miles down the road the headlights came left, then in my direction, then right and then it went dark. Were they at a farmhouse? I didn't know the town or area well enough to know. I turned my headlights off and because it was the winter solstice there was enough light to keep on the road. As I drew near I realized the county cemetery was to my left. They were in the cemetery. Holy shit. I pulled over and turned my car off. Now what? My SLR camera was in my car but I would have to use the flash to take a picture, which they would see. I didn't have my gun so I couldn't make a citizen's arrest. Besides, if the cops were in on this I would be the next one buried in this cemetery

I needed to see what they were doing, although I knew. I did have my swiss army knife. Yah right. A Swiss army knife against two young cowboys. Why hadn't I brought my gun? A gun. I had an idea. I saw that they had shovels and they were throwing dirt into an already prepared plot. They were about 30 feet from their truck. If they were Texans, I knew they had a rifle in the cab behind their heads. They were talking and laughing and had the radio in the truck blaring some cowboy catterwallin'. I crept up to the passengers side and looked in the cab. Sure enough, there was a rifle behind the seat. I very quietly stood on the step and reached into the opened window so as not to turn the interior light on by opening the door. I lifted the rifle off the hooks and pulled it out through the window. I was 90% sure it was loaded. My military training kicked in and I soon figured out it was a shotgun. The two men were too far behind the open windows for me to use the door as a support so I lifted the rifle and walked towards the back and used the truck bed to rest the rifle on.

I shouted "Hey, what are you doing?" I wanted them to come for me so they'd be closer and I could claim self defense it it came to that. I went for the tallest one first. I aimed for his stomach so he'd bleed out but aimed too high and after squeezing the trigger I got his head. The blast sent him spawling into the grave. The other man turned around and made himself a wide open target so I was able to shoot him right in the solar plexus. He also fell in the grave.

I really like this rifle. I think I'll keep it. I opened the door to the truck and found a box of shells for future use.

I went over to the grave and looked in. Both men were laying in the arms of the young girl I had seen Scott take to her doom. Comeuppance was mine that night. I went back to my car and drove back to Waco, pretty damn satisfied.

Once I was in my house I sat in the living room thinking like a detective in case I was questioned about the killings. My alabi would be that I was home. I had gone out to Sonic for food and had the receipt and wrappers to prove it. They were in my car and would remain there with the pretense I am not good at cleaning my car.

I wondered how the Satanists would react once the news hit that two men and a woman were found dead in an open grave. I had seen that the dead girl's chest had been cut open. They probably cut out her heart. They probably all ate a piece of it. I had read that it was part of a sacrificial ceremony.

The Satanists wouldn't report it and if the police officer I had seen at the killing was assigned the case, he wouldn't report it. He would just treat it like any other case. Detectives would question their family members and friends and hopefully someone would know at least one of the men had gone to B&s's house. Then it hit me. The pastor of that C of C was in on all of this. Also, the FBI would surely be brought in on the case. The whole town of 500 people could be investigated. The only tie I would have was if the FBI from Atlanta would notify the FBI in Texas about Texas allegations of Satanic activity and that Riverton, Waco and Dallas had been cities I lived in. That would probably only happen if the news went national.

I decided not to worry, besides, I had taken out two horrible human beings and had gotten justice for the girl. She had a mother and maybe a father and family who would be devastated. I had done a good thing and if I was to be arrested and imprisoned I would not feel ashamed.

CHAPTER 96

I spent Christmas with Wayne. We attended church events and went to the singles dinner put on by our group leaders, who had married. We took his mom and sister out for dinner that evening and I was allowed to call Kali. Her foster mom and her had made a sweatshirt for me with wording that said, "I Love You Mommy" on it. It was left on my porch Christmas morning. I had given Kali her gifts at my previous visit at CPS. Ugh, it sucked. It just really sucked.

On the day after January 1, I got a summons to court in Waxahachie. I called my attorney there to talk about it. He said I would not take the stand and he was going to ask for the charge to be dismissed. I figured Scott would be there and was very surprised he wasn't. Because he hadn't shown up, there was no case to try. I asked my attorney if it was dismissed and he said not exactly, it was just shelved for now. OMG, so when will it get resolved, "Maybe never," he said but this is a good thing.

"Oh really," I said, giving him a side eye. He said it would be in limbo until Scott got around to getting the Texas courts to bring charges. The FBI had dropped all charges in Atlanta. I had spent an afternoon in the Waxahachie county jail the day I posted bond. Once my payment cleared, my attorney got me out by 3 pm. He explained to me that because I had posted bail it meant I wasn't a flight risk and because Kali was in foster care there was nothing for the judge to sentence me for. Georgia had let me go so he said, Texas would too...probably. Oh great. Well, I decided not to worry if my attorney wasn't concerned.

My Waco attorney, however, was very concerned about our mock hearings. He said I looked terrified and intimidated answering his questions which he asked in a very intimidating way, and he worried how I would be up against my adversary. He said that's what it will be like on cross examination. I was still so beaten down and broken, our session ended with me in tears. He made a point of telling me Lurch was a terror in court and would practicaly tell the jury to hang me. He said Cruz would also make me out a child abuser. Oh for joy.

In mid January I got a summons to CPS. My attorney had notified me to definitely be there as Scott had also been summoned and whatever CPS said to do was extremely important.

I came without Wayne, but what I did come with was an engagement ring from him. Scott also showed up but without his girlfriend.

After everyone had gathered around the conference table Cruz went around the table and asked for evaluations. Lurch was there and said Kali should be placed with Scott's mom in Riverton.

Kali's social worker gave a report on how Scott and I were meeting our goals. She reported that Scott had missed many sessions and had refused the psychiatric evaluations and had missed all the parenting classes. She told them that I had attended every class, had met weekly with Kali's child psychiatrist and had passed all the psych texts. Scott was asked if he had a place to live and if he was working? He said he had a room rented in a boarding house in Riverton and they would live there; that he had daycare set up for her during the day.

I was asked how I would provide for Kali if I got custody and I showed my engagement ring and said I would be married by the time of the trial and we would live in Glen Haven in a new home and she would attend Glen Haven Elem., a new school with an A1 rating. I told them my fiance was an engineer at the Glen Haven Nuclear Power plant and made enough money so that I could be a stay-at-home mom for Kali.

Next was the foster mom who told the group she thought Kali needed to be with me.

Cruz said he would give his opinion during the trial but did say that he knew the SW had had to stop meetings with Scott when Kali demanded he confess to what he had done to her and he refused to do so. Kali's Child Psychologist reported the same as Cruz.

Scott was very angry and upset about everyone's report and almost knocked his chair over standing up and slamming his fist on the table.

"I have to work and it's not fair that I can't make it to all these appointments." Scott whined. His attorney motioned him to sit down.

Cruz said, "Mrs. McConnell has to work as well but she is making all her appointments."

"Well, I work out of town and she doesn't," he whined.

"That's your choice Mr. McConnell. Why don't you try to get work in town?" Cruz said, "OK, this meeting is adjourned."

I looked across at my attorney and we both smiled as we got up and filed out. The only fly in the oil was Lurch.

The hearing was only a week away and I really wanted the charges dropped in Waxahachie beforehand. I knew Scott's attorney would bring it up at trial, arguing that if I did get primary custody, I could still be sent to jail, leaving her alone.

CHAPTER 97

It was a good thing I had an understanding boss. I had eventually told him my predicament and he sympathized and allowed me time off to make all the appointments set up by CPS and the court.

Jury selection took place the last week of January and my attorney and I tried to seat as many women as we could. We had to weed out quite a few people though as many said they thought depriving a child of their father was egregious. 'Well what do you think about incest and torture, you idiots,' I said to myself. On that theme many of Scotts potential jurors were weeded out. Scott sat glaring at me the whole day. 'What a sweetheart he was,' I thought. 'The fucking spoiled brat con artist, pedophile abuser.'

Once the jury was selected the trial was scheduled for the next Monday, Feb. 4th. My friends would be flying in from Atlanta Friday night so they would have Saturday morning to meet with Steve and go over his questions.

I was so glad to see them but I was such a nervous mess that I wasn't a good hostess.

Saturday afternoon after we left Steve's, we went out to dinner but we were all somber. My daughter's life was on the line. They both knew Kali and Joy had been her caretaker for almost two years and was very close to her.

I wanted to bring them in on my plans for Lurch but didn't want them implicated. On Sunday evening after we got back from church I told them I was going to the store for pantyhose for the trial the next day and would pick us up some ice cream. Wayne was working overtime in Glen Haven and wouldn't be at the trial. Steve thought it best he not make an appearance, a decision I didn't agree with, but Steve held the reins to this rodeo.

As soon as I left the house I drove to the street Lurch lived on. I was nervous as I drove past his house afraid he'd be peering out the window or lurching around his front yard. My new shotgun was in the trunk and it was loaded. He lived in Waco's toniest neighborhood and being 80 plus was probably asleep by now. The phone book listed his and his wife's name so he wouldn't be alone.

I decided to give up and go home after I bought pantyhose I didn't really need and ice cream I didn't want.

Back home Gail and Joy were in the twin beds talking when I came in. I went in to sit with them and we prayed a long time before I got up to go to my room. I felt really bad about dragging them into this.

The next day we solemnly rode to the courthouse and we all held hands going up the stairs. We sat on the hard benches at the back of the rotunda.

Soon Scott, his mother and his girlfriend came up the stairs and sat on the other side. She was very pretty and Scott's mother and her were soon in conversation while Scott put on his familiar facial scowl.

I hadn't heard anything in the news about the three dead people in Riverton which was good. I'm sure all the residents knew about it and wouldn't I love questioning them about that. Bertha and Scott most assuredly knew about it. If they did suspect me they wouldn't tell the police because that could open up the coffin revealing all their dark secrets.

Steve soon arrived and told me to follow him into the courtroom. My hands were peeling again, I was so nervous. Soon the courtroom filled up with looky lous. Anyone testifying had to stay outside.

Scott came in with his attorney and he made it a point to stand and glare at me before he sat. Lurch came in and had his own table off to the left and Cruz walked in and sat next to him.

The judge came in and after we all sat back down he called the attorneys, Lurch and Cruz up and they talked, probably about their golf game on Wednesday afternoon.

They finally all ambled back to their seats and the judge called in the jury. I really didn't want to look at them in case they were giving me the stink eye.

Opening remarks were first and Scott's attorney went to stand in front of the jury and predictably called me a kidnapper, a fugitive from justice, a woman not to be trusted with her daughter's welfare. As he spoke some jury members looked over at me to examine me for the signs of insanity and instability he was accusing me of. I hoped that what they saw was how I felt; a mom maligned by a psychopath and the Texas judicial system.

Steve was up next and I have to say I was very disappointed in his delivery. He didn't say anything about the abuse Scott had subjected me to in front of our daughter, the sexual abuse from him and Bertha and her coven or his DUI's (he had four by then), He did say that Devil worship would be brought out during the trial and asked that the jury keep an open mind. It wasn't what he said, it was how he was saying it. He looked like an actor who hadn't coordinated his actions with his words, like he hadn't rehearsed enough. He looked awkward.

Next up was Lurch who, while crossing in front of me to address the jury, deliberately stepped on my foot. I let out a yelp and all eyes looked my way. Both the judge and my attorney gave me stern looks. Oh great, now I look crazy.

Lurch said that in his opinion, because I wasn't from Texas and given custody would flee to CA. never to return and Kali would be deprived of her father. He was in favor of Scott and his mother getting custody. As he lurched his way back to his seat I was tempted to stick out my keg and trip him. Ugh.

Scott's girlfriend was called to the stand by his attorney. At his suggestions she gave a glowing account of how good a father he was to her three girls. My attorney and I looked at each other with the same 'Oh my god, he has three girls to molest.' look on our faces.

Steve's cross exam did get her rattled when he asked, "Has Scott ever hit you or slammed you up against a wall or choked you?" This got her looking nervously at Scott while an obvious deer in the headlights flash of fear crossed her eyes. "Well no, we have had arguments but they are usually caused by me," she said like a true domestic violence victim. Scott had a big grin on his face as if to tell her she said exactly what he wanted her to. She was from Riverton and could possibly be involved in the cult.

By then it was lunch. Steve said he would take us all out to eat when we reached my friends in the rotunda. I was hoping it would be a nice restaurant but he drove us to a sandwich shop. Just as well, I'm sure the retainer I had given him was used to pay the bill.

"I'm sorry you guys have to sit out," I said as we looked at the menus.

"I'm going to put both of you on the stand this afternoon so let's go over the questions I'll ask." Scott said.

They went over how they were going to answer and after a few tweaks, he was satisfied they would be good character witnesses.

We finished and went back to the courthouse. Scott and his attorney were seated while Bertha and girlfriend were seated in the rotunda. Steve said Bertha would be up next. This made me practically apoplectic. I knew what that woman was capable of and I hoped Steve would get that out of her.

Scott's attorney allowed Bertha to give a narrative about how Kali told her she hated me and didn't want to live with me. She said she had to cut visits short when I came for visitation when she had custody of Kali before the divorce because I would make Kali cry. I nervously looked at the jurors' faces to see if they were buying the old hags crap. Too hard to tell. Steve did make objections but they were all overruled

On cross, Steve took out of his stack of evidence the picture Kali had drawn that showed a huge Bertha chasing after a tiny Kali with a knife dripping in blood along with a picture of Bertha wearing a wolf mask with a truly terrifying look and entered them into evidence. Scott's attorney looked at them and objected but was overruled and I watched the jurors closely as the looks of alarm crossed their faces after being handed the pictures. Steve said "Remember when I told you ritual abuse would come up in this trial?, Well this is just the beginning." Take that witch, I muttered under my breath.

Next up were my witnesses. Both Joy and Gail said they had known me the two years we had lived in Georgia. They said I had been an active member of our church and had been there every time the church was open for services. They said I had been in the choir and had sung solos. More importantly Joy told the jury Kali had told her about what her father and grandmother and spider man had done to her. Joy also testified that on one occasion right after we had moved into her home, Kali had tried to show Joy's daughter, who was a year older, the Doctor game. Joy's daughter ran to her mom and told her what Kali wanted to do. Joy sat Kali down and Kali told her about the game. Joy told her that was a very bad game and to not do it. I was at work when that happened. I had told Kali many times not to do the game but hearing it from someone else finally got her to stop doing it. Kali told Joy and I that Bertha said they could always see her and that I would be hurt if she didn't try to play the game with other children. As Joy told all this to the jury they all had startled looks. Neither Scott's attorney or Lurch cross examined them.

There was a break in the afternoon and after Scott went out I saw him immediately take his mom aside to talk. She left immediately afterward, I hope because she was afraid she'd be arrested.

Steve had also gotten the leaders of the singles group at my church to speak on my behalf. After they testified the first day was over. Whew, I had made it through the day without fainting. I drove my friends to the airport and went home praying I would get custody.

The next day, entering the courtroom without my friends for support, I felt vulnerable and scared. While walking up the stairs I saw Katherine, the SW from Dallas who I had ditched the day we ran. She was smoking a cigarette and observed my approach with an unmistakable look of disdain. I stopped to apologize before she testified. I really needed her on my side.

"Hi Katherine, are you here for my case?" I asked.

"I'm not here because I want to be, but yes I'm here for Dallas CPS in spite of the fact McLennan CPS resents us."

"I want to apologize for..," she stopped me by putting up a stopping guard palm. "We're not supposed to talk before the trial."

I nodded and proceeded up the stairs. I will be so pissed if she doesn't tell the jury I was a victim of the stupid Texas laws and the incompetence of her boyfriend cop who couldnt get the DA to bring charges instead of the Waxahachie Grand Jury.

When I got up to the rotunda Steve was standing by the double door and motioned me over. We went in together and sat down. I had told him I was out on bail in Waxahachie but no court date had been set. I also gave him Billy Bob's card, my Waxahachie attorney, and told him he felt confident he could get the case dropped. Steve said Waco probably didn't even know about it because Waxahachie is in Dallas County and if Scott brought it up then Steve would question whether Scott knew Georgia FBI had dropped all charges and Texas FBI hadn't arrested me the six months I had been back. He said Lurch was our problem.

Soon the peanut gallery and Scott's attorney came in minus Scott. Cruz was over at his desk filing through paperwork. There was a woman sitting next to him I hadn't seen before. I looked at the clock and it was straight up 8 am.

The judge was announced and we all stood. After swearing in, Steve sat and began writing a note. He slid it over and relief filled my being. It read, "This judge does not tolerate absences." I smiled.

After seating the jury, the judge reached for a paper and read from it. "This morning at 4 am, Guardian Ad Litum for Kali, Mr. Don Desantis (Lurch), passed away at Waco General from a heart attack. He will be replaced by Guardian Ad Litem, Martha Cleary."

Scott turned and gave me a 'Don't you dare get up and cheer look.' I had to put my hand over my mouth pretending to be shocked but I was hiding a broad grin. Commupence had murdered him so I didn't have to. There was a pause, then the Judge addressed Scott's attorney. "Mr. Jay Jordan, can you tell the court why the chair next to you is empty?"

"Your honor, may I approach the bench?" The judge motioned with his finger to approach. There was a whole lot of gesticulating by Scott's attorney while the judge sat stone faced. Their tete a tete finally ended and the judge said, "Court will be in recess until 9 am." Steve rose and asked the judge if he could approach. "No you may not," and got up and walked out.

Steve immediately walked over to Scott's attorney and came back with an answer. "Scott has car trouble." As he was sitting I said as quietly as I could, "Are you kidding me?"

Steve said, "Normally we could ask for a mistrial but this isn't criminal, it's custody."

"Damn it, I was hoping he had gotten his 5th DUI and was being taken to jail." I said. It did give me a chance to tell Steve I had run into Katherine outside and asked Scott to make sure she told the jury that she believed Scott had molested Kali and that night before I ran she was planning on taking Kali into protective custody and not allowing him to take her at the Grand Jury hearing in Waxahachie. He nodded. He did say he was going to do something I asked him not to but he did anyway. He said when I took the stand he was going to question me from the back of the courtroom.

"Why are you going to do that, I'll be humiliated," I said.

"I want you to talk as loud as you can. You are still having trouble standing up for yourself and I don't want the jury to think you are so emotionally crippled you won't be able to care for Kali. I want you to tell the jury why you ran."

"Well be sure and ask me why I did," I countered.

We filled up the remaining hour going over questions he would ask and how I should answer cross examination questions.

Scott finally showed up, much to my disappointment. The court finally came to order and the new Att. Ad Litum was sworn in. With the help of Director Cruz she wheeled in a TV and announced to the judge that an interview with Kali had been taped that she wanted to show. She listed the people who had been present at this taping. Lurch, of course, Scotts attorney, the judge, Kali's SW, and Steve. I looked at him, surprised, "You didn't tell me about this," but he motioned for me to be quiet.

The interview started with Kali and her SW seated while the men took turns asking her questions. Lurch was first. All his questions were an attempt to get her to say how scared she had been while with me on the run and how much she had missed her daddy and all her family and friends that she was separated from. He failed. She said she had not been afraid because she was with her mom who loved her and took care of her. She said she didn't miss her daddy or her grandmother because they did bad things to hers. That's my girl!

Next up on the video was Steve to ask his questions. He got her to say she had told a worker at a house (the shelter in Dallas) about the abuse her daddy and grandma did to her and not her mommy. She said "The bad people told me they would stab my mommy if I told her."

Steve then asked "And how did you know stabbing people could hurt your mommy?"

"Because my grandma stabbed the baby Sam and his mommy and they didn't wake up." There was an audible gasp amongst the jurors. It made me start to cry but I did so quietly.

Scott's attorney was next. "Did your mommy tell you to say those things about your daddy and grandma?"

Kali yelled "No, my daddy was there when baby Sam was killed but my mommy wasn't so how would she know about it?" Nice try Jay Jordan. He was obviously counting on the latest Psychology Today articles that most children had been brain-washed by parents in custody cases to accuse a parent of abuse that didn't happen.

Next was Kali's SW who asked her who she wanted to live with and she said,

"My mommy, I want to be with her, I want my mommy," she shouted and this made her break down crying. Director Cruz shut down the questioning and court recessed for a break. I sat crying throughout the break. I couldn't believe what they were making my daughter go through without me.

Women are penalized for having a dangerous, crazy ex husband who puts their child in danger when they show up and harass their ex wives. The children have to be taken from the mom because the system refuses to imprison abusive hus-bands. The argument is always, 'Well how can he pay child support if he's in jail?' Hell, the men all lie and say they don't have a job so the judges tell them they have to pay $35.00 a month. That's what this stupid judge ordered at our divorce hearing. He ordered me, the abused, to pay Scott $200.00 a month. I hated this judge, hated my ex and thoroughly hated the state of Texas.

CHAPTER 98

We broke for lunch and I wanted my mommy. I had no one to comfort me as I sat alone half heartedly eating the PB&J I had brought while sitting in my car.

Scott came down the courthouse steps surrounded by his girlfriend, his attorney and a man who I realized was his cousin. He searched the parking lot looking for my car and when he saw me he grinned then made a pouty face like he was victorious in his imaginary popularity contest.

Unlike you my boyfriend is working you asshole so keep your eyes on your own business.

After lunch when Scott was called to the stand he gave his boohoo performance trying his hardest to squeeze out tears. He talked forcefully and bitterly while he glared and pointed at me with accusations of ripping his heart out.

It took all my strength to not stand up and scream at him, listing all the horrible things he had done to me and Kali. He put on quite the performance for the jury and spun intricate tales about how I started every fight we had, how he found me in a Waco nightclub parking lot having sex in the backseat with a black man, knowing Texans have a deep seated dread and hatred for blacks. All made up lies. He spun yarns about me being drunk and passed out with Kali running around with a dirty diaper whenever he got home from work. The usual bullshit narcissistic, psychopath, teenage napper, pedophile killers come up with. God I wish I had kept his syringes, and cocaine and the kiddie porn mag I had found of his. Steve would have blown him out of the water with those. On cross he did bring up the four DUI's Scott had acquired since living in Texas and Scott, of course, accused Steve of making it all up. Steve entered into evidence the arrest records and after showing it to Scott, he gave it to the jury to have a look-see. Scott began clearing his throat and gulping loudly like he always did when caught in a lie. He knew his case didn't look so good after that. Steve pounded him on his living arrangements. Scott said he was living in a boarding house and had a room there. Scott walked back and forth as he talked to the jury "So, you want us to believe that you can care for a six year old girl while you both live in a boarding house? So tell me, are there community meals at the boarding house and by any chance is this a boarding house for men or is it a halfway house for alcoholics and pedaphiles out of jail?"

Scott mumbled "No," and Steve punched him again with,

"Is there a playground there, is there a kitchen in your room, is there a private bathroom or does Kali have to go down the hall to use the community toilet?"

Again, Scott muttered "No." nervously coughing and keeping his head down.

"What's that Mr. McConnell, please speak up so we can all hear you." I looked at both the jury and Scott's attorney and they all looked disgusted.

"Does Kali have her own bed or does she have to sleep with you?" Scott just shook his head and looked down.

OK, now it was my turn. My legs felt like rubber sticks as I made my way to the witness chair. Steve did what I asked him not to and went all the way to the back of the courtroom and began shouting questions at me. I thought for a second about telling him to get closer but didn't want the jury to think we weren't a united front.

"Now Miss O'Tool, I want you to tell the jury the circumstances leading up to you refusing to hand your daughter over to Mr.McConnell and his mother." Talking as loudly as I could without sounding screechy, I told the jury about the abuse starting in Hawaii and culminating in Waxahachie where I was sent to the Women's Shelter in Dallas because Waxahachie didn't have one.

When I stopped to catch my breath, Steve called out, "And what happened at the shelter?"

I continued telling how Kali had started crying and said "Mommy, I have to tell you something," "Yes baby what is it?" "Gramma sticks pins up my bottom and so does granpa'." Then she said, "Don't tell them I told you because they will kill you." I immediately stood up and took Kali downstairs to tell the Shelter Director. The Director quickly got the Shelter Child Psychologist, who then called CPS and they all went into a room with Kali. When they came out an hour later they called me into the room and told me Kali had been the victim of Ritual abuse and pedophilia.

I looked at the jury and crying, I said, "When the Grand Jury in Waxahachie and Riverton refused to convict them and was told my daughter would have to be relinquished to foster care, I had no choice, I had to run to protect her both from her abusers and the state of Texas that failed to protect her." By this time I was crying loudly so the judge stopped the proceedings for lunch.

When I was cross examined, Scott's attorney tried to whip up indignation but I could tell a switch had flipped in his being and he realized he was counsel for a psychopathic pedaphile and his devil worshiping family. He half heartedly asked his pre rehearsed questions but he knew the jury was siding with me and didn't want to hear him denigrating a victim.

However, one thing he did ask was if Scott had come to the house I was living at and asked to get back together. I truthfully answered yes, realizing Martha Cleary, Kali's attorney, would not release her to me knowing Scott would soon be banging on my door, frightening Kali.

When I sat back down, Steve said, "You know your ex came to your house intentionally so he could let CPS know that he knows where you live. He knows they are convinced he is dangerous and would not allow Kali to live with you so in a way, he got what he wanted and that's to destroy you. If he can't have her he doesn't want you to either." I went home alone after court, shell shocked.

Steve said closing arguments would be the next day and a verdict, in all likelihood, would be read by Friday. I called and asked Wayne to come with me to court if he could but he said he couldn't. I spent the evening in prayer and fasting.

In court the next day, both attorney's had given their final arguments by lunchtime. The jury would go into deliberation in the afternoon. Steve told me to go to work and he would call me there if a ruling was imminent. I went to work, glad I had something to do that would take my mind off this continuous nightmare. Plus, I could get a call there;

The day ended and he hadn't called. He said to go to work on Friday and that the verdict would probably be decided by the afternoon.

I was so jacked up on adrenaline, I made more sales than all the other 10 sales reps combined. My boss said I deserved the rest of the day off so I hightailed it to the courthouse.

As I waited in the rotunda I tried my best to stay positive. I really felt like finally, this saga in my life would come to a conclusion. I watched emotionless as Scott, his girlfriend and spider man all reached the top of the stairs and sat down. My temptation was to go over to his girlfriend and tell her to take her three daughters and run for her life. But for now, I needed to concentrate on saving Kali's.

Steve arrived and sat down next to me. "I want you to be prepared for the verdict going to CPS. Because the jury and CPS know Scott knows where you live, they will be afraid you will run to California as soon as you get her, again denying her father his rights and also opening you up to another kidnapping charge."

I didn't get a chance to reply because just then everyone was called into court. A verdict had been reached.

Scott kept turning his head and looking at me so much his attorney must have told him to stop because after that he did. As the jury filed in, all five women jurors looked at me and smiled after being seated.

The judge asked the Foreman to read the verdict and a man stood and said, "We the jury, find that CPS shall retain custody."

Scott jumped to his feet, almost knocking his chair over and bolted out the door. I stood and shook Steve's hand and we walked out together. Director Cruz caught up with us and said

"Just keep attending all the meetings and there will be another hearing six months from now."

As we reached the parking lot, Steve stopped at his car and turned and said, "At least we succeeded in keeping Scott and his family from getting her." I nodded and drove home, emotionally spent and very sad the madness would continue for another six months.

CHAPTER 99

I kept to myself when I returned to work. It was humiliating that I didn't get custody and I didn't want my coworkers to find out so I avoided my coworkers. However, I knew if I had gotten it, Scott would keep coming around. He eventually would get unsupervised visits and if those went well, overnights. Over my dead body, I thought.

On my next psychiatry meeting I discovered I had an ally. Dr. Goodman revealed to me that Scott had missed all his appointments for the past 2 months. He speculated it was because previous sessions had ended up with Kali wanting an apology from him and for him to say he had molested her. When he refused she would cry and beg for him to leave.

This news, plus Kali's accusations from the court videotaped interview should have gotten Scott arrested in at least two counties. I asked Dr. Goodman why he wasn't and he said, "The testimony of children under five in the state of Texas is considered invalid." To which I said, "Well that's got to change Dr. don't you agree?" I asked. He wouldn't answer.

I continued on, "Lawmakers here don't give children any rights." I didn't want to get on his bad side by saying it was up to the Drs. like him to convince the lawmakers to take molested children seriously. He was a child psychiatrist for Christ's sake, and it was up to him to protect the children he counseled by informing the ignorant lawmakers to fix the laws concerning children's testimony. I'd bet most of the children he got from CPS were victims of incest or molestation by a relative or family friends.

Another ally I had was Kali's SW. After a meeting with Kali at CPS I went into an employee breakroom to get a snack from the candy machine when Peggy came in for coffee. After some small talk she came around the table separating us and said, in a whisper, "You are my hero, you protected your daughter and I've told the Director you should get full custody with her dad only getting supervised visits." She squeezed my arm and said, "You hang in there, this will all end soon." She smiled then left.

As I was headed for the trash bin to throw away my wrapper the Director came in. I stiffened in fear but managed a "Hello," feeling like a kid caught with my hand in the cookie jar.

He acknowledged me so I took advantage of this rare opportunity and I asked him as casually as I could, "I found out from a coworker that I can attend a four year college paid for by the VA. I want to become a Social Worker and was wondering what Texas college you would recommend."

He took a sip of the coffee he had poured himself and said, "Texas A&M in Stephenville has a good program. There's Baylor here but it's harder to get into. Excuse me, I have a meeting to get to. "

I'm normally not that quick on my feet but I was glad I had conveyed to him I would be sticking around Texas and was also wanting to be like him.

I think it worked because three weeks after I had spoken to him, he called me at work and said he wanted to meet with me in his office. Upon entering, Kali's SW was present and after we all sat down he said, have a proposal for you. If you agree to marry and move out of Waco, I will arrange with the judge that you get full custody with Mr. McConnell getting supervised visits with Kali at Dr. Goodman's office. This means you will have to bring her to Waco twice a month for his visits. We know you are engaged. Do you have plans to marry soon?"

"We were planning a summer wedding, but I can talk to Wayne about getting married sooner and Kali and I could move to Glen Haven where he works," I said

"Perfect," he said as he stood up, "let me know when you get that all taken care of and I'll set a court date." Kali's

SW was grinning as she and I left the room. Once we were in the hallway, she hugged me and said, “Your nightmare is almost over.”

“Thank you for supporting me,” I replied as I headed for the exit, feeling great relief. Now all Wayne and I had to do was get his annulment from his wife.

CHAPTER 100

When Wayne came over that Friday night I filled him in on the Director's solution. He surprised me when he said, "What a coincidence, I filed this afternoon in Glen Haven and can get a court appearance for annulment in one month. We would be able to marry immediately after the hearing."

I was puzzled why everything going so smoothly didn't make me overjoyed or relieved. I realized that I had become numb, like in perpetual shell shock. What can go wrong, when will the other shoe drop?

"What about your mom?" I asked him, hoping to catch a shoe before it hit the floor. "She can move to Glen Haven with us." I offered.

He shook his head no, "I'll keep visiting her on the weekends like I've been doing for 10 years and you and Kali can come with me or stay here."

"Perfect, ok, I will make all the arrangements." I said. Ok, this could be fun, so why wasn't I happy? Did I love Wayne? Or was it that I still loved Scott? Now why on Earth would I still love that monster of a man? Was it because it seemed like his psyche, the inner depths of his soul were crying out in pain, to me, for help. I couldn't help him, I had tried, bút I needed to help myself.

Wayne and I announced to our singles group of our impending wedding plans on the following Sunday. One of the members, Cindy, said she would talk to her parents about having it at their home while they would be in Europe all summer. She said she would be caretaking it and they wouldn't mind. I knew her parents and her mom was in the choir with me. After the service they both approached Wayne and I and offered their home. Cindy said her boyfriend was finishing his training as a Youth Pastor and could officiate. I talked to Kali's SW about Kali attending and she said she would get permission.

The wedding was small due to the size of the house. Kali was there, wearing the dress I had made her. I had made my dress as well and wore a small brimmed ivory colored matching hat. A friend from the church choir sang, "After the Sunset" and it was a sweet ceremony. I only felt a sting of humiliation when Kali was driven off by her foster mom.

I had accomplished getting married, now I needed to move to Glen Haven. On Monday I took the marriage certificate to Director Cruz and left a note on it saying I would be moving to Glen Haven in two weeks. I also said I had given notice at work and would like child support going to Scott discontinued at the hearing.

Director Cruz called me at work and said before the hearing Kali's SW needed to go to Glen Haven to check out the house. He said he could have her come out in two weeks. If she ok'd it he could get a hearing a few days after. He said the hearing would be a formality but Scott would probably be there making objections. I called Steve to give him a heads up about the meeting.

I moved to Glen Haven two weeks after the wedding, the day before the SW came. She checked for smoke detectors and all the other requirements a foster parent has to go through. Afterward she interviewed Wayne to make sure he wasn't a weirdo or dangerous. Before leaving she said we passed inspection.

We got a phone call midweek that a hearing was scheduled for the following Monday. I said it would just be me because Wayne was a Foreman and government inspections of the power plant were that week.

I drove to the once dreaded Waco courthouse and walked up the steps with Steve who was waiting for me. This had been a long uphill battle, for me at least, and I never wanted to be here again.

We were alone in the courtroom until Director Cruz and Kali's SW came in and sat at the table to the left of us. Soon after Scott came in, by himself.

Steve leaned over towards me and said, "I talked to Scott's lawyer who told me Scott hasn't paid him so he dropped him as a client." We both smiled.

After several minutes of silence the bailiff and recorder came in and then the judge. We all did the perfunctory stand then it got down to business. The judge asked Director Cruz to stand and make his request.

Cruz gave a statement that after eight months of required classes and psychiatric testing and monitored visits, it was the opinion of CPS that Mrs. Kiftin Wellborn be given sole custody of Kali McConnell and Mr. Scott McConnell be given supervised visits once he makes up all the classes and visitations he had missed.

The judge then gave Scott the floor and he railed and whined and accused and cried until finally the judge told him to stop. When Scott kept complaining he was the victim here, the judge said loudly, "Mr. McConnell, stop or I will have my bailiff arrest you." That shut him up.

After that dramatic display, the judge asked if I had any objections to the request made by Director Cruz, I stood and gave an emphatic "No, your honor."

"Then, I grant you full custody, effective immediately," said the judge. And just like that, it was over, not with a bang, not with a whimper, but a huge sigh of relief.

Poor Scott. He jumped to his feet and charged for the door. He brushed right past Kali and a SW who were standing outside the courtroom waiting for me.

I scooped up my baby girl and was on the highway within minutes headed out of Waco, hopefully forever.

CHAPTER 101

Kali and I laughed and sang the whole way to Glen Haven. I told her about the new school she would attend and the pretty river that went through town. I told her about the dinosaur museum and how much I loved her.

She had met Wayne at the wedding but had no time with him there so I told her he had a little boy her age that lived in Sweden with his mommy. I told her he was funny and kind and would love her like I did.

When we got to Glen Haven I drove her straight home and made us lunch. We sat out on the front porch in the swing and I was truly happy for the first time since that first day Scott had hit me, eight years earlier. It had been a nightmare existence for too long. Kali was my life and my joy and I finally had her home. She said she was happy too and that was what I needed to hear.

Wayne came home that evening and took us on a tour of Glen Haven. It didn't take long, the town was so small. Back at home I made dinner while Wayne and Kali talked. He was so good with her, making her laugh and being silly. After we ate Kali and I unpacked her little Rainbow Bright suitcase I had gotten for her in Hawaii and that she had with her all along. She took out a photo album her foster mom had put together for her. It had drawings of her and I together but I noticed there were none of her and her father.

It was Spring and school was out for the summer so Kali and I had glorious sunny days together.

The neighbor who had brought cookies for Wayne and I came over after seeing us walk by her house. After I let her in she told me about a passion play musical the county put on from May until November every year and told me she had a part in the play. After I told her I was a singer she told me auditions were happening in the next three days and said they were open so Kali and I should try out. Kali loved to sing as much as I did so the following day we went to the address Shirley had given us for the auditions. Before going we practiced singing Amazing Grace and went downtown.

The Promise was the name of the play and it was put on by a for profit production company but the amphitheater it was performed at had been built by the county Glen Haven was in. Church and state, I knew didn't exist in Texas. The amphitheater had been designed by Peter Wolfe, a renowned set designer from Dallas who I had heard about when I had lived there.

The auditions were in an old theater and there were benches along the wall where there were eight or so people sitting, waiting to be called in to audition. Kali and I found two seats and I filled out the forms I was given by an attendant. There were other children there and Kali and a little girl were soon playing with the doll I had brought for her. I found out from the woman sitting next to me that these were paying parts and the pay was contingent on what role you got. Speaking parts paid more. I didn't care, I just wanted something for Kali and I to do together.

We were the last ones called in for the day and I sang first. When I finished they asked if I could act and I told them I had been in the Boston Opera Company. Next was Kali. I worried she would be nervous and shy but was blown away when she sang the song acapella loud and in perfect pitch. The two producers were also very impressed. They handed her all the song words and taped music for a part they needed to fill and asked her to learn the songs for the first rehearsal which would be in a week.

We left so excited and I took her for ice cream and a little tour through the dinosaur museum, then home to get dinner ready for Wayne.

Shirley came over the next day and when we showed her the songs Kali had to learn her eyes widened and she said, "OMG, that's a lead role. The principals are a grandfather and his two grandchildren, a boy and a girl. Why don't I drive you up to the amphitheater so you can see what a big deal this play is."

"Great, let's go," and we drove up a steep windy hill at the North end of town. At the top of the hill we came to a huge parking lot that hàd spaces for large buses. Shirley said they were for the tour buses from Dallas, Ft. Worth, Waco and San Antonio that brought people to the play. Wow.

We parked and got out and walked a long distance until we reached four big ticket and concession buildings spaced 50 ft. apart. Once at one of the buildings we were looking down at a huge amphitheater with over 2,000 seats, an orchestra pit and a three story set replete with a water moat, a mountain, three levels of stages and multiple rows of lights and curtains. We walked down one of the four aisles of seats and went around the orchestra pit to the stables. They were for the camels, the horses, sheep and goats that were part of the play. Now I really wanted for us to get parts, mainly something to help us forget about our last year of separation.

Once back home I made dinner and Kali and I listened to the music tape. The songs were incredible but so was Kali. She had all but one song out of ten memorized by the next day. Her part had three solos. She got the part of the granddaughter the next week and I also got a speaking role.

Rehearsals began and lasted an entire month and soon we were performing Wed. and Fri. evenings and two shows on Sat. and Sunday. Our days were filled with exploring and reading until school started. Kali was put in the advanced classes and soon made many friends.

I also began school at Texas A&M in Stephenville. My major was Social Work. I would be done with classes in time to get back to Glen Haven to pick Kali up from school. I also had Kali see a Ritual Abuse Psychiatrist in Dallas. His wife taped their sessions. She told him everything without me in the room. After seeing him six times, she refused to talk by the seventh, which he said was normal. He did give me one warning at our last meeting. He said, "If she doesn't have this resolved it will appear as acting out around her late 20's, early 30's so be sure to keep her in therapy." Those words would come back to haunt me years later.

CHAPTER 102

Life was good but change would soon come. One day, after the performances were over in November, there was a knock on the door. It was a Friday afternoon at the beginning of Christmas school recess.

Wayne was at work so I answered it. A pretty blond woman was standing there with a young boy. She looked very scared and I knew immediately who she was. "Does Wayne Wellborn live here?" she said.

"Come in out of the cold," I said. "Yes, he does and you must be Katya and your son Christian?" I motioned for them to sit. Kali came in from the back yard and I said, "Why don't you take Christian outside to play," to which his mom nodded.

"Are you just visiting?" I asked.

"No, I am moved here," she said with a thick accent. "I know who you are but I don't accept divorce so Wayne and I are still married. I am coming back to live with him." She looked scared but defiant.

Just then, Wayne pulled into the driveway. He saw an unfamiliar car out front so quickly came into the house. When he saw Katya, I thought he was going to faint.

Katya stood up and began to cry. We both made a move to comfort her but I realized she wanted nothing from me so held back. He sat her down on the couch and sat beside her.

I probably should have gotten angry or scared but all I could think of was getting them both something to drink and possibly eat. I even closed the hall door to give them privacy. I went about starting dinner and made enough for all of us.

Somehow my brain went into 'helping them be together' mode. I had spoken with Katya many times about coming back over to the U.S. She probably found out we had married from Wayne's mother. I felt like an interloper. How odd. Perhaps I had only loved Wayne because he had helped me get Kali back. I had these thoughts while boiling potatoes and marinating the steaks I had been thawing out. I always made doubles so Wayne would have home cooked lunches prepared so had enough for everyone.

I checked in the backyard and told Kali and Christian to come in as it was getting dark. They came in the kitchen door and I told them to sit at the dining table. Christian spoke broken English so Kali felt it her duty to translate for him, like a kidspeak thing. I poured some sweet tea for them and asked Christian if he was hungry. Kali made eating motions with her hand and he shyly nodded yes. We all laughed. Christian asked, "Where momma?" I pointed toward the living room and he said, standing, "I go to her." He went into the living room and I could hear Wayne let out a year's pent up gasp, then I heard crying all around as the boy kept saying, "Pappa, pappa."

Kali looked at me and said, "What's happening?" I tried to explain to her who Katya and Christian were and she just stared at me with a look that said, "So are they moving in and we're moving out." I sat down and took her hands and said, "I've always known Wayne still loves his wife and son so if we have to move out, we will get our own place here in Glen Haven."

"Ok, I'm hungry, when are we eating?" It's not that she didn't like Wayne, she just didn't know him well enough to be upset if he disappeared out of her life.

I told Kali to wash up and change her pants that were dirty. She came back out to the kitchen and helped me set the table. Spoken like a true mature adult she asked, "Do you think they'll want to eat with us?"

"I don't know, all we can do is ask," I said. "Ok, I'll go ask them," and before I could object she sailed through the swinging door and shouted, "My mom's making dinner everyone," and without waiting for an answer she bounded back into the kitchen. I went out to the living room myself. I approached Wayne and Katya who were holding hands and said, "I would be honored to have you and Christian have dinner with us." Wayne looked pleadingly at her and she said, "You are very kind." We broke bread together and afterward Katya said, "We have hotel room here and I want husband to be with me." Wayne looked absolutely flummoxed but I could tell he wanted to be with the woman he deeply loved and their son. I looked at him and nodded yes. He looked relieved and hugged me as they all headed out the door.

CHAPTER 103

Our annulment went through within a month and Kali and I found a 2 bedroom, 2 bath apartment. Wayne had given me $7,000.00 to send me on my way. I was at peace. I had my baby back and I no longer had to deal with the rigors of married life which I already had become weary of. My year spent talking to Katya in an effort to reunite with Wayne had succeeded. It was time and effort well spent and I realized that met goal gave me deep satisfaction.

Kali thrived at school and was very popular due to her star status at the play which brought in great publicity and revenue for the community.

I continued with my schooling and got a paper published in a Social Work textbook. As a SW major, I interned at a foster care facility in Stephenville and met a young girl there named Rebel. The name triggered a memory. Kali had said there was a girl Bertha and spider man had abused named Rebel and Kali said they had gotten her from a foster care place in Steven. Kali said she heard them talking about it. She might have meant Stephenville. I asked and was told there was a girl there named Rebel who had been sent to a couple in Riverton for Christmas one year but they had stopped the visits after Rebel told them the man had taken her to the woods and 'touched her where she peed' and the woman was abusive to her, almost drowning her in the tub and wearing scary masks. I asked why they hadn't been arrested and was told they thought Rebel made it all up! I requested a visit with Rebel and she told me she had stayed with some people in Riverton but couldn't remember their names. She said, "I never wanted to go back there because the man made me do bad things. The old lady there was really mean to me and at a party on Christmas they made everyone take their clothes off and there were big cameras there."

I was furious that Bertha and spider man hadn't been arrested. "Noone believed me so I stopped telling anyone but they won't make me go back there anymore." I couldn't believe she had not been believed. She must have been under five when she reported. What a bunch of incompetent idiots ran the state of Texas.

I seriously contemplated offing Bertha and spider man but when I drove to Riverton and saw my pastor there at the church, he said they had moved away and no one knew where to. Yeah, they hitailed it out of town after the murders of the two men assigned to bury the sacrificed woman and had abused Rebel during Christmas of the past year. Good riddance.

CHAPTER 104

After living in Glen Haven for two years, I made plans for moving back to California to try to reconnect with my family. Both for my sake and Kali's.

Scott had quit showing up for supervised visits immediately after I got custody. Kali and I had dutifully made the long drive to Waco three times, but by the fourth Dr. Goodman said he had canceled any further visits.

I transferred to a California college and my mom flew out to help us move back. I rented a UHaul and we headed West. I cheered when we crossed over the Texas state line into New Mexico.

We didn't have a time crunch so we stopped at places of interest where I could rekindle my passion for photography. My mom was a good sport but I sensed that old discomfort between us. I believe she was afraid disaster would befall her just being in my presence.

Once back to where she lived, all brothers but one came to see us. Kali was nine by then and happily soaked up the attention. I knew though, in my heart, that my brothers only came because they wanted to please our mother. Once she was gone, I knew they would have nothing more to do with me. In their eyes, I had disgraced them and everything Kali and I had gone through was my fault. I knew they would never forgive me for putting our mother in jeopardy and causing her unimaginable stress.

After she died, two years later, all I feared came to pass. There was not one family at my college graduation.

Was all I had gone through to save my daughter worth it? Absolutely!

CHAPTER 105

There was only one other person I wanted dead at that time after finding out Bertha and spider man had died.

I think you know who it is.

He had accumulated 8 Dui's by then, three of those arrests he got in the new state he was living in. He had also been arrested twice for carrying an unregistered gun. So far he's gotten a year in jail for all his stupidity. I was also sure he was still beating women and raping and torturing children.

There was another reason I wanted him gone. Kali had found him on the internet at age 16. Why? Why would she want to do that? Had she forgotten what he had done to us? Or had the torture and brainwashing that had happened to her from infancy up to age four taken root in her soul? I learned from reading books on Satanism that because she had helped kill baby Sam and was forced to marry Satan in a ritual they told her she was evil just like them and always would be. I had also learned that there are trigger words spoken by her trainer (her father) that would awaken the evil in her every time he spoke to her on the phone. By the time she was 18 he called her frequently. Time would tell if Dr. Mongatzes' prediction of her falling prey again at around age 30 would come to pass. She was an adult now and there was nothing I could do about his influence on her. There was something I could do about him, however.

As I sat waiting, I pondered whether losing my freedom was worth this killing. What if there was a chance he had changed. Not likely. What if my daughter would never get the chance to love him into goodness and would hold it against me that I ruined that chance? What if she allowed him into her life and he molested his granddaughters? His charm was already wearing her down.

I decided this was an assignment by nature for the sheer fact I alone knew his heart and how now he was again a danger to Kali and my grandchildren. He was the patient and I was the doctor. I saw it as my duty to extricate the infection of evil he gave Kali. I needed to break their bond. I knew I was risking my freedom because the broken justice system inevitably throws the book at abused women who kill their ex's. If they had done their jobs and arrested and jailed the male abusers, women wouldn't have to resort to killing them, often in self defense.

It had been long enough and I knew in my being Scott was still out there doing harm.

I had made the long drive to where he lived and now I sat in my car waiting. I hoped the homemade silencer would work. If it didn't, I was confident I could escape. I still had my license from when my name was changed and had rented the car with it. I had gotten a new credit card in that name as well. I would take him out then use the passport I had used to book a flight to the Maldives. I had heard it's beautiful and they don't extradite. My life would mirror that first movie we saw on our first date where the last scene shows the woman relaxing on the sand of a tropical island after having disposed of the man.

He lived near a freeway entrance so making my getaway could be easy. I was parked facing the freeway entrance when a car pulled into his driveway. I snapped awake and watched. A young woman got out on the passenger side and came around the car and headed for the door. Scott got out and ran towards her grabbing her by the arm. She turned and swung her purse at his face. She missed and he threw a punch that caught her in the jaw.

I was so mesmerized I realized I had lowered the rifle between my legs. Here was proof he was still abusing. Now I raised it again and continued watching.

The girl reached for and grabbed her bag lying next to her. She opened it and took something out. What was it? It was pepper spray, or mace. She sprayed him in the face as he gropped around blindly. "I'll kill you," he screamed.

"Not if I kill you first," she hissed and reached in her purse again and brought out a pistol. Shoot him, shoot him, I whispered loudly as I drew a bead on his head as backup. I truly felt like I was covering for her. If she couldn't succeed, I would.

She pointed the gun to his head and screamed a name, "This is for Amanda," and pow, she shot him in the head. As he lay on the ground she arose and screamed, "And this is for April," and shot him in the chest. She crumpled to the ground sobbing.

I knew I couldn't help her as a witness. I instead waited until the ambulance, the police and the woman were all gone and I got out, put my rifle in the trunk and said quietly to myself, 'Comeuppance at last' and drove to the airport to catch my flight to the Maldives, not as a fugitive but as a tourist.

EPILOGUE

As for women being abused by their mates, then let down by the cops, the courts, CPS, et al, that has not improved in the 30 years since I went through my hell dealing with them.

The custody judges are still uneducated about abuse, especially Narcissistic abuse predominantly carried out by males. Judges still don't accept the fact of the profound emotional damage it does to a child who sees their non abusive parent being constantly brutalized and not being given a voice to tell about abuse being done to them.

Custody laws are still a total maze of confusion; there are still no houses and apartments provided to children and their protective parent because Women's Shelters are always full and there are limits as to how long they can stay. The abusive parent often ends up with more rights than the protective parent in the futile ongoing effort of CPS to unify the family and provide mandatory access for abusers to the children they have brutalized.

State and county jurisdiction laws can make it oftentimes impossible for witnesses, doctors exam reports, CPS findings to be admitted into evidence because of mileage limitations. For example, McLennan County CPS, in Texas, and custody courts will not recognize abuse reports if the reporting county is over 100 miles away from the custody county. Custody laws should be state wide and not county based. They also don't believe the testimony of children under age 5.

Foster homes are not screened adequately and the children placed in them are not monitored enough. Abused children often report, once out of the foster care system, that their foster parents' abuse was just as bad as their biological parents. My Kali told me her foster father was very mean to her. He would punish her by making her stand in a dark closet with her arms outstretched for long periods of time. He often hung up on me when I called if Kali began crying, cutting our half hour mandatory talks down to minutes.

We need to do better. We can change the system and it starts by educating in the schools from the get go about abuse, about predators and abusers and the red flags to look for to avoid them. The fact that there are evil people should not be sugar coated for children. Adults in charge of children, including parents and teachers make the mistake of thinking it does harm to inform them of sexual predators and what abuse is. Isn't it better to tell them what constitutes abuse before they are abused. A no brainer. We need to do away with memorizing history dates in schools and teach how to make it in a wild and dangerous world. Schools should include teaching compassion and love but also teach that daddy coming into your bedroom at night and getting into bed with you is wrong and tell them that if that's happening there are people to talk to about it and will get it stopped. Same with daddy and mommy or a sibling hitting you and that threats of secrecy are also wrong.

I hope changes are made before my body stops working. We can't continue on the way we have been.

Time will tell if Kali can effectively process all the traumas she endured in her formative years between birth and six. It's too soon to tell but I will let you know when those chapters are written closer to my passing. That may not be for another 25 years.

I can say that so far, from the time she left home up to 2022, it has been a tumultuous journey. Dr. Mongatzes predictions of problems starting in her late 20's have come to pass. I hesitate to report on those eight years. I guess I'm waiting for a happy ending before I talk about it. Who knows, maybe before I do I will get my Comeuppance.

RESOURCES

Pedophilia & Empire: Satan, Sodomy and The Deep State: Chapters 1 - 20
Chapter 8: America's Military Pedophilia Scandals - Daycare Scares and "Satanic Panic" (Amazon/Kindle)
By Joachim Hagopian
E[11]
Operation Paperclip:
The Secret Intelligence Program That Brought Nazi Scientists To America
By Annie Jacobsen

Restoring Survivors of Satanic Ritual Abuse:
Equipping and Releasing God's People For Spirit Empowered Ministry
By Patricia Baird Clark

Ritual Abuse in the Twenty-First Century
Psychological, Forensic, Social, and Political Considerations
Editors: Randy Noblitt & Pamela Perskin Noblitt (26 author compilation, 2008)

The Ritual Abuse Secrets of the Illuminati
By ArchAngel (Survivor from the
(Rothschild/Illuminati bloodline)

Breaking the Circle of Satanic Ritual Abuse
Recognizing and Recovering from
the Hidden Trauma
By Daniel Ryder, C.C.D.C., L.S.W

Childhood Ritual Abuse: A Resource Manual for Criminal Justice and Social Service By J. Adams (2000)

Drawn Swords: My Victory Over Childhood Ritual Abuse
By J. Adams (1999)

Our Life Beyond Mk Ultra
By Elisa E (Amazon/Kindle)

The Rituals Part 1: Book 5A from
"The Making of the Monarch" Series
(Amazon/Kindle)
By M. K. Ultra

Ritual Abuse - Torture Within
Family/Groups I Office of Justice
Programs
http://www.ojp.gov>ncjrs>abstract

Institutional, Ritual Abuse, SRA Support on #RemovingChains
https://www.removingchains.org

U. S. Department of Health & Human
Resources
Child Welfare Information Gateway
Organizations for Adult Survivors
of Abuse
OrganizationUpdates@childwelfare.gov

Australia

BRISSC (Australian Resource Org.)
https://www.removingchains.org › i...
https://www.google.com/url?sa=t&source=web&rct=j&url=https://www.inverse.com/article/47055-why-are-canadians-suing-over-mk-ultra/amp&ved=2ahUKEwiQnLCK18j2AhVxRN8KHR7EC-G8QFnoECA4QAQ&usg=AOvVaw2wa92ICaTHNvwpm-rQ6N3K1

Canada

CIA Mind Control Survivors Seek Restitution From Canadian Government
https://www.google.com/url?sa=t&source=web&rct=j&url=https://www.inverse.com/article/47055-why-are-canadians-suing-over-mk-ultra/amp&ved=2ahUKEwiQnLCK18j2AhVxRN8KHR7EC-G8QFnoECA4QAQ&usg=AOvVaw2wa92ICaTHNvwpm-rQ6N3K1
https://www.inverse.com › article

Great Britian

RAINS (Ritual Abuse Information
Network and Support) Great Britian
https://www.google.com/url?sa=t&source=web&rct=j&url=https://www.thesurvivorstrust.org/faqs/rains-ritual-abuse-information-network-and-support&ved=2ahUKEwjG3-iiysj2AhXpYd-8KHe1SDjoQFnoECAkQAQ&usg=AOvVaw1hTcWakLJDTJ1i6o-vAdhfO

Made in the USA
Las Vegas, NV
26 July 2022